Renegade Lady

By Dawn Martens & Emily Minton

Renegade Lady by DAWN MARTENS and EMILY MINTON

Copyright © 2013 Dawn Martens and Emily Minton

Published 2014

Cover Art by Kellie Dennis at Book Cover by Design
www.bookcoverbydesign.co.uk

Edited by **Brandi Gilvaja**. Main edits by **Kendra** @ Catdipity Kendra's Proofreading, Line Editing, and Reviewing. Proof reading by **Evette Ashby**

Formatted by **Angel Steel**

Renegade Lady is a work of fiction. All names, characters, places and events portrayed in this book either are from the author's imagination or are used fictitiously. Any similarity to real persons, living or dead, establishments, events, or location is purely coincidental and not intended by the author. Please do not take offence to the content, as it is FICTION.

Trademarks: This book identifies product names and services known to be trademarks, registered trademarks, or service marks of their respective holders. The author acknowledges the trademarked status in this work of fiction. The publication and use of these trademarks is not authorized, associated with, or sponsored by the trademark owners.

Acknowledgements

Emily's Acknowledgements:

I want to thank all of our freaking bad ass betas **Maureen, Ahren, Tee, Lindsey, Hayley, KC, Melody, and Skye**. You guys are amazing. I adore each and every one of you. **Brandi**… You freaking rock. You're the alpha reading queen. Thank you so so so much for everything.

Evette Reads, you rock girl. There is no way I could've done this without you. Thanks for being my sounding board and my friend. I know I call you my personal assistant, but you're really my savior.

Kendra, Kellie, and Angel: Thank you guys for making the final product the bomb!

To all our **bloggers**: Each and every one of you ROCK! You are the backbone of the writing community. We appreciate you more than you will ever know.

David, Jess, and Bailey: I know you guys have to pick up my slack, when I'm lost in book word. Thanks for not complaining too much. I promise to make lasagna and meatloaf for you soon.

Dawn, thanks for being by my side. You make working a freaking blast. Love you, chicky. (But, next time, no more discussions of anal sex.)

To my **readers**: Thank you for taking this wild ride with me. I hope you enjoy reading it as much as I enjoyed writing it.

Dawn's Acknowledgements:

I def need to thank my mega bitch **Brandi**. She is my sister queen reader. When she read this as our Alpha Reader, and loved it, even declared she wanted to be a Pimptress too, haha, I knew this book was a good one. Thanks B for being awesome.

To my first round of beta readers **Maureen, Ahren, Tee and Skye**, thank you for all the feedback, all the notes you gave helped us to build this story more, made it longer, and just overall, made it that much better.

To my second round of beta readers **Lindsey, Hayley, KC, Melody** – Thank you!! You ladies read this sort of books all the time, and love them, so having your input on Lady made us sigh a huge sigh of relief.

To **Evette** for helping Emily and I with this! Appreciate it! And thanks for being an awesome assistant, even though I don't really take advantage of it lol, but I'll try harder! ;)

To my best friend **Nikki**, this is 5 books I've put out. Where the hell is yours woman! You've been working on it longer than I started writing! Ha, get to it! Love you! And I hope we get to meet in person before Nash and Ava get married ;)

To **Emily**, you have made writing together so flippen enjoyable. Seriously, you friggen rock.

To my **hubby**, I love you! Thanks for keeping the kids busy when it got close to deadline time so I could make sure this was finished. I know books and reading are not interesting to you, but every day you ask about my books, and support me. That means the world to me.

And last, to my **readers**, thank you for loving my work, and supporting me as an author. Emily and I are going to be working hard, to try and get Broken done before this baby comes out, that way, you don't have to wait forever and a day for us to get back to writing. While I have this baby I will be on hiatus, so I appreciate you awesome people in being patient with us.

Dedication

This one is for all the old ladies out there. Hope each and every one of you have your own Kidd. — Emily

This book is for my girl, Brandi, just because. — Dawn

WARNING:

Renegade Lady contains adult situations some readers may find offensive. This is a raw and gritty story involving under-age rape, explicit sex, graphic language, violence and drug use. Not intended for readers under 18.

Renegade Lady
Renegade Sons MC Book One

Jenna "Ice" Chandler grew up as part of a motorcycle club. She considered it her home, until one wrong move made it her prison. After months of abuse, she is rescued by Chipper, who takes her to Big Clifty, Missouri, home of the Renegade Sons MC.

Kiddrick "Kidd" Jones is the president of the Renegades. He knows there is something special about Ice the moment his older brother, Chipper, brings her into the club, but stays away, because she is too young.

When time comes for Ice to take her place in the club, she has two choices, become an old lady or a club whore. Not believing in love and knowing a man can never be faithful, she decides to earn her spot on her back.

With each passing year, Kidd's feelings for Ice grows and the urge to make her his becomes stronger. Frustrated and jealous, he finally decides it's time to make her his.

Will Ice finally thaw out and give love a chance, or is Kidd fighting a losing battle?

Renegade Sons Motorcycle Club
"Never Forget and Never Forgive"

The Renegade Sons Motorcycle club was founded by Charles "Gun" Jones, Clyde "Digger" Bell, and Kenneth "Killer" Thompson on March 23, 1973.

The three brothers by choice were all members of the 42nd Infantry division out of Fort Campbell, Kentucky, also known as the Renegade Sons. Each man had done at least two tours in Vietnam, each believing they fought for something bigger than their self. A fact they were all proud of.

After returning home from Vietnam, the three men realized that they fought and bled for a cause that many of their country men did not believe in. They realized that they had watched their fellow soldiers, their brothers, die in vain. Even though the men were scattered across the United States, their anger at the situation led them back together. That same anger led them to establish the Renegade Sons.

Part One

The Beginning

Prologue

Jenna

I stare at the ceiling while Timmons pounds into me. I bite down hard on my lip, so hard I can taste blood. He slams in one more time and grunts loudly into my ear before rolling onto his side. He lays there for a moment, breathing hard, then climbs from the bed.

I can hear him getting dressed, but I never take my eyes off the ceiling. I just lay there and count. I usually make it to around thirty before he leaves the room. One Mississippi, two Mississippi, three Mississippi…. He's pulling on his jeans. Thirteen Mississippi, fourteen Mississippi… I hear the swish of his shirt. Twenty Mississippi, twenty-one Mississippi, twenty-two… There's the shuffle of his boots. Twenty-eight

Mississippi… Finally, the door opens and he walks out.

As soon as I hear the click of the lock, I roll off the bed and run to the trashcan. I barely make it there before the bile comes spewing out. When I'm done, I crawl back to the bed and pull myself onto it. Once there, I curl up into a ball and pray that God will send someone to save me today. I'm still praying when sleep takes over my body.

"Get the fuck up!" Timmons shouts, waking me from my nightmare filled sleep. He reaches down and grabs me, pulling me from the bed by my hair. I land hard on the floor, causing pain to ricochet through my already aching body. I slowly push myself up onto my knees and do my best to look at him through my swollen eyes.

"Get the fuck off the floor and follow me," he says after giving me a swift kick to the ribs.

I rush to get up, doing my best to ignore the pain. I walk behind him, every step causing a stabbing sensation to shoot up my side. He finally stops when we reach the middle of the common room. He takes a seat next to my dad and pulls me into his lap. "Jenna, your Dad has something he needs to talk to you about."

I don't respond, just simply nod my head. I learned during my first night with Timmons that things go better if I just keep my mouth shut. Being quiet doesn't keep him from hurting me, but this way I can't say something to make him mad. When he's mad, his beatings turn brutal.

Dad leans towards us, putting his hands flat against the table. "Timmons and I have been talking. He seems to think it's time someone took hold of your reins. After that shit you pulled coming in here after your mom died, I've decided he's right."

I close my eyes, hoping he doesn't see the anger flashing through them. Scene? What scene? All I did was come to the clubhouse to tell him that Mom was dead. Yes, I was crying and screaming, but who wouldn't be after they just found their mother OD'd on the kitchen floor?

"Do you understand what I'm saying to you, girl?"

I look back to my father and shake my head. I don't understand. I don't understand anything that has happened to me over the last few weeks. How a father could allow his own daughter to be raped and beaten by a monster like Timmons, I will never understand.

"What I'm telling you is that Timmons is claiming you. You're his old lady now. There's nothing you can do to change it. Best start listening to him if you don't want to be hurt," he states matter of fact.

Hurt? Can he not see the bruises covering my body? What about the dried blood that stains the disgusting nighty Timmons makes me wear? "But I'm only sixteen," I whisper out, even though I know I should keep my mouth shut.

Timmons' arms tighten around my waist, causing a sharp pain to course through my ribs. "It doesn't matter how fucking old you are. You're mine, and pleasing me is the only damn thing you need to be worrying about anymore. Understand?"

I have to swallow a gasp of agony, but force myself to answer. "Yes, sir."

Dad looks from me to Timmons. "I can't tell you how to treat her. She's your old lady now, so it's your choice. But if you don't lay off taking your fists to her, she won't make it more than a week or two."

Timmons body tightens next to mine. "Like you said, she's my old lady. I'll do whatever the fuck I want to her," he says in a near shout.

Dad raises his hands, palms up, in an attempt to calm down Timmons' anger. "You're right. She's none of my business anymore. I won't say shit about it from now on."

Timmons leans towards Dad, causing my head to nearly hit the table. "You better not. 'Cause if you keep getting in my business; I'll get in yours. I'm sure you don't want the boys from Big Clifty knowing your secrets. Be a real shame if they found out you've been using their cocaine to feed that nasty little habit you got. You know what I'm talking about, right? The coke that should have been in Cali by now."

Dad's face turns red, and I can tell he wants to come across the table and lay Timmons out. Instead, he sits back and scowls. "You got what you wanted. Take her and get the hell away from me."

Timmons chuckles as he stands us up. I look back towards Dad while Timmons pulls me across the room. He's staring at me with a look of regret on his face, but he keeps his mouth shut. I guess his secrets are more important than his daughter. Before Timmons pulls me into the hallway, he shouts across the room, "Come on Rig! Let's go have some fun with my old lady."

CHAPTER One

Chipper

Anger fills me as I walk through the Mateland, Missouri chapter of the Renegade Sons MC's clubhouse. I didn't want to come to this shithole, and now that I've seen what's going on, I can't wait to get my ass out of here. There're a ton of reasons I gave up the VP chair, and being away from home is one of the biggest. I can't believe all the shit I'm seeing. There are drugs everywhere-- every-fucking-where. One of the club whores is literally snorting coke off the fucking floor. Never seen anything like it in my life.

I've been here nearly two hours, and I've yet to see a member sober enough to talk business with. I should be home taking care of my sick wife, instead of having to deal with a bunch of fucked up dipshits. My Dad is the President of The Renegade Sons MC. He knew some shit was going down with the Mateland Renegades Chapter, so he sent me here to talk to Killer, the Chapter President. Dad wants me to find out what the fuck is going on with the missing cocaine. It was supposed to have been transported to California last week, yet no one there has seen it. But after being here two hours, it isn't hard to figure out what happened to that shit.

"Yo, Chipper. Are you still lookin' for Killer?" One of the prospects quips from behind the bar.

"Yeah, is he back yet?"

"Yep, just came in. I saw him walking down the back hall with a few bitches," he says as he wipes down the counter. I can tell by the tone of his voice that he knows some serious shit is going on, and he's smart enough to know that he doesn't want to get on my bad side. I've talked to him a few times today, and he seems like a good kid; a little green, but all prospects are. Maybe I should take him to Big Clifty and let him see what it means to be a true Renegade Son.

"What's your name?"

"Reese," he says, sticking his hand out for me to shake.

I shake his hand and look back towards the coked up members. "How long's this been going on?"

He shrugs. "Not sure man. I just signed on a few weeks ago, and I've been on the road since then. I just got here this morning."

"It wasn't like this when you were here before?" I ask.

"Today's my first time inside the clubhouse. I signed on as a prospect after meeting a few of the members at Sturgis," he explains.

I motion my head towards a guy throwing up in the corner. "Is this what you signed up for?"

A look of disgust crosses his face. "Hell no. I got an old lady and a daughter. I planned on bringing them here after I got settled, but I don't want my little girl around shit like this."

"So, you're not planning on sticking around?"

"Doubt it. I figure I'll work for a while then head back home." He shakes his head. "Sad though, I liked the idea of being a part of something bigger than myself."

I smile as soon as the words leave his mouth. "If that's true, then head on down to Big Clifty. It's about thirty minutes south of Kansas City. I think you'll find what you're looking for there. I'll be heading out soon. You can follow, if you like."

I don't bother waiting for him to reply before I start to walk towards the hall. I figure Killer took a few chicks to his office, but he's going to have to kick them to the curb. We need to talk, and what we don't need is an audience. I make my way down the hallway, but stop when I hear a whimper. I swear, it sounds like a baby. If these crazy motherfuckers have a kid in the middle of this shit, I'm going to kill a few of these stupid sons of bitches.

16

I continue to the office, but stop when I reach the room next to it. What I see makes me want to put a damn bullet into Rig and Timmons' heads. Both of the stupid fuckers are buck ass naked and hammering into a girl. From the looks of it, she seems to be a damn kid. There's no fuckin' way the girl can be over eighteen. What the hell? This is wrong! I storm into the room and snatch Timmons off of the frail girl beneath him.

Dick swinging around, he stumbles back. "What the fuck?" he says, slurring, high as a kite.

I pull out my piece, grab him by the hair, and push the barrel of the gun into the center of his forehead. "That's exactly what I want to know."

"What the hell is going on, man?" Timmons asks again as he tries to pull away from the cold steel hovering between his eyes.

I jerk his head back towards me. There's no way in hell that I'm letting this fucker go. "Like I said, that's what I'd like to know."

Rig pushes the kid off his dick, and she falls towards the floor. "Chipper, you need to chill the hell out."

I look down at the girl, and for the first time, I can get a good look at her face. Both of her eyes are black and swollen. I'd bet she can't even see shit through either of them. Blood steadily drips from her nose, and there's no doubt in my mind that the damn thing is broken. Her body is covered in multiple black and blue bruises, and I wouldn't be surprised if she didn't have a broken rib or two. When I lower my eyes down her body, I finally zero in on the blood that's pooled between her legs.

"How old is she?" I seethe out, grinding my teeth.

"Don't worry about it, Chipper. She's good. She's Timmons' little plaything," Rig says with a smug smile. He looks towards her and nudges her with his foot. "You enjoy it. Ain't that right, sweet thing?"

Fury over-boiling deep within my belly, I smash the butt of my pistol into Timmons' temple, and he instantly goes limp. I toss him to the floor and point my gun at Rig. "Timmons' plaything?" I say in disgust. "Does she look like she's enjoying it to you?"

Rig takes a step back. "Like I said, you need to chill out. This isn't club business. It's between her and Timmons," he says, motioning towards the girl.

I ignore him and take a step towards the kid. "Darlin', how old are you?" I say as softly as I can, hoping I won't scare her more than she already is.

"I'm sixteen," she says in a faint whisper. Her voice is so weak that I worry she may be hurt even worse than I originally thought.

"Do you think you can walk?" I ask her.

She hesitates for a second then slowly nods.

"Okay, darlin'. I want you to stand up, get your clothes on, and walk out to my bike. It's the white 'fat boy' with the Renegade emblem on the tank."

She slowly stands up, no doubt trying to avoid as much pain as possible. She stumbles towards a piece of purple material on the floor, and when she slides it over her body, I realize it's a nearly see-through nighty. "That all you got, babe?"

"They took all my clothes when they gave me this," she says, running her hand over the nighty with a look of disgust slowly rolling over her battered face.

The finger on the trigger of my piece tenses. I quickly pull off my cut and jerk my T-shirt over my head to toss it in her direction, transferring the gun from hand to hand and never taking the thing off of Rig. She hurriedly snatches the cloth from the ground and clings to it for dear life. "You put that on and go to my bike. If anyone tries to stop you, tell them Chipper has claimed you as his."

She nods again, then quickly pulls on the shirt and rushes as fast as she can out into the hallway. I wait until she's gone before I look towards Timmons. It's time for his stupid ass to wake up, so I give him a hard kick in the ribs. It takes a few more blows before he regains consciousness. "Get your ass up. Now."

He pushes himself up with his hands, shakes his head, and looks towards me. "Man, you need to put the gun away. There's no need for you to kill anyone. If you want the girl, take her. No one here will stop you."

A slow smile spreads across my face. "You're right. I'll take her, and ain't nobody gonna stop me, but you're wrong about the other shit. I feel like killing someone, but first I gotta figure out which one of you fuckers needs to go down."

As soon as the words leave my lips, Rig starts to rush me. Without a second thought, I put a bullet in his head then quickly turn the barrel towards Timmons. His entire body begins to shake as a small pool of piss gathers at his feet. As much as I want to blow his fucking head off and paint the walls with his brains, I restrain myself. He's Killer's son, and Killer is Pop's best friend. Shit's bad enough as it is, but it will get infinitely worse if I kill Timmons.

"I'm not gonna kill you, asshole," I growl out. "But I am gonna teach you a lesson, and you can relay this message to the rest of your fucking club. No underage kids--ever. I don't give a fuck who they are. No one touches a kid, and Renegade Sons do not beat or rape women. If I find out that members are continuing to do that shit, this club will be torn the fuck down."

I spend the next few minutes working him over with my fists and making sure that he hurts every bit as bad as the kid he was just abusing does. By the time I'm done, half the damn club is standing in the hallway watching the show go down. I look towards them until my gaze lands on Killer. As soon as our eyes meet, I toss Timmons' weakened body to the floor.

Lifting my finger towards Killer, I ground out, "Your son is a piece of shit. Judging by what's going down in the club, so are you."

He starts to say something, but I cut him off. "Save your excuses for my father. I'm done here."

I look towards Brew, the Mateland VP, before motioning to Rig's body. "Clean this mess up."

With those words lingering in the air, I leave the room and head out of the club. The first thing I see when I barrel through the thick double doors of the compound is that the girl is standing exactly where I told her to. I can tell just by looking at her that it's taking everything she has just to stay on her feet. As soon as I reach my bike, I swing onto it and look towards her. "Come on, darlin'. Climb on. Let's get you home."

She shakes her head and looks up at me with tear filled eyes. "I don't have a home anymore."

Her words cut me straight to the heart. "You do now."

Jenna

The man that saved me, the man I prayed for, pulls his bike

into a rest stop. When the engine shuts off, he looks back at me. "Jump off, darlin'."

As soon as I slide off the bike, my legs begin to buckle. He catches me before I hit the ground. "Easy girl, you got enough bruises already."

I nod my head and slowly back away from him. I look around at the deserted rest stop, and my fear starts to build. "Why did we stop here?" I ask in a shaky voice.

He swings his leg from the bike and takes a step towards me. "I can't stop somewhere that has people around with you wearing nothing but my shirt, and I knew you'd want to clean up a little. Also, I thought you might be hungry, so that's why we're here. They've got vending machines, so you can get you some chips and a drink. It ain't much, but it'll fill that hole in your belly."

I haven't eaten anything since early yesterday morning, and just the thought of food has my mouth watering. "Thank you."

He lifts his chin and turns to walk into the building. I trail behind him, my hunger overriding my fear. He motions towards the bathrooms. "Go ahead and get cleaned up. Ill grab you something from the machines."

I rush to the bathroom and do my best to scrub away the filth covering me. As soon as I'm done, I walk out of the bathroom and see the guy that took me away from Timmons talking to another man. As soon as I lay eyes on them, I freeze. Visions of what Timmons and Rig were just doing to me earlier re-play through my brain. The fight or flight instinct immediately kicks in, and without another thought, I start to run.

I barely make it a few feet away from them when a pair of strong arms surrounds me. I immediately start to fight him. I scratch at his hands while biting into his arm. It takes a few minutes before I realize that he isn't fighting back. He's just restraining me and doing his best to avoid hurting me. Finally, I admit defeat and go limp. Tears tumble down my face as harsh sobs begin to rock through my body.

My captor places his lips near my ear and whispers, "Shhh now, sweetheart. No one's going to hurt you."

I look over my shoulder towards the unfamiliar voice and see that it's not the man that helped me. "Who are you?"

Still whispering, he replies. "I'm Reese. I'm gonna make sure you get somewhere safe."

"I never told you my name either, did I, darlin'?" the man that saved me asks as he steps in front of us.

I shake my head in the negative.

"I'm Chipper," he says. "Now, it's your turn."

"I'm Jenna," I hesitantly reply.

"Okay, Jenna. I know you're scared as hell, and I don't

blame you, but I promise you, there's no reason for you to be scared anymore. I swear that you're safe with us."

Slowly, Reese releases me and takes a step back. Chipper walks towards me and hands me some chips and a drink. "Why don't you eat, and then we'll talk."

I take the food and walk to one of the wooden picnic tables at the front of the rest area. While I eat, I watch the two men talking. Both seem angry, and I'm not sure why. I don't think it's me that they're pissed at though. I hear Timmons' name said a time or two, and each time, Chipper seems to grow more agitated.

Two bags of Fritos and a Dr. Pepper later, Chipper leads me back to his bike. "We got to talk, darlin'."

"Okay," I whisper out.

"I know you've been through hell, and you probably don't feel like talking about this shit right now, but I need to know how in the hell you got to the Mateland clubhouse."

I look towards the ground and stay quiet, fearing the truth may cause him to send me back.

"I wouldn't ask if I didn't have to know," Chipper says in a calming voice, just as Reese walks up to stand beside him.

Chipper's gentle voice soothes some of my fears, but not all of them. I know I have to tell him something; I just have to choose what I say carefully. "My mom died. My dad didn't want me anymore, so he gave me to Timmons."

"Why did he do that?" he asks, sounding both confused and pissed.

Again, I stay quiet, but he doesn't. "Darlin', you don't have to be scared to tell me the truth. I'm not part of that club. I'm a Renegade, but I'm part of the original charter." He points towards the patch on his vest.

When I look at it and see the words Big Clifty, my heart starts to pound. I remember Timmons' words about drugs and the Big Clifty MC and know my Dad screwed over the wrong people. I quickly think about my options and decide to tell the truth, but not all of it. "My Dad got into some trouble with the Renegade Sons. He gave me to Timmons to protect himself."

"Fuck!" Reese hisses out.

"Who's your dad?" Chipper asks in an anger filled tone.

"David Brewster." I say, giving my father's middle name and praying he doesn't realize that my Dad is actually Brew, the Mateland VP.

I hate lying to the man that fought for me, but I don't have a choice. I know if he takes me back, I'll die. If he figures out who my dad is, then he'll probably feel obligated to take me back. So for now, I'll stick with half-truths.

"Any kin to Brew?"

Hearing my Dad's name sends bile up into my throat. I now have no choice but to flat out lie. "Brew? I'm not sure who that is."

I look back towards both men and see Reese's eyes flash. I can tell he knows I'm lying. I just hope he doesn't call me on it.

Chipper shrugs. "He's one of the brothers, but if you don't know him, I doubt you're related."

I stay quiet and look back to the ground. "What are you going to do with me?"

We stand there, no one saying anything for a long time. I can feel Chipper's stare while I wait for his answer. "Well, that's up to you. I can give you some money, and you can try to make it on your own. But I gotta be honest with you. It's hard as hell for a kid to be alone in the world, but there's another option."

I look up to him. "What's the other option?"

"My old lady's not been feeling too good lately. You could come home with me, help her around the house and shit. Stay with us for a while and decide what you want to do after you heal up."

I know I should take whatever money he gives me and run. I've learned the hard way never to trust a man, but for some reason, Chipper makes me feel safe. That's something I haven't felt in a long time, not ever really. Finally, I whisper out, "I'll go with you."

CHAPTER Two

Kidd

I'm sitting around the table with my Pop, the reigning
president and founding member of the Renegade Sons MC,
waiting on Chipper to get his ass home. He's been in Mateland
for two damn days now, and we still don't know exactly what's
going on down there. All we know for sure is that the Mateland
MC has been fucking up big time. The boys in California haven't
been getting their cocaine or weed shipments on time for the past
month. The last shipment they did receive was short; more than
short, actually. It was nearly cut in half. The Cali crew have
been pretty cool about it so far, but there's only so much shit
they'll take without making the boys in Mateland pay.

I've tried talking to Pop about it more than once, but he
isn't really saying anything. Then again, I'm not really sure what
he can say. There's no way you can explain away the shit that's
been going down lately. I and every other member of the club,
knows that Pop is the reason this bullshit has went on as long as

it has. He's close with Killer, the Mateland MC President. We all know their relationship is the only reason the charter wasn't cut loose years ago, but friends or not, the club has to come first. If Pop can't do that, then he needs to step his ass down. I don't want his position, but I will take it if I have to.

I'm pulled from my thoughts when Mindy comes in with two huge plates filled with creamy mashed potatoes, a huge rib eye, and one of her famous chocolate chip cookies. I look up at her and grin as she sets a plate in front of me. She sure is one hell of a woman. There's not one fuckin' green thing in sight. Her famous chocolate chip cookies are just icing on the cake.

I'm not ashamed to admit that I love this woman with all my heart. She's the sister I never had. "You didn't have to cook for us, darlin'. We could have sent one of the prospects to pick something up."

She lays her hand on my shoulder and smiles. "I love to cook, especially when I'm cooking for two of my favorite men."

I want to argue with her, to tell her she should be resting, but her smile seems so genuine that I end up smiling back and grabbing my fork. Chipper is one lucky son of a bitch to have a woman like Mindy. She's everything an old lady should be; sweet, sexy, and above all else, loyal.

I'm not sure what's going on with her, but she hasn't been herself lately. She's been sleeping a lot more and has lost some weight. I wanted to go to Mateland, instead of Chipper, because his ass should've been home taking care of Mindy, but Pop held me back. No doubt, he's worried I'd blow that fuckin' club up if I saw shit I didn't like.

I'm just about done with my plate when the front door crashes open. A second later, I hear Chipper yelling for Mindy. I can tell by the tone of his voice that something isn't right. I look to Pop, and we both jump up and head towards Chipper.

When we reach the club's common room, I see Chipper holding Mindy in his arms. I look around and notice a few of the members staring at them with surprised faces. At first, I don't see what the problem is, but then a movement behind Chipper catches my eye.

What I see shocks the shit out of me. There's a young girl standing silently behind Chipper, and judging by her size, I can tell that she should be at a pep rally, not a fucking MC. When I finally zero in on her face, my shock turns into fury. The little thing is covered in random streaks of dried blood from her head down to her toes. Her face is bruised and swollen. Her legs are bare, and the only thing that she's wearing is Chipper's shirt.

Before I can open my mouth and ask what the fuck's going on, Pop beats me to it. "What the fuck happened?"

The girl starts to shrink away, but Chipper puts his arm around her and pulls her close to his side. "It's okay, darlin'. You're safe here," he says quietly.

He then turns to his wife. "Mindy, can you take her and find some clothes, clean her up, and get a room ready for her? Make sure it's close to my old room. I got a lot of things to talk to Pop about, so we'll all be sleeping here tonight. But tomorrow, she'll be coming home with us."

"She's going home with us?" Mindy asks, looking as shocked as the rest of the room.

A determined look crosses Chipper's face, and then he leans down and whispers into Mindy's ear. Whatever he said leaves her looking like she's seen a ghost. She looks up to him and places her hand on his cheek. "Okay, love. I'll take care of your girl."

"Come with me, honey," she says softly, reaching her hand out to the shaken girl. The kid hesitates and looks to Chipper. As soon as my brother nods, she takes Mindy's hand.

As I watch her walk away, something comes over me; something I can't quite figure out. Even though she looks like she's had the shit beat out of her, her eyes unsettle me... there's just something about them. Something that calls to me in a way that I don't understand. Shaking off my thoughts of underage girls and their haunted eyes, I turn to Chipper to see that he's staring at Pop with anger etched onto his face, and I know he's about ready to blow.

"Pops, you're fucking lucky I had to get that girl outta that damn club, or I would have blown every last one of them bastards apart," he says angrily. "Do something about that fuckin' club, or I will!" he shouts.

Pops steps forward. "What happened?"

"What happened?" he shouts even louder. "I'll tell you what happened. Nearly every damn member was strung out on coke. There's no leadership, nothing's getting done. It was a complete cluster fuck."

"What about the girl? Who is she?" I ask, not giving Pop a chance to respond.

Chipper jerks his head towards me. "She's a sixteen year old kid that was being raped by members of the fucking club. Renegade Sons raping a kid…" He shakes his head. "It's a fucking disgrace."

Anger boils up inside me. We may be bikers, often crossing the line between right and wrong, but we don't rape women. We sure as hell don't rape little girls. "Who?"

"All I know is that her name is Jenna, and she doesn't have anywhere to go."

I shake my head in frustration. "No, I meant who the fuck was raping her?"

Chipper's body grows rigid as he looks towards Pop. He stares at him for a moment before looking back to me. "Rig was, but he won't be raping anyone else. I planted a bullet in his brain."

I can tell he's not telling me everything, but I don't get the chance to ask anything else before Pop motions for Chipper to follow him into his office.

Jenna

The woman, I'm assuming, is Chipper's old lady, leads me into a room at the back of the clubhouse. It's a lot bigger than the rooms at the Mateland MC, and it's sure as hell a lot cleaner. There's a bed in one corner and a small table with chairs in the other. It looks a lot like the rooms at the women's shelter that me and mom would stay in when she didn't have money for rent.

To say I'm scared is an understatement. In fact, I'm terrified. I can't stop myself from worrying that at any moment, someone is going to say that I have to go back to Timmons. I'm his now, right? He said I was his and that no one would ever be able to help me. They can't just take me away from him, can they?

"Here're some clothes. They may be a little big on you, but they'll do until we can get you something else," the woman says, handing me a pair of dark blue sweats, a black Harley T-shirt, and thick white socks. "Sorry, but I don't have any panties or a bra for you. We don't really keep women's clothing here, so you're going to have to go commando for a while."

"They're fine. Thank you," I whisper, taking the bundle

from her.

She gives me a sad smile and motions towards a door near the back of the room. "The bathroom's over there. While you take a shower, I'll grab you something to eat."

I nod and walk to the bathroom. As soon as I step into the room, I lock the door. I know that if someone really wants in, there's nothing I can do to keep them out, but the lock makes me feel a little safer. I can't forget that these are bikers, just like my dad and his brothers. There's no way they're going to help me for nothing. Everything always comes at a price with them.

I get out of my clothes as quickly as I can, throwing the purple nighty in the trash, and glad to be rid of the nasty thing. I fold Chipper's shirt, setting it beside the sink before stepping into the cool shower. I turn the stainless steel handle all the way over and put the hot water on blast, doing my best to let it scald the filth of Timmons and Rig off of me, the filth I couldn't fully get off at the rest stop. Grabbing the soap, I spend the next ten minutes scrubbing every inch of myself. By the time I'm done, my skin is red and burning, but I do feel somewhat better. I rush to dry off and get dressed, then run a brush through my tangled hair.

I'm just stepping out of the bathroom when Chipper's woman walks back in. She's carrying a plate piled high with food. "Good, you're done. Now, you can eat."

She motions me towards a chair and hands me the plate. "I

wasn't sure what you liked, so I brought you a little bit of everything."

"Thank you," I say as I sit down.

She stays and quietly watches me as I eat; each bite causing my jaw to ache even more. I'm not complaining though. I know that I'm lucky Timmons didn't completely break my jaw. He sure tried hard enough to. The proof of that's all over my face.

As soon as I set the plate on the table next to my chair, she gently grabs my hand. "My name is Mindy. I guess you already figured out that I'm Chipper's old lady."

I nod. "Yeah. I kind of figured that."

She laughs. "What's your name, sweetie?"

"Jenna."

"You want to tell me what happened to you, or do you want me to wait and hear it from Chipper? He told me a little, but I'm sure there's more to it."

In truth, I don't want to tell anyone what happened, but she's been nice to me, so I figure I owe her something. "Some guys were hurting me, and Chipper stopped them. He saved me, really. Problem is that I didn't have anywhere to go, so he brought me here."

"Hurting you?"

I know she wants me to tell her more, but that's just not

something I'm willing to do right now. Instead, I ask her the question that's been bothering me since Chipper and I pulled out of the Mateland MC parking lot. "What's he gonna do with me?"

A puzzled look crosses over her face. "What do you mean, do with you?"

I shrug. "Is he going to send me back?"

"There's no way my husband would send you back to a place where you were being hurt. Don't worry about that," she says, placing her other hand on top of our joined hands. "Where are your parents?"

"My dad...." What can I really say about my dad? It isn't like I can tell any of them my dad is the Vice President of the Mateland crew. "My dad doesn't want me. He never really did."

"And, your mom?"

"My mom is dead," I say, my voice sounding harsh even to my own ears.

"Do you have any other family?" she asks, giving my hand a soft squeeze.

I shake my head. "Not really. I know my mom's parents live out in Montana, but I've never met them. As far as I know, Mom hadn't talked to them since before I was born. I don't know anything at all about my dad's parents."

"No aunts or uncles?"

"Not that I know of. It was always just me and Mom," I say, trying in vain to think of someone, anyone that would care enough to take me in. "I have no one."

"That's not true."

I jerk my eyes up to meet hers. "Yes, it is. No one cares whether I live or die."

She gives my hand another squeeze as a soft smile crosses her face. "When my husband brought you here tonight, he was claiming you as his."

I shake my head in denial. "No way. Nuh uh. You're his old lady! He can't claim me!"

"I meant that he claimed you as family, so that means you're my family too. I've always wanted a daughter."

Her words are like a balm to my soul. "I always wanted a real mother." I say quietly.

CHAPTER Three

Jenna

I'm sitting at the kitchen table, looking out the window and reflecting on how much my life has changed over the past few weeks. I've been in Big Clifty for nearly a month now, and I still can't believe that I've been saved. First of all, I have a real home with Mindy and Chipper. It's not a huge place, but it looks like a mansion compared to the shitholes that mom and me lived in.

Secondly, my dad and Timmons aren't even looking for me, although I'm pretty sure they know where I am. All that really matters is that they haven't come to get me yet, and I'm starting to think that they never will. To be honest, I never really thought Dad would come for me, but a big part of me feared that Timmons would. I guess he didn't want me as bad as I thought he did, thank God.

Timmons and Killer were the only two members of the Renegade Sons I knew before I went to the clubhouse. They used to stop by my Mom's every once in a while looking for Dad. Killer was an okay guy. He never bothered me when he came over. I've been afraid of Timmons since I was just a little girl, though. I can't really explain why, but I just knew there was something weird about him. Then five years ago, he started making me touch him. I was only eleven years old at the time, and he was in his late twenties. That's when I realized that he wasn't just weird, he was a complete sicko.

When I first walked into Mateland MC, I was a virgin. Timmons stole that from me the first night. I was sure nothing could have hurt worse than that, but he proved to me that I was wrong. The other things he did to me made the first rape seem like a walk in the park, especially that first week when he kept me locked in his room, only coming in when he wanted to hurt me.

Eventually, he decided that he'd share me with Rig. I hate to admit it, but Rig wasn't all that bad. He never used his fists on me, and he made sure I had food and water. That's a hell of lot more than I can say for Timmons. To him, a fist in the face was a love tap.

Rig took the time to show me around the club. I was surprised to see other girls the same age as me there; a few of them I even knew from school. They'd quit a while back, and I hadn't seen them since. I naively assumed that they had moved away, but I never even considered the thought that they were stuck in this hell hole right along with me. As soon as I saw them, I wanted to do something to help them, but how could I when I couldn't even help myself.

Rig occasionally let me talk to some of the girls when I behaved well. He said that they could teach me the ropes, but what they really taught me was to run if I ever got the chance. The longer I stayed at the club, the more I learned. A few of the girls were even younger than me; the youngest one barely being thirteen. She looked like a little kid, but her eyes were dull and void from the loss of her innocence. Some of the girls claimed they were there willingly, and even went as far as to say that they loved their old man, but more than a few were being held against their will, just like me.

Before the night Dad gave me to Timmons, I had my life mapped out: turn eighteen, get my mom and me out of the little trailer we lived in, and run as far away as we could. But, finding Mom dead on the kitchen floor changed all of that. I should have been smart. I should have packed up and ran away from that piece of shit town as soon as I laid eyes on her cold, lifeless body. Instead, I made the ultimate error of running straight to my Dad, which has, so far, been the biggest mistake of my life.

Losing hope as the weeks passed, I didn't think I'd ever get out of that clubhouse. The day Chipper found me being raped and humiliated by two disgusting men, I knew I was going to be free. I wasn't sure how, and I never would've thought he'd be the one to do what he did, but I knew in my gut as soon as I saw him that he was my savoir. Chipper not only saved me, but he also gave me a home and a family; a place where I felt safe and loved for the first time in my entire life.

It took some getting used to at first, because I'd never had a true home or a place where I felt that I was wanted. It was all so new to me, and in the beginning, I was convinced that it would all come crashing down at any given time. I was scared to death of all of the bikers, because something inside of me just knew that one of them would try to hurt me. But the truth of the matter is that no one ever did. In fact, Chipper's younger brother, Kidd, has even become one of my best friends.

Kidd was there when I first arrived, and he has made a point to come over to Chipper and Mindy's nearly every day since. I may be only sixteen, but I'm not blind. That man is just... wow. He has dark blonde hair and clear blue eyes, pretty much every girl's dream. He may be nearly ten years older than me, but there's something about him; something different from all of the rest. Just being around him puts my nerves at ease.

Last night, I finally told Mindy that I had a big ol' crush on Kidd, which is something I thought would never happen after what Timmons did to me. I thought she would be shocked or even a little mad, maybe even scream at me for falling for a twenty-six year old man, but she didn't. All she said was that I had to wait till I turned eighteen before I even thought about being with him.

Mindy told me all about Kidd; how he stepped up and took Chipper's place as VP. Chipper is seven years older than Kidd, so everyone always assumed he'd take Gun's place as president when the time came. Mindy says that Chipper stepped down to spend more time with her. I think there's more to it than that, but I don't know what yet, and honestly, it's none of my business.

I'm still thinking about Kidd when Mindy walks into the kitchen and pulls me out of my thoughts. She smiles as soon as she sees me, but her smile doesn't fully reach her eyes. I can tell she isn't feeling well again today. "Hey, sweetie. You want some breakfast?"

I shake my head. "Nah. I'm not hungry."

She walks over to me and pushes the hair from my face. "If you're not hungry, why are you sitting in the kitchen?"

"I got up, and you were still sleeping. I figured I'd sit in here until you woke up. I didn't want to turn on the TV and disturb you." I shrug, not wanting to tell her that I heard her getting sick last night, and I knew she needed to get all the rest she could. She also needs to get to the doctor, but there's no damn way I'm going to say that. I've heard her and Chipper fighting over going to the doctor too many times.

He wants her to see someone, someone that knows a little

more than the quack at the clinic in town, but she refuses. She says that if something was really wrong with her, then her doctor would have figured it out by now. Mindy is a smart woman, but I'm siding with Chipper on this one. I'm just too nervous to voice my opinion about it.

She bends down and places a soft kiss on my cheek. "That was sweet of you, but you could've turned on the TV. I can sleep through anything. It wouldn't have bothered me."

I smile back and stand up. "Do you want me to make you some breakfast?"

She shakes her head. "No, I'm the mom here, remember? I'm the one that cooks."

"I made my mom breakfast a bunch of times."

Her brows tighten and anger flashes in her eyes. "I know you did, but that's not happening here."

Mindy was not at all happy when I told her about my mom. She didn't like that Mom had me do all the cooking and cleaning around the house. I tried to explain that my mom just didn't feel good most of the time, and it wasn't her fault, but Mindy refused to listen. Ready to change the subject, I smile. "Fine, Mom. What do you want to do today?"

A smile flashes across her face as soon as I say mom. She loves when I call her that. At first, it felt kind of foolish to be calling a woman I've only know for a little while Mom. She seems to like it though, and she's been a way better mother to me than mine ever thought about being.

"Why don't you go watch some TV? I'm going to stick a pot roast in the crock pot for dinner tonight, and then we can veg out on the sofa."

I smile and place a kiss on her flushed cheek. "Sounds good to me," I say as I make my way to the living room.

Kidd

I walk into Chipper and Mindy's and see Jenna sitting on the sofa watching TV. I smile as soon as I lay eyes on her. I can't seem to stay away from the kid. She just draws me to her in a way that I don't really understand. She's a pretty little thing. You can see she's going to be a beautiful lady someday. She's got shoulder length black hair that sometimes looks blue in the right light, and she has the biggest eyes that I've ever seen. They're the color of freshly brewed coffee and look a little too big for her face. Her body is long and lean. She's the tallest sixteen year old girl I've ever seen. Even so, there's no denying she's just a kid. There isn't a womanly curve on her body. How some sick fucker could touch her, I'll never know, but I can guarantee that it won't happen again.

Jenna's still quiet most of the time. Who wouldn't be after what she's been though? But when you get her to open up she's funny as hell. Her laugh, I swear, I've never heard anything more beautiful in my life. I've never had a little sister, but I think if I did, she'd be just like Jenna. "What'cha watching, kiddo?"

Her whole face lights up when she sees me. "Charmed. Cole is like such a babe. You want to watch with me? I'm a girl and all, but even I think Phoebe is pretty hot."

I shake my head and shoot her a smile. "I don't think so. I was hoping you might want to go for a ride."

"Yes!" she shrieks before jumping up and running towards her room. Within seconds, she's back, carrying her shoes in one hand and her jacket in the other. "I'm ready."

I laugh before answering. "Don't you think your shoes would work better if you put them on your feet?"

She smiles again and places her shoes on the floor. She quickly pulls them on her feet then stands back up. "Now, I'm ready."

Before I can respond, Mindy walks out of the kitchen. "Where are you two going?"

I walk over to my sister-in-law and place a soft kiss on her forehead. "I figured I'd take the kid out for a ride, maybe go over to Drexel and grab some lunch."

"Hey, I'm not a kid." Jenna shouts from behind me as she walks closer to us. "I'm almost seventeen."

Mindy laughs at Jenna before responding. "You'll be seventeen in four months."

"Like, I said, I'm almost seventeen," Jenna says with a smile.

Mindy and I both look at her and laugh at the same time. By the time we're finished, Jenna's face is red. I can't tell if it's from anger or embarrassment. Either way, I can tell it's time to hit the road. I reach out and curl my hand around her neck and pull her towards me. "Come on, Jenna. Let's get going."

Before we walk out the door, I have to listen to Mindy's rules. Jenna better be wearing a helmet, I better not go over the speed limit, and I have to have her home before dark. I guess I'm not the only one that's grown attached to the girl.

After promising Mindy that I'll keep her girl safe, Jenna and I jump on my bike and make it to Drexel in less than an hour. As we walk towards Mimi's café, I hear Jenna's stomach growl. I chuckle and look down to her. "You hungry, girl?"

She smiles. "I wasn't, but I am now."

I wrap my arm around her shoulders and lead her into Mimi's. "That's good, cause this place has the best damn food I've ever ate."

"I thought you said that Mindy made the best food you've ever ate?" she asks with a giggle.

"Well, I did. As far as Mindy will ever know, it is. If she

thinks I've been bragging on someone else's cooking, she may stop inviting me over for dinner every night."

Jenna swings her hip into my leg, giving me a little nudge. "I won't tell her that you said her cooking sucked."

I step back and put my hands up in front of me. "Hey, now. I didn't say that."

She giggles again and walks to a table. "Since you're nice enough to bring me to eat the best food ever, I won't rat you out."

I chuckle as I join her at the table. As soon as I sit down, a cute little brunette walks up to the table. "Hey, guys. What can I get you two?"

Jenna starts to look through her menu, but I jerk it away from her and hand it to the waitress. "Give us two country fried steaks with mashed potatoes and gravy. Oh, add two sweet teas too."

"Alright, I'll be back with your drinks," she quips before bouncing back to where she came from.

I watch the waitress wiggle her tight little ass as she walks away, and for a brief moment, I wish that I hadn't brought Jenna with me.

"I wanted a burger."

I jerk my eyes towards Jenna, and thoughts of the waitress

and her sweet ass fade away. "You don't come to Mimi's for a burger. You come for her country fried steak."

Jenna's eyes narrow in my direction as she places her hands flat on the table and leans towards me. "But, I wanted a burger, onions rings, and a big ol' chocolate milk shake."

"Too bad. I'm buying, so I get to order you whatever the hell I want to."

"Fine, but it better be good," she says before sticking her tongue out at me.

Within minutes, our food is on the table and we're devouring it. When I notice that Jenna's plate is nearly empty, I shoot her a big smile. "You still wanting that burger?"

She shakes her head and smiles. "Nope, but I could still use a chocolate milk shake."

I look back to her empty plate that just moments ago held enough food to feed a small army then throw my head back and laugh.

"You eat any more and you'll bust a gut," I say as I stand up and reach inside my jeans. I throw some cash on the table and motion for Jenna to follow me. "Come on. Let's get out of here."

CHAPTER Four

Jenna

I'm standing in front of my mirror, putting on make-up and thinking about Kidd. He's taken me riding a few times over the last couple of weeks. Spending time with Kidd is awesome. I have so much fun; more fun than I've ever had before. We don't do much other than go out to eat and ride around town on his bike, but it is still a blast. Just being with him is amazing. I only wish that he'd quit looking at me like a kid and see me for the woman I am. I know that most people wouldn't consider a sixteen year old a woman, but I figure I've been through more than most grown-ups ever have.

I've just finished putting on my lipstick when Chipper walks into my room. "Are you ready yet?"

I lay my make-up bag on my dresser and turn to him. "I sure am."

We're heading over to the clubhouse for their annual Easter egg hunt. When Mindy first told me about it, I was shocked. As far as I know, my Dad's club never did anything with the families of their members, but Mindy says the Renegade Sons always make time for their families. They do Christmas parties, Thanksgiving dinners, Fourth of July cook outs, and even let the kids come to the clubhouse to trick-or-treat.

Chipper looks up and down my body, and then narrows his eyes at me. "Where the hell is the rest of your dress?"

I look down at my skirt and shake my head. What? I'm wearing a blue skirt that stops right above my knees and a white sweater that's covered with small blue flowers. "What's wrong with my skirt?"

"There's nothing wrong with your skirt, hon." Mindy says, as she walks into the room.

He turns to her and points to my legs. "It damn near shows her ass."

She giggles back at his frustrated face, sounding like a school girl. "No, Dad. It doesn't."

Chipper starts to argue more, but Mindy narrows her eyes and quickly cuts him off. "She looks pretty as a picture, doesn't she?"

He stares at Mindy for a few more seconds then turns back to me and pastes on a fake smile. "She sure does."

"Then that's all that matters. Our girl sure is a beauty, huh?"

Mindy walks over to me, grabs my hand, and leads me from the room. Chipper follows begrudgingly behind us, mumbling about his little girl flashing her legs. I look towards Mindy and see a smile cross her face. She leans towards me and whispers, "Don't worry about him. He's just worried that some of the guys will notice how beautiful you are, but you could be wearing his old Iron Maiden tee-shirt with baggy jeans, and they'd still notice you."

I smile back at her then walk towards the door, not caring if any of the guys at the club look at me; which is a bold face lie, because I'm secretly hoping that Kidd notices me.

During the ride to the clubhouse, I imagine what his face will look like when he sees me. I know I might not compare to the other women in his life, but I think I look pretty exceptional today. I hope he thinks so too.

As soon as I get out of the car, I see Kidd. He's sitting at one of the picnic tables with a blonde chick straddling his lap. Seeing him with her brings a rush of tears to my eyes. I turn away, hoping to wipe the evidence of my hurt away before anyone notices, but I know that I failed when I feel Mindy slide her arm around me. "Don't let them see you cry, sweet pea. Wipe your eyes, put a smile on that pretty face of yours, and pretend it doesn't matter."

I lean into her, placing my head on her shoulder. "It shouldn't bother me."

"Bullshit. You can't control your feelings."

I look towards her and smile sadly. "He thinks of me as his sister. Why can't I think of him as a brother?"

She squeezes my waist and smiles back to me. "Like I said, darling, you can't control your feelings."

I feel her body tighten as she looks over her shoulder to see who's coming up behind us. Kidd's walking towards us with a big smile on his face, the blonde trailing close behind. When he gets close, he grabs me and pulls me in for a bear hug. He then leans down and kisses Mindy's cheek. "How's my girls?"

Mindy grabs my hand and pulls me back towards her. "We're good. Jenna just got some dust or something in her eye, so I was helping her get it out."

He looks at my face then places his thumb under my eyes and wipes my tears away. "Did you get it?"

I'm so focused on the feeling of his fingers on my skin that I don't answer, but Mindy does. "Yeah, we're all good now."

He starts to say something, but stops when the blonde walks over and wraps her arm around him. "Hey, baby. You going to introduce me to your friends?" she says while shooting me an evil glare.

"This here's my girl, Jenna," Kidd says, giving me a wink. Then he looks towards Mindy and smiles. "And this is my sister-in-law, Mindy."

The blonde ignores Mindy and zeroes in on me. "So, you're his niece?"

Hearing myself labeled as a member of his family causes my stomach to roll. I love when Mindy and Chipper call me their daughter, but I don't want Kidd to think of me as his niece. I stay quiet, hoping someone else will explain the situation to the bitch that's still giving me the evil eye.

Luckily, Kidd does. "She's not really my niece. More like a little sister."

His words send bile into my throat. I look up to see that the blonde is now smiling at me in a way that sends chills down my spine. "How nice. A little sister," she says, emphasizing the word little.

Mindy pulls me closer to her, gradually pushing me slightly behind her back. She smirks at the woman and says, "Yeah, but she won't be little too much longer. Ain't that right, Kidd?"

Kidd looks between Mindy and the blonde, a puzzled expression crossing his face. He's about to say something, no doubt ask what in the hell's going on, when the woman beside him goes up on her tiptoes and whispers in his ear.

His eyes flash bright, and a smile that I've never seen on him before spreads across his face as he looks towards the blonde before turning back to us. "You guys have fun. I know I'm going to." Without even saying goodbye, he turns away and walks to the clubhouse with the blonde on his arm.

Mindy and I stand there quietly for a while longer before she pulls me to the clubhouse. "Come on, girl. Shake it off, and let's have some fun."

Kidd

I throw my head back and pump the last of my release down the chick's throat. I look down at her and start to run my fingers through her hair, but stop when I realize it's a dingy blonde color and not the shiny black hair that I'd been picturing in my mind. Fuck! What the hell is wrong with me? Jenna is sixteen years old; way too fucking young for me to even be imagining having my dick in her mouth.

I push the girl off my junk and stand up. I jerk my jeans up, zipping them as I take a step away. Looking down at her, I feel nothing but disgust and can't keep the snarl off of my face.

"Thanks."

I start to walk away, but stop when the blonde lays her hand on my arm. "No reason to run off, baby. We could make a night of it."

I shake her hand off, not bothering to look at her. "Sorry, I got other things to do."

She snorts and says, "Yeah, like running after your little

sister."

I stop and turn to look at her. "What did you say?"

It's one thing to admit to myself that I'm fantasizing about Jenna, but it's completely different when someone else notices that I am.

"You heard me. This big biker boy wants a little girl instead of a woman," she says, sticking her chest out to show me her generous cleavage. "What's your problem? Can't handle the real thing?"

Without thinking, I rush towards her and grab her around the neck. Slamming her into the wall, I place my face inches from hers. "You're gonna shut your mouth right now, or you'll never walk out of this club alive."

Her face starts to turn a deep shade of red as she panics and claws at my hands. "Let me go," she gasps out.

Ignoring her pleas, I squeeze her throat tighter to make my point even more clear. "If I ever hear that you've said that shit to anyone else, I will find you. When I do, I'll bury your ass. Do you understand me?"

She does her best to nod, barely choking out the word yes. When I feel that she gets me, I let go of her throat and walk away, doing my best to shake off my own shame. I've got to get away from here before I do something I'm gonna regret; something that'll cause Jenna even more pain, and God knows she's been through enough of that.

I stomp out of my room and head straight to the common room, hoping a drink can wash away my anger. I step up to the bar and shout at the prospect handing out drinks. "I want a bottle of Jack and a glass."

Before he can even get my much needed bottle to me, Pop comes up and tells me that he needs to talk. I abandon my drink and follow him to the office, only to see that Chipper's sitting on the couch, looking pissed as hell. I look towards Pop and ask, "What's up?"

He motions towards Chipper and replies, "He refuses to go back to Mateland. Says he has to stay around here to take care of his wife."

Thinking back on how pale Mindy looked earlier, I agree. "I don't blame him. Everyone knows that Mindy hasn't been feeling great here lately. She doesn't need to be alone right now."

"The stray he brought home last time he was in Mateland could take care of her. It's not like she's doing much else," he growls out.

Hearing Pop call Jenna a stray sends my already simmering anger to its boiling point. "She's not a fucking stray! She's a kid."

"If you had your way, she'd have been sent back by now,"

Chipper says as he jumps up and gets in Pop's face. "What the fuck happened to you? When did you get to the point that you don't even care about an abused kid? When did you get so damn cold?"

Pop snarls at him. "I got enough to deal with without dealing with her shit too."

"How many times have I told you to let me deal with it? Let me kill the motherfucker," Chipper shouts. "I promise that not one fucking soul will be able to track it back to you."

"What the hell are you talking about?" I shout, trying to gain their attention. "I thought you said you put a bullet in Rig."

Pop and Chipper turn to look at me. Both of them seem shocked that I'm standing here, so caught up in their argument that they forgot I was in the room. "Again, what the fuck are you talking about?"

"Nothing," Pop answers.

I raise a brow. "Didn't sound like nothing to me?"

"Yeah, nothing," Chipper mumbles as he sits back down.

Pop ignores him and walks over to his safe. He pulls out a few stacks of cash; at least ten grand. He walks over to me and pushes it towards me. "I want you to go Mateland. Get their shit straight and set someone up to run the club. Killer will remain president, but someone else will hold the power. Make sure whoever you pick can keep their ass out of trouble and their nose clean."

I shake my head and motion towards the money. "What the hell's that for?"

Pop pulls in a deep breath then looks towards Chipper. Finally, he replies, "It's gonna take some cash to get them out of this mess. I'm not sure how much, but I know that's just a drop in the bucket. I'll send more in a few weeks, but I don't want you carrying too much with you when you first get there."

I finally take the money, wondering what in the fuck I'm getting into. "When do you want me to leave, and how long do you want me to stay."

"You leave tonight, and you stay until you get their shit straight."

Chipper gets up and walks towards me. He places his hand on my shoulder and leans close to me. "Be prepared, brother. There's some serious shit going on inside that club."

With that, he walks out of Pop's office. I look towards Pop and start to question him, but stop when I realize that I'm not going to get any straight answers from him. He's so far up his own ass, there's no point in trying to set him straight. Where Killer is concerned, Pop's ain't going to tell me shit, so I decide to find the prospect that Chipper brought back from Mateland and get some intel on my own.

It takes me a few minutes to find Reese. When I do, I see

that he's helping his daughter open up all of her plastic eggs. I look around, wondering where his old lady is off to, but naturally she's not anywhere in sight. Knowing that slut, she's probably spreading her legs for one of the members' right this very moment, while her baby girl is having the time of her life playing with little plastic eggs. Bitch. Members don't fuck other member's old ladies, but prospect's old ladies are fair game. Well, only when they're down with it. Reese's woman, Roxy, is always up for a roll.

I've asked myself more than once in the past few weeks why in the hell doesn't Reese get shot of the bitch? Looking at his daughter, I have my answer. I continue my way toward them, crouching down to see her stash. "Did you get a bunch of candy?"

"I got a lot." The gap-toothed red headed girl smiles up to me. "I even got twenty whole dollars in the golden egg that the Easter bunny hid in my Dad's pocket."

I reach out and tousle her hair. "That's great, Pebbles."

She scrunches up her nose. "My name's not Pebbles. I'm Rosalie."

"You look just like Pebbles Flintstone to me, so you'll always be my Pebbles."

Reese chuckles as he bends down to give his girl a kiss on the top of her head. "Why don't you go show Mindy and Jenna your candy, yeah?"

"Sure, Dad," she says, before giving him a quick hug around the neck. She then runs towards the picnic tables that all the old ladies are sitting at.

We watch her run away and laugh at her excitement. I look back towards Reese and smile. "She's a cute little thing."

"Sure is. I can't believe she's nearly ten." He looks at me with a proud smile on his face. "I know she's too old for all this Easter bunny shit. She doesn't believe in it anymore, but I wanted to have just one more year."

"I understand" I say, nodding.

"I saw that face you were wearing when you walked up. I know you didn't come over here to talk about my kid. What's up?"

I shake my head then tell him about my upcoming trip to Mateland. I ask him what his take is on the shit that's going down with the Mateland MC. Reese ends up telling me everything that he knows about the MC, which isn't much, but it's enough to make my stomach clench. Underage girls, drugs, and trouble with the local police are just a few of the shit storms that the club's dealing with. All in all, it's too much shit for one person to handle.

"Fuck!" I say, running my hands through my hair. "What in the hell am I going to do?"

"Nothing on your own. You need to take a crew with you. Men that know how to use their fists, but aren't afraid of using fire power when needed."

"What about you?" I ask.

He looks towards his daughter, anxiety flashing across his face. "I'd go man, but things didn't go very good the last time I left Rosalie alone."

I take a second to consider my options then lay my plan out to him. "What if she stays with Mindy and Chipper while you're gone? You could come back every few weeks and talk to her on the phone every day."

"I could do that, but I don't know if Mindy's up for taking care of her."

"Jenna will be there too. She'll help."

He finally nods in agreement. "That could work."

Within ten minutes, we've got it all settled. Mindy quickly agreed, seeming to be excited to have another kid in the house. Chipper seemed a little reluctant at first, but he relented as soon as he saw the excitement on Mindy's face.

Jenna walks up, holding Pebbles hand, just as Reese and Mindy are ironing out the detailing. "What'cha talking about?"

A huge smile crosses Mindy's face as she explains. "Rosalie is going to be staying with us for a while."

"That's cool." Jenna says, looking down to Pebbles. "You can share my room with me."

Pebbles seems excited about staying with Jenna, but her apprehension comes through when she looks at her dad. "Where are you going?"

Reese lays his hands on her head. "I'm going with Kidd on a road trip."

"How long will you be gone?"

He crouches down in front of her. "I'm not sure, but I'll come home to visit you as much as I can."

She continues to question her dad, but I don't hear a word she says. Instead, I'm stuck on Jenna's reaction. She looks like she's about to cry. It's the same look she had on her face earlier. I see Mindy grab her hand and give it a squeeze, and I know it's more than just a piece of dust in her eye.

I walk over to her and drop my arm around her shoulder, pulling her into my side. "What's wrong, baby doll?"

"Where are you going?"

I have to tell her, because I know if I don't, someone else will. I hate having to bring up bad memories for her. "I'm heading up to Mateland."

As soon as the word leaves my mouth, her face turns white. "Why are you going there?"

"I can't tell you that."

She nods. "How long will you be gone?"

I bend down and kiss the top of her head. "Not long, I promise."

Jenna

Kidd said he wanted to take me out for one more ride before he left. It was fun, but it was also sad. I know it could very well be the last ride I ever take with him.

"I'm gonna miss you," I say as I climb off of his bike for the last time.

"I won't be gone long, darlin'," Kidd says, smothering me in a warm bear hug.

"I don't know why you're the one that has to go," I say for the hundredth time in the last two hours. Not only is Kidd, my best friend, leaving me, but he's going to Mateland. I don't know much about what's going on, but the little I do know is from hearing Chipper and Mindy talk. Neither one of them is happy about sending Kidd four hours away to handle someone else's shit, especially Mateland's shit.

My biggest fear is that Kidd will figure out who I really am while he's there. If he learns about my dad and figures out that Timmons claimed me in the past, he may have to send me back.

I don't think he'd want to, but I'm not sure he'd have much of a choice. He's loyal to the club to a fault. Even though mom and I were kept away from the club, I still know for a fact that the club doesn't interfere with a member's personal life. If Kidd didn't give me back, he would be sticking his nose somewhere that it didn't belong and going against everything he believes in.

I have to fight myself to keep from begging him not to go. I don't want to lose Kidd, and I don't want to see the look on his face when he finds out about my past. I've grown to love Kidd over the last few months, but Mindy says that it's just puppy love and I'll grow out of it as I get older. But deep down, I know she's wrong.

I also know Kidd doesn't feel the same way as I do. He thinks of me as a sister. Hell, he even introduced me as his little sis today. I can't help but wish that his opinion will change of me someday, but I know that's not going to happen if he goes to Mateland. I pull in a deep breath and try to be brave. "Will you call me?"

He gives me a tight squeeze. "You know I will, baby doll.I'll do my best to call you at least once a week. If I'm lucky, it won't take but a month or two, and then I'll be home."

I nod and pull away from him. "Well, go on then. Quit being such a cry baby."

A sad smile crosses his face and he lifts his hand to wipe the stray tears from my face.

"See-ya soon, Jenna."

As soon as he starts to ride away, I run into the house and go straight to my room. I plant myself on my bed and break into sobs. I'm crying so loud that I don't hear my door open. I don't even notice Mindy until she sits beside me. She pulls me into her arms and whispers, "Quit crying, sweetheart. He'll be home before you know it."

I shake my head then burrow deeper into her arms. "You don't understand. He's going to send me back."

She squeezes me so tightly that she takes my breath away. "There is no way Kidd would ever do that."

"He won't have a choice."

She pulls back and places her hands on my face, moving it so she can look into my eyes. "What are you talking about?"

"I'm Timmons' old lady," I say between sobs.

"What?" She asks in a near shout.

"Timmons told everyone that I was his old lady, so Kidd will have to send me back to him. It's club rules," I try to explain, still crying.

Mindy's body starts to shake with anger. "Jenna girl, you listen to me. You are sixteen years old. You're not old enough to be anyone's old lady. If Timmons so much as mentions that he's claimed you, Kidd will kill him."

I shake my head, not understanding. "But there are a lot of girls there who are my age. Some of them are even younger. They wear tattoos with members' names on them and everything," I say, motioning toward the 'Property of Chipper" tattoo that Mindy proudly displays on her arm.

The anger on her face is replaced with shock. "Oh, sweet Lord."

She jumps up and starts to pace the room. "Did Chipper know about this?"

I don't get a chance to respond before she answers her own question. "Of course, he didn't. If he did, the club would've been burned to the ground."

I stay quiet as she continues to pace back and forth alongside my bed. I want to tell her to calm down, especially since she doesn't need to be so upset. It isn't good for her. She's been so sick the last week that she's barely gotten out of bed. I'm not sure what's wrong with her, but whatever it is, it has to be bad. Thank God, Chipper finally convinced her to go to the doctor. She went in and had some tests a few days ago, and she has to go back Monday for the results. I want to go with her, but Chipper said he's going. For some reason, they don't want me there. At first, it hurt my feelings, but then I realized they were trying to protect me. That's when I really got scared.

Mindy walks towards me, bringing my thoughts back to the situation at hand. "Don't say anything about Timmons to anyone. Let Kidd deal with it."

"What if he has no choice but to send me back?" I ask, fear running thick through my voice.

She shakes her head. "That won't happen."

"But, what…." I start to ask again, but she quickly cuts me off.

"If anyone tries to take you from me, we will run so fucking far away that no one will ever find us," she says defiantly before pulling me from the bed and into her arms.

CHAPTER Five

Kidd

I spend most of my ride to Mateland thinking about Jenna. Getting away from Big Clifty might be a good thing, 'cause Lord knows that I need some space from her. She's too fuckin' young for me. The fucked up part is I still want her. The more I'm around her, the more I feel the need to claim her. Fuck! I feel like a damn pervert just thinking about that shit.

I also spent a good portion of time thinking about Mindy, and hoping she'll get better while I'm gone. I don't know what in the fuck is wrong with her, but I know it ain't just a damn cold like she says it is. Colds don't last for months and months on end. Every time I've looked at her over the last few weeks, I think of Ma.

After Ma died, Mindy took care of all of us. Her and Chipper were already together when Ma first got sick, but he hadn't claimed her yet. After Mindy spent months cleaning up

Ma's puke, there was no fucking way Chipper was going to let her go back to being a club whore.

Chipper has always had a thing for older women, so it wasn't much of a shock when he fell for Mindy, who is ten years older than him. They tried for a long time to have kids on their own. They even tried In-Vitro, which cost them out the ass, but no matter what they did, Mindy never could get pregnant. After it was all said and done, Mindy just had to come to terms with the fact that she'd never have a baby. Having Jenna in her life is a blessing for her, really. Jenna ain't really much of a kid, but at least Mindy has someone to mother now.

When I finally reach the MC, the guard at the gate gives me hell about coming in. I swear the motherfucker had to get permission in the compound before he opened the gates. I'm the fucking Vice President of the original club. I have more power than any of these dickheads here. Someone my age being the VP of a club is kind of fuckin' rare, but that's beside the point.

Chipper held my seat before me, but he stepped down a few months before he came to Mateland. He said it was too much shit for him, especially with Mindy being sick. Having the VP duties, he missed a lot of time with her over the years, and he didn't want to miss any more. Pop was pissed, because he wanted Chipper to be the Pres when his time is up, but Chipper didn't give a fuck. He refused to listen to Pop and seems happier for it.

When the motherfucker finally lets Reese, Preach, and me through the gate, I jump off my bike and stomp to him. "You ever lock me out of one of my clubs again, I will put a bullet in your fucking brain. Do you understand what I'm saying, brother?" I shout with a sneer.

"This is Killer's club," he says with more attitude than I like.

I grab him by his cut and pull him towards me. "I'm next in line to hold the fucking gavel. This clubhouse, and every other one that flies under the Renegade Sons flag, is mine."

With those words, I send my fist into his face. I then turn around and walk into the clubhouse. There's a party going on, but I don't see anything that pisses me off; none of the shit that Chipper and Reese told me about. Sure, there are a few brothers smoking weed, but no coke or heroine are to be seen. There's also plenty of club pussy wandering around, but none that looks like the underage variety. Then again, we sat outside of the gate for nearly twenty minutes just waiting to get in this bitch. A lot of shit could disappear in that amount of time.

As I walk further into the clubhouse, I see Brew and Killer sitting over by the bar. Brew has a woman between his legs, not giving a fuck that he's getting sucked off while he's chattin' it up with his president; the same president who's fingering a chick that's sitting on top of the bar and moaning like a bitch in heat. I shake my head at their behavior. These old men are sick fuckers.

At least in my club, the men don't talk the shit with each other while fuckin' with a whore.

I walk over to them, my men following close behind. I yank the hood of my sweatshirt down off my head. "Hey boys," I say, sliding up to the bar and shouting for a whiskey. They don't stop what they're doing with the women as they turn their heads my way.

"Hey, my boy. How was the road?" Killer says, giving my shoulder a hard smack with his free hand.

Killer and my Pop are friends, have been for years. They started this club together. Along with Timber's dad, who runs a charter down in California; the same charter this club has been fucking around. The three of them were in the same unit in Vietnam back in the day. My Pop says you don't know what real friends are until it's you and them against a sea of bullets.

"You know me. I love to ride. How's the Old Lady?" I say, just to see if it'll piss him off. Of course, it doesn't. I'll never understand how some men can fuck around after they choose to spend their life with one woman. Sure, I get that a man needs some relief when he's away from home, but making use of road pussy is completely different than fingering a rabid bitch, especially when your wife's just right down the road.

"Lanie's good. She's home with the kids. You'll see her while you're here. She says to let you know that she'll be making some of her bacon wrapped meatloaf for you on

Sunday," he says then motions to the woman on the bar. "But this bitch here's keeping my dick warm tonight. Ain't ya, sweet cheeks?"

"Yeah, Killer baby. Lanie's pussy ain't good enough for you tonight," she says, moaning out. Killer laughs, but it's not a pleasant sound. He yanks his fingers outta her, then grabs her arm and jerks her down off the bar.

"Looks like this bitch needs to find out what her mouth is meant for, because it's sure as hell's not meant to be spewing out shit about my old lady. We're gonna hit the sack. Feel free to enjoy whatever you want, Kidd," he says, dragging the girl with him.

I hear Brew chuckle, "That bitch'll be gone by sunrise. He'll fuck her good, then she'll be eighty sixed if she's lucky, dead if she not. My guess is he'll kill her after what she said about his old lady."

I have no doubt Brew's right. In fact, I'm surprised Killer didn't punch the girl's lights out as soon as the words left her mouth. I would have. Club girls don't get much shit from the members. We treat them all pretty good, but they have to learn to follow rules if they don't want to get hurt. One of the most important rules is that whores never talk shit about a member's old lady.

I hear Brew find his release and can't help but chuckle. The old fucker must give the girls here lock jaw, considering how long he's been pumping into her.

"Ok, girl. Get goin'. Men are talking now," he says, zipping his pants and slapping the girl on her ass.

I just shake my head at his shit, then tap the bar for another whiskey.

"Heard Chipper has himself a kid now?" He asks quietly, picking up his glass.

"Yeah, Jenna, sweet kid. Pretty fucked up though. If Rig wasn't dead, I'd be shoving my gun down his throat about now," I say with a nod.

"Yeah, he was a sick fuck. Is uh, is the girl doin' good? Being treated right there?" he asks hesitantly.

"Yep, Chipper and Mindy have claimed her as their daughter. Mindy loves her to death, and so does Chipper, but she's running his ass in circles. He's just not sure how you're supposed to treat a teenage daughter," I say chuckling, and remembering the times that Chipper was pissed right the fuck off about some of the clothes Jenna would wear.

Brew puts his head down, looking almost sad and remorseful. "That's good, that's good. She needed someone to look after her."

"Yeah, she did. Did you know her? How she came to the club and all?"

He shakes his head slowly. "Nah, man. I don't know shit about her."

"I heard her bastard of a father gave her to Rig. Can you imagine anyone being such a sorry son of a bitch?"

Still looking down, Brew shakes his head. "I'm sure he regrets it now."

Without waiting for me to respond, he stands up and claps a hand on my back. "We'll talk business tomorrow. Tonight, have some fun. There's a new piece around here somewhere, name's Sarah. She's only been here a day or two. You should get you a piece of her before she becomes used goods."

I'm calling for another shot when I hear a voice come from behind me. "Hey, handsome. I haven't seen you around here before." I turn my head to look at her and notice a stunning blonde with big green eyes standing behind me. My dick goes instantly hard.

"What's your name, beautiful?" I say reaching towards her and bringing her into me.

"Sarah, my name's Sarah."

Jenna

I wake up to the sound of my new cell ringing. I smile as soon as hear it. I know that Mindy and Chipper are both still in bed, so that only leaves one person that would be calling me; the person I've been missing like crazy for the last month. I grab it off my nightstand and stick it to my ear. "Hey, Kidd."

I hear him chuckle before he responds, "Hey, baby girl. Did I wake you?"

"No," I lie. "I've been up for a while."

"It's six thirty in the fuckin' morning, and you've been up for a while?"

"Well, maybe not that long."

He chuckles again. "Well, I know it's early, but I got shit to do today. Knew if I didn't call now, I wouldn't get a chance to later."

"You can call me anytime. You know that."

"I ain't got much time, so tell me what I've missed."

"Nothing much. Timber came over for dinner last night. He taught me how to cheat at poker. When you get home, I'm going to whoop your ass."

This time he flat out laughs. "Not sure it's a good idea to tell me you're gonna cheat."

"Maybe not," I admit. "We also watched Harold and Kumar go to White Castle. It's the funniest movie I've ever seen. He told me that he'd take me there someday, and he's supposed to bring his old Cheech and Chong movies with him next time he comes over. He says they're even better."

Kidd is quiet a moment before he responds. "You been spending a lot of time with Timber lately?"

"Yeah, he's cool. Not as much fun as you, but then again, no one is."

"That's right, and don't you forget it."

Before I get the chance to respond, I hear a muffled voice say, "Come back to bed, baby. It's cold without you."

As soon as the words register in my mind, my stomach starts to roll. Oh my God! He's got a woman in his bed, and he's talking to me on the phone. For a second, I'm pissed, but then I remember that he thinks of me as his sister. With that thought weighing heavily on my mind, my anger begins to fade and deep sadness takes its place. All of the excitement I felt when I answered the phone is completely gone now.

"Jenna, I got to go. There's some pressing business I need to take care of," Kidd says, while the woman in the background giggles.

I shut my eyes and try to stop the tears from coming. "Bye, Kidd."

"Bye, baby girl. Talk to you soon."

I click the off button, drop my phone on the nightstand, and lay back down. "I don't love Kidd. I don't love Kidd." Maybe if I say it enough, it will be true.

CHAPTER Six

Kidd

I'm sitting in Killer's office with him, his son Timmons, and Brew. I'm trying to get a straight answer about what's been going on with the drugs, but none are coming my way. "I've been here for nearly three months, and I still don't know shit about what happened with the coke that was supposed to go to Digger's crew. I'm telling you for the last time, I want an answer and I want it now."

Killer sits forward and places his elbows on the table, a look of total defeat is written across his face. "I know, Kidd. I've been looking for the same answers you are, but I ain't finding them either."

Brew jumps from his seat, sending his chair crashing against the floor. "I've told you both more than once, Rig was lead on all three shipments that were short. Since he's been dead, every load has been flush. He had to have something to do with the missing coke. I don't know why you won't fuckin' listen to me."

"And, I've told you before, it's just too fucking convenient of an answer. Blame it on the dead man, doesn't work for me. Plus, I met that bastard a time or two. I don't think he was smart enough to pull this shit off."

"I might be able to help you with that," Timmons mumbles out, shooting daggers my way.

There's just something about this motherfucker that rubs me the wrong way. I've known him my whole life, and never really thought much of him, but now I can't stand being in the same damn room as him. "What's that?"

"He'd grown pretty tight with one of our prospects. The kid went with Rig on his last two runs to Cali. He helped him get ready for the other. This kid was slick. He'd only been here for a few months, and we were already thinking about making him a member."

Killer looks towards his son. "You talking about Tug?"

Timmons nods. "Yeah. He talked Rig into riding through Tennessee, instead of straight through."

"That's right. Rig told me that Tug was helping him map out the trip. He said the kid told him it'd be better to change up our normal route, said backtracking through Tennessee would be safer. I didn't understand why, but didn't fucking think about it. Just wanted to get the shit there without any issues," Brew says, looking almost relived.

My eyes cut back to Killer. "Where's this kid?"

He shakes his head. "Found him dead a few days after Chipper left, OD'd in his bed."

"Well, now you have your answers. You can head back to Big Clifty," Timmons says with a sneer.

I shake my head. "I won't be going anywhere for a while. We still got shit to settle here. This club isn't pulling its own weight, so it'll be a while before I leave."

"What the fuck do you mean by that?" Brew asks, picking his chair up and sitting back down.

"Just to get your asses in the black, I had to put nearly hundred grand of Big Clifty's cash into this club. That shit ain't right. You know the rules. Each charter covers their own ass. Until Mateland can do that, I'll be here."

"Gun didn't say shit about that to me," Killer says, sounding confused.

I shrug. "Maybe not, but he did to me. He also told me that I needed to pick a man to stand in for you. You'll still be president, but the one I choose will hold the power."

"No fucking way!" Killer growls out. "I started this club! Ain't nobody taking it away from me."

"You helped Pop start the club, and you also voted him in

as President. You and Digger are founding members, but Pop is in control."

"I'll talk to Gun about this myself. If he thinks he can pull this shit on me and get away with it, he's fuckin' wrong. I'll tell Digger and find out what he thinks about this shit. Maybe we two founding members might need to see about taking that control away from Gun," Killer threatens.

I nod. "You can do that, but you might reconsider. Digger's not real happy with you right now. In fact, I'd say he's really fuckin' pissed."

"What the fuck are you talking about now?" He shouts.

"Digger made a trip to Big Clifty the week before I came here. See, he wanted Pop to cut your charter. Actually, he wanted Pop to approve his club going to war with Mateland. Seems he's tired of your shit," I say with an edge to my voice. "Took Pop nearly three days to convince him not to sic his boys on your ass."

All color drains from Killer's face before he responds, "Digger wouldn't do that to me."

I nod again, "Yeah, he would. Your club fucked up big time. Your fuck up cost him money, and more importantly, it cost him connections. You made him look bad, you know Digger. He doesn't like to look bad."

Digger got his name during his second tour in Vietnam.

Pop says Digger put more men in their graves than the rest of their entire unit combined. Pop got his name because he was a crack shot, especially with a long range shotgun. Killer, on the other hand, got his name for the killer weed he seemed to always have.

Killer's quiet for a moment before replying, "Fine, do whatever the fuck you have to."

Jenna

I smile at Timber as I climb off his bike. "Thanks for everything. I had a blast."

"Anytime, Jenna girl," he says, sliding off the bike. He wraps his arm around my shoulder and leads me into the house.

It's been a wonderful day. Timber showed up this morning right after breakfast and told me to go get dressed, but refused to tell me what he had planned. An hour later, we pulled into the parking lot at the Kansas City zoo. When I saw the zoo sign, I got so excited that I nearly fell off the bike.

I couldn't believe he would take me to a zoo. Bikers don't go to the zoo, do they? A few weeks ago, I told him I'd never been to one. He said everybody should go to the zoo at least once, for no other reason than to see the tigers. I didn't think much more about our conversation, but obviously, he did.

By the end of the day, I realized he was right. The tigers are badass.

As soon as we step inside of the house, the smell of vomit hits my nose. I immediately pull away from him and run towards Chipper and Mindy's room. She's laying in the bed, eyes closed but not asleep. "Did you have fun, sweetie?"

I walk to her side and go down to my knees. "You've been sick again?"

"I'm sick every day," she says in a weak voice.

I reach for her hand and bring it to my face. "You should have called. I would've come home."

She finally opens her eyes and turns her head towards me. "You haven't been anywhere but school in weeks. When you're at home, you're either taking care of me or watching Pebbles. With Pebbles spending the day with her mom, I wanted you to have some fun. I wasn't going to ruin your day."

"You could never ruin anything."

She lets out a shaky laugh. "You won't say that when you see the mess I made in the bathroom." A look of shame crosses her face before she whispers out. "I'm sorry, but I just didn't have the strength to clean it up."

"I don't mind. I'll get it for you."

She pulls her hand back and rubs it across my cheek before

letting it drop back on the bed. "I just hate that you have to do all this for me. I'm the mom. I supposed to be taking care of you."

"I don't mind it at all. I'd do anything for you. Don't you realize how much I love you?"

"I know you do, Jenna. I love you too, sweetie." With those words, she closes her eyes. Minutes later, she falls asleep. I sit with her, until I know she's completely asleep, before I make my way to her bathroom and start cleaning.

By the time I'm done cleaning, I'm sweaty and smell like vomit, but I don't mind. I would do anything for Mindy. I quietly make my way out of her bedroom, and am surprised to see Timber leaning up against the wall. "I thought you went home," I whisper.

"I couldn't leave you alone," he says, pushing off the wall and wrapping his arms around me.

As soon as I feel his touch, I break into tears. He bends down and hooks his arms under my knees, then picks me up and carries me to the couch. Once he's settled in beside me, I bury my face into his neck and cry myself to sleep.

Kidd

I'm staring out the window, wondering why I haven't called

Jenna for the last month. For some reason, I keep avoiding picking up the phone. Our last conversation pissed me the fuck off. She's spending way too much time with Timber. I can tell they're getting close, and I don't like it one fucking bit. Jealousy is an emotion I'm not accustomed to, and it's one I don't like at all.

Last time I called her, she was telling me about him taking her swimming at the strip pits in Amoret. The thought of him seeing her in a bathing suit made me fucking furious, yet the sound of her excitement when she was telling me about their time together made me sad. I was glad she was finally getting to have a little fun, but I hated that it was with someone other than me.

Being away from Jenna has been a good thing. I haven't been thinking been about her every minute of every fucking day. She still crosses my mind more than she should, but I've been too busy to dwell on what that means. I'm just hoping my time here breaks whatever hold she has on me.

"Whatcha thinking about, babe?" Sarah says as she walks to me and wraps her arms around my waist.

"Nothing important." I lower my mouth to hers, trying to wash away my thoughts of Jenna. Sarah's a good woman; one of the best I've ever met. I didn't think I'd ever find someone like her, especially here. Even as great as she is, she still can't take away my fantasies of Jenna. I hate what Rig did to her, but here I am thinking along the same line. There's no fucking way I would ever rape or beat her, but I have to wonder if wanting a seventeen year old in my bed is any better.

"Whatcha got planned today?" She asks.

I shake my head. "Club business. Nothing I can tell you about."

"Got time to join me back in bed before you go?"

I'm just about to agree when my phone rings. I stick a finger up. "Hold that thought."

I look down to the phone and see Jenna's name flash across the screen. This is the first time she's ever called me, so I know something's wrong. I immediately take a step back from Sarah and place the phone to my ear. "What's up, baby girl?"

"She's dying," Jenna says, between sobs.

"What the fuck are you talking about?"

"Mindy's going to die."

I take a deep breath and close my eyes, doing my best to hold my pain in. "Again Jenna, what the fuck are you talking about?"

"I'm not supposed to tell you, but I'm scared."

Anger courses through me. "What the fuck do you mean, you're not supposed to tell me?"

"Gun doesn't want you to know. He says you got shit to

do, and there's nothing you can do to help Mindy."

Motherfucker! My Pop is a damn bastard. "Tell me what's going on. I thought Mindy was doing okay."

Her crying becomes louder before she says. "I don't know everything. I just heard her talking to someone at the funeral home yesterday. She was planning her own funeral. Who plans their own funeral?"

Bile starts to make its way up my throat as I say. "I don't know, baby girl. Knowing Mindy, she's probably trying to make things easier for you and Chipper."

"It doesn't matter what she does. Nothing's going to be easy about losing her. I love her so much. I can't lose her," she finishes on a whisper.

"I know, baby girl."

"I've been so scared, so afraid, and I needed you really bad, but you never called. Why didn't you call, Kidd?"

I close my eyes again, trying to block out the pain of my own betrayal. I was so caught up in trying to avoid my feelings for her that I left her alone when she needed me the most. "I'm sorry, Jenna. I've been busy, but I should've made time."

I hear murmured voices before she whispers. "I gotta go. Your Pop's here. If he finds out I'm talking to you, he'll be pissed."

She doesn't even take the time to say goodbye before hanging up. When I hear the line go dead, I toss the phone on the bed and shout, "Fuck!"

"Was that Jenna, babe?" Sarah asks quietly. She knows about Jenna. I couldn't help talking about my girl. Most of the time, it's just me relaying silly shit she's been doing, but sometimes it's me telling Sarah how much I miss my baby girl. I always make sure to tell her that Jenna is like a little sister, but Sarah's not an ignorant bitch. She has to know it's more than that.

She hasn't really said much about Jenna. In fact, this is the first time she's ever even said her name, but she knows how Jenna came to the club. She heard about that shit going down before I even got here. She also knows how important Jenna is to me and my family. Every time I've brought my baby girl up, Sarah just smiles and listens. But there is something in her eyes, a spark of jealousy that I don't like.

"Yeah, I need to try and finish shit here and get home as soon as I can." I say, getting up and walking to the door.

"When it's time for you to leave, do you think I could come with you?" she asks quietly.

After hearing Jenna just now, I don't know if I should bring Sarah home. There's just too much shit going on. If Mindy's dying, it should be just the family, not some stow away. "I'm not sure that's a good idea."

"Please, Kidd. I don't want to be thrown back to these boys here. You know they won't go gentle on me."

She's right. Some of the brothers were pissed that I chose Sarah. They were even madder when I told them I didn't share. They've been chomping at the bit to get to her, so gentle will be the last thing they'd give her. "You can come, but you got to know that I'm not sure this thing we got going on will last long after I get home."

She shrugs. "We can just see what happens when we get there."

"Yeah, babe," I say walking out.

CHAPTER Seven

Kidd

After nearly a year away, I'm finally home, but not because the shit is fixed in Mateland; not even fucking close. That's a dream that may never come true. Those fuckers are so screwed up, I'm not sure anyone can fix it. My only hope is Brew, the current VP, will continue where I left off and get everyone's ass in line.

The reason I'm heading home is because of Mindy. She's dying. Fucking cancer. I swear even the thought of that word makes me want to throw up. She's been going through treatment for nearly a year, but nothing has helped. If anything, it's just made her sicker. Last week, the doctor finally laid it out for her and Chipper. She can continue chemo and she might have two more months, but she would be sicker than hell for every day of those two months, or stop treatment and maybe live a couple more weeks. If she's lucky, she'll still be weak, but nothing like when she's taking treatment.

Mindy chose the no treatment route, and Chipper had a shit hemorrhage. He didn't give a shit what it took. He wanted every day he could with her. Mindy stood her ground though, and stopped the chemo. Can't say that I blame her. Needless to say, Chipper's not taking it well, and neither is Jenna. She puts on a brave face for Chipper and Mindy, but she spends every night crying on the phone with me.

If it wasn't for the kid, I may not even know how bad it had gotten. I knew she had cancer, but the last time I had talked to Chipper, he said she was on the mend. As soon as Jenna told me the truth about Mindy's condition, I called an end to my time in Mateland. My Pop was pissed as hell when I told him my decision, but he can be pissed all he wants to be, because I sure the fuck am over this shit. I still can't believe he hid this shit from me. I know he wanted me to stay on a little longer, but I don't give a damn. Pop may put the club first, and in most situations I do too, but not when my sister-in-law is dying. Fuck no!

When I pull into Chipper and Mindy's driveway, a young woman runs out the door. I can't figure out who she is. I know I've seen her before, but I'm not sure where. One thing I do know is that she's a fucking knock out. Just watching her walk towards me has my dick going hard.

As soon as I slide off my bike, she jumps onto me, wrapping her arms around my neck and her legs around my waist. Instinctively, my hands go to her ass and my dick turns to stone.

She looks into my eyes and smiles. "I'm so glad you're home!"

The sound of her voice sends shock waves through my system. No way. No fucking way is this the kid. I pull my head back and look into her face, and my cock starts to ache. "What the fuck happened to you?"

A confused and hurt look crosses her face, and she slides her body down mine. I can only hope she didn't feel how hard my cock is. "I asked you a damn question. What the fuck happened to you?"

"What do you mean?" she whispers, taking a step back.

I start to answer, but the words get stuck in my throat. How in the hell do you ask someone how they went from being a cute kid to the most fuckable woman you've ever seen in less than a year? I mean really, it's not something she could miss. Her once shoulder length black hair now hangs down to the middle of her back. I swear the shit looks as soft as silk, and I would give my left nut just to run my fingers through it. The eyes that seemed too big for her face last time I saw her now tilt seductively and fit perfectly into the most beautiful face God ever made. The coltish body she once had is filled with womanly curves that many women would pay out the ass to have. Hell, I'd pay out the ass to just touch them. No! There's no damn way she missed this. So instead of explaining, I just motion towards her. "You. What the hell happened to you?"

She starts to open her mouth, but shuts it when a weak voice answers for her. "She grew up."

I look towards the house and see my sister-in-law standing on the porch. My body seems to turn to concrete and the heat that Jenna sent my way is instantly gone, replaced by a cold fear that I haven't felt since my mom died. Mindy, the sweetest woman in the whole damn world, is now just a shadow of her former self. Her once robust body is now merely flesh and bones. The beautiful red hair that my brother loved so much is gone, and her big green eyes are hollow. Fuck! I should've come home sooner.

"You gonna keep staring me, or are you gonna come give me a hug?" she says with a smile that doesn't quite reach her eyes.

With those words, I come unstuck and rush towards her. I take her in my arms and hug her, doing my best not to cause her any pain. "How's my girl?"

"Dying," she says matter of fact.

"Don't say shit like that," I say, stepping away from her.

She reaches for my arm and gives it a squeeze. "No reason to beat around the bush. We all know that it's coming, so no need to pretend."

"Chipper should be here soon," Jenna says, stepping onto the porch. "Let's get you inside."

She takes Mindy's hand and leads her inside, then looks back to me. "You guys go on to the living room, and I'll grab us something to drink."

I watch Jenna's ass as she walks towards the kitchen and join Mindy on the couch. "When the hell did she grow up?"

Mindy laughs before she replies. "I'm not sure. I swear she went to bed one night and woke up looking like that."

"It sure in the hell shocked the shit out of me."

"I'm sure it did more than just shock you," she says with a smile, motioning towards my lap.

"Shut the fuck up."

She laughs again. "You should have been here the first time Chipper saw her in a bikini. I swear I've never seen him move so fast. One minute he was sitting beside me, and the next he was running across the room with a towel."

I nod. "Can't say I blame him."

"That was nothing. He completely freaked out when she went out on her first date."

"Date?" I bark out. "Who the hell's she dating?"

Mindy shrugs. "No one right now, but she was seeing some guy from school. They broke up a few weeks ago. "

"Good," slips out before I can stop it.

Mindy's eyes jerk to mine and a stern look crosses her face. "She's nearly eighteen. You got a little while before you can go there. When you do, it better be for more than just a quick ride. I won't be here then, but I can guarantee that I will come back and haunt your ass if you hurt my girl."

I shake my head and do my best to deny her words. "I don't know what you're talking about."

She leans towards me and speaks in a voice that's barely above a whisper. "That girl has been hung up on you since she first got here. You may have thought of her as kid, but you were every bit as hung up on her. I always knew that once she grew up, you would claim her. She's yours, and you're hers. Just make sure that you do it the right way."

I start to respond, but am cut short by a knock on the door. Jenna rushes into the room and swings the door open. When I see who walks through, my gut clenches and I grab Mindy's hand. Giving it a squeeze, I hope that she'll understand.

"Hey, baby," Sarah says, walking towards me with a smile on her face.

I stand up and look towards Jenna just in time to see the color drain from her face. She looks towards me and the pain reflected back to me in her eyes lends truth to everything Mindy has just told me about Jenna's feelings. It also makes me realize that Mindy was right about mine. Jenna is mine, and I'm hers.

I feel Sarah paste herself to my side and know there's no way I can avoid this. It's not her fault that my life changed as soon as I pulled into my brother's driveway. Sarah's a nice woman and she's been good to me. I can't just kick her to the curb the same day she uprooted her whole life to move across the state with me.

I stare at Jenna for a moment more before making a decision and placing my hand onto Sarah's back. I look back towards Mindy and force a smile. "This is Sarah. She's going to be staying with me for a while."

I feel Sarah's body jerk, and she whispers, "For a while?"

I ignore her and continue with my introduction. "This is my sister-in-law, Mindy."

Then, I turn towards Jenna. "This is my… this is my Jenna."

Jenna

As soon as dinner was over, I rushed to my room. I just couldn't stand being around Kidd and that woman any longer. I know he's not my boyfriend, but I still hate to see him with anyone else. Just the thought of him with her breaks my heart. I barely make it to my bed before the tears start to fall. I'm crying so hard that I don't even hear the door open.

"Are you okay, sweetheart?" Mindy asks, walking into my room.

I rush to wipe the tears from my eyes and paste on a fake smile. "I'm fine, just a little tired."

She closes the door and walks towards my bed. "You weren't tired before Sarah showed up."

I shrug. "I stayed up last night. I guess it finally just hit me."

She sits on my bed and grabs my hand. "You know it's not nice to lie to a dying woman."

Anger bubbles up inside me. "Don't joke about that."

She releases my hand and lays down, throwing her arm around my waist. "Okay. I'm sorry. I know it bothers you."

"Thank you," I whisper out.

We lay quiet for a moment before Mindy starts to talk about the elephant in the room. Actually, I guess it's the elephant in the other room. "Kidd didn't mean hurt you."

"I know."

"You don't need to worry about her. She isn't his old lady. She's just a hanger on. She'll never last."

"Yeah," I say, even though I'm not sure that she's right about that. It only took a few minutes of being around them to know that the woman is in love with Kidd. I can't really say for sure how he feels, but I can tell he cares for her.

"Sweetheart, you're still young. Give it a little time, and everything will work out."

I nod and grab her hand, pulling her arm tighter around me. "I love you, Mom."

She places a soft kiss on the back of my head. "I love you too, sweetheart."

We lay like that for a long time, neither of us saying anything. I think she just needed to be close to me, and I know I just needed her. I don't know what I'm going to do when she's gone. That's something I don't even want to think about, but looking down at the frail hand holding mine, I know it's going to happen soon. I start to close my eyes when I hear the door open. Mindy and I turn around and see Kidd standing in the doorway. "Is this a private party or can anyone join?"

Mindy lets go of my hand and slides out of the bed. "I think it should be a party for two, and I don't think I need to be one of those two."

With those words, she walks towards Kidd. When she gets near him, she lays her hand on his shoulder and smiles. Then she walks from the room, shutting the door behind her. I look from the door to Kidd, hoping that he can't tell I've been crying.

"Won't your girlfriend get mad if you leave her out there by herself too long?" I ask sarcastically. As soon as the words leave my mouth, I start to blush. I know I sounded like a jealous girlfriend, but I couldn't help it.

Kidd shrugs. "If she does, she'll get over it. Nothing comes between me and my girl."

Hearing him call me his girl brings a smile to my face. I finally look up to him and smile. "I'm glad you're home."

"I am too, baby doll," he says as he walks towards me. He crawls into the bed and lays down beside me, pulling me flush to his front. "I missed you, Jenna."

"I missed you too," I whisper out, trying to concentrate on the feeling of his body next to mine.

"Tell me what's been going down while I was gone. I heard you've been dating," he says, sounding harsh.

"I went on a date or two, nothing serious."

"Do you like this guy?"

"Who?"

He blows out a breath, tickling the back of my neck. "The guy you went out with."

"Not really. He's just some boy from school. He was kind of boring." I shrug, my shoulder sliding across his chest. "He has an old car. Some kind of muscle car. He thought it was the shit, kept bragging about how fast it went. I asked him if he ever drove a Harley, and he said that he wasn't in to motorcycles. I knew then he wasn't the guy for me."

He chuckles, and I can feel the vibrations through my body. "You're right. When you get a man, he'll drive a Harley."

"Yes, he will," I agree, visions of Kidd on his Harley running through my head.

After that, we lay there quietly. Him holding me, and me enjoying being close to him. Finally, my eyes start to get heavy. I'm just falling to sleep when his lips brush the top of my head. I spend the rest of the night dreaming of his kiss, but in my dreams, his lips are on mine.

Kidd

I leave Mindy and Chipper's with Jenna on my mind. I cannot believe how fuckin' much she's changed. She's still the same Jenna, just a more mature version. The fascination I had with her before is nothing compared to how I feel now. I thought being gone as long as I was had helped me get over my feelings for her. Well, maybe not get over her, but at least lessen the need I had for her. Instead, the minute I see her again, I want her more now than ever.

Sarah senses my mood shift as soon as we step outside. "What's the matter, baby?"

Fuck, I need to break this to her, but I don't know how. Over the past eleven months, I've grown to care for her. Do I love her? Hell, no. But I do care enough about her not to want to cause her pain. I knew I shouldn't have ever brought her here. When she asked if she could come along, something inside of my head kept telling me to say no. It's like it just knew something has always been missing, and now I know what it is. It's Jenna.

"We'll talk at the clubhouse," I grunt out.

She shifts in her seat and asks, "I thought we were going home, baby?"

She's right. I planned on moving her into my apartment; a place that I don't stay at very often and that no one from the club ever goes. I guess somewhere in the back of my mind, I thought I could keep her there and away from Jenna. Now, the thought of having her in my home seems wrong. "Yeah, I changed my mind. We'll talk at the clubhouse."

I walk to my bike without saying another word. I can feel her stare boring onto my back, but she stays quiet too.

Ten minutes later, I pull through the gate to the compound and park in my spot. Sarah pulls in beside me as I'm sliding off my bike. She follows me quietly to my room, passing the brothers I haven't seen in nearly year, but I don't stop to talk and they don't call out. Guess my body is giving off the 'don't fuck with me' vibe.

I unlock my door and lead Sarah inside. I walk to the bed and sit, leaning forward, and put my head into my hands. Shit, what can I say? There's no nice way to explain this to her, and she deserves nice.

I feel her walk over to me, but I don't look up. She sits down beside me and places her hand on my leg. "Baby, what's going on? Something wrong?"

I snort. "You think? Of course, something's wrong. My sister-in-law is dying."

"But that's not what you're so upset over, is it?"

I stand up and start pacing the room. "When I brought you here, I thought we could give it a go. You're a great woman, and an amazing friend. You're a fucking firecracker in bed; everything a man could want."

I stop pacing and look at her. "It's not your fault. You didn't do anything wrong, but you're not the woman for me."

"Who is?" she asks, jumping from the bed. "That kid? She's what all this is about?"

I can do nothing but nod. "I'm sorry, but the minute I saw her, I knew this wouldn't work out."

"What the fuck are you going to do, hook up with a seventeen year old?"

I shake my head. "No, she turns eighteen in four months. I

can wait that long, but the minute she's legal, I'll be making her mine."

Sarah says nothing. She just continues to look at me like I'm a piece of shit. Why shouldn't she? I am a piece of shit after all. "Sarah, I'm so sorry."

"You talk about her all the time. Your baby girl," she says, venom lacing through her voice. "You had to know you wanted her, so why the hell did you bring me here?"

"I told you, I thought we could give it shot. I didn't think my feelings for Jenna were anything more than me looking out for her, but fuck, the feelings I shouldn't have had for her before I left are still there. Only they're stronger now. I just can't keep ignoring them."

She starts to shake her head. "You can't do this to me. You were supposed to make me you're old lady."

"That's not fucking true," I shout, starting to get angry. "I never made you any promises. I made sure you knew that before I brought you here. I told you I didn't know how long this shit between us would last."

"No! You just said that. You didn't mean it. You love me, and I refuse to let you throw me to the side for some little bitch."

My anger explodes and I grab her by the arm. "I never once said I loved you. I wouldn't, because I don't. There's only one woman I love, and if I ever hear you talk about her like that again, I'll lay your ass out."

She pulls away and steps back. "Fine. I won't say shit about your precious baby girl, but I ain't leaving. I have nowhere to go. You told me I could work at The Kitty Kat. Let me strip for a few months. You can at least let me stay until I can save up some money."

I stare at her for a moment before my anger begins to fade. This is my fault. The least I can do is give her a little time to get shit straight. "You've got four months."

CHAPTER Eight

Kidd

Mindy's gone. I can't believe it. We're lucky she lasted as long as she did. We ended up having a lot more time than the doctor thought we would; a little over three months. Thank God I came back when I did. I'm not sure I could have ever forgiven Pop if I hadn't gotten to talk to her one last time. Seeing her lying in the hospital, taking her last breath, was the hardest thing I've ever done, but it was also a privilege. It was a privilege to have had her as my sister in this life, a privilege to be her brother-in-law, and a privilege to share in all the goodness that was Mindy.

As I turn to walk away from the casket, I see Jenna standing in the corner of the funeral home crying. I know there's nothing I can do to take her pain away, but I still walk towards her and pull her into my arms. "I'm so sorry, baby girl."

She buries her head into my shoulder and lets her pain out. Her body convulses with sobs, and I can feel every ounce of the grief that she has coursing through her body. Even though she's only known Mindy for a little over a year, I know she's hurting every bit as much as I did when I lost my mother. "She loved you, Jenna. You were the daughter she always wanted. You made the last year of her life the happiest she'd ever lived."

She draws in a labored breath, then pulls her face back and looks up to me. "She was the best mom ever, and I'm just not sure I can live without her."

I give her a tight squeeze and place my forehead on hers. "You can, and you will. It'll just be hard for a while. As time goes on, you'll get to a point where you can look back at the time you had with her for the gift it was."

"It wasn't a gift. It was a reward," she whispers out.

"A reward?"

"Yes, I think God sent her to me. She was my reward for all the bad shit that's happened to me in my life." Her tears start to come faster as she continues to talk. "I would go through it all again, just to have my Mindy back."

Hearing her talk about the past, even not going into detail, kills me. I hate that my girl had to go through all that shit. If I could, I'd dig Rig's ass up just to kill the motherfucker again. I pull my head back and kiss her forehead. "She told me once that you were a gift from God."

"She told me that too. She said that she used to pray that

she could have a baby, but it never happened. Then, I showed up and she knew that I was the baby she had prayed for." She looks up to me and a sad smile crosses her face. "She said that God knew how much she would've hated changing diapers and wiping snotty noses, so he sent her a child that could take care of her own bodily functions."

I let out a quiet chuckle and start to respond when I see Sarah walking towards us. I let go of Jenna and take a step back. I don't want to, but I also don't want Sarah starting any shit here. She's been pretty good about everything so far, but I can tell she's ready to explode.

It only took her a few minutes of seeing me with Jenna for her to realize that Jenna meant more to me than she ever would. I should've sent Sarah home right away, but I hoped she'd help me keep my hands off Jenna. Needless to say, a woman doesn't like being used as a stand in for the one you really want.

She stops a few feet from us and places her hands on her hips. "Are you ready to sit down yet?"

"I'll be there in a minute."

"I'm ready to sit down, now," she says, drawing out the now.

"Well, I'm talking to Jenna right now."

Her eyes cut to Jenna then back to me. "I can see that, but I think it'd be better if she was up there with Chipper. Don't you?"

I can see the anger working in her eyes, and I know that I either go with her now, or she's going to throw a bitch fit in the middle of Mindy's funeral. I can't let that happen, so I turn to Jenna. "Baby girl, why don't you go on and sit by Chipper?"

"Are you not going to sit with us?" she whispers.

I don't get the chance to respond before Sarah butts her big ass in. "No, we're going to sit in the back."

Jenna looks up to me, tears in her eyes. "I really wanted you to sit with us."

Again, Sarah answers her. "Well, I'm sorry honey. There's not enough room for Kidd and me in the front row, and I'm Kidd's woman. I need to be there to comfort him today. A man needs his woman when he's upset, not some little girl."

I reach out and grab Sarah's arm, jerking her to me. I bend down and whisper in her ear, "Shut the fuck up, or I swear I'll have you packing your shit and heading back to Mateland before the day's over."

"I have nowhere to go," she whispers angrily.

"Then you'll do what I said and shut the fuck up," I say before turning to Jenna. "Go on up to Chipper. I'll talk to you after the service."

She doesn't respond, just walks away. She's only a few

feet away, when she looks back to me. The look on her face is full of pain. Not the same pain as she had earlier, but a different kind completely. The kind of pain that someone feels when their best friend betrays them. She shakes her head sadly and turns away, and I know that everything between us has just changed.

I jerk my head towards Sarah and growl out, "You've got two weeks, and then I want your ass gone."

Jenna

Setting up the house after Mindy's funeral sucks. All the old ladies brought a ton of food yesterday, so at least I didn't have to cook, but I still had to get everything set up. Feeding nearly a hundred bikers isn't easy, especially when all you want to do is lay down and cry. Timber and Reese are helping me out, since Chipper is drunk and crying. Wish I was too. It'd be nice to dull the pain I'm in.

As I'm setting the last casserole on the table, I see Roxy slip onto the couch beside Chipper. She's been trying to chat him up for months. Let me tell you, that bitch has some nerve. When Mindy was still alive, she used to come over here all the time. She said she was here to help, but not one time did she lift a finger to help me take care of Mindy. Instead, she'd try to hit on Chipper. One time, I heard her tell him they could make it quick. She said he wouldn't last long since he hadn't been getting any from Mindy. I braced, hoping he wouldn't be like my Dad and jump at the chance, and instead he got pissed and told her to back the fuck off. He also told her to never step foot in his house again. I guess she didn't listen.

Roxy was pissed when it happened, but she still wanted Chipper. I could see it in her eyes every time they were around each other. Now, she thinks his wife's funeral is the perfect opportunity to get him. The bitch is unbelievable. She just doesn't get it. Chipper loved Mindy. He wouldn't cheat on her. He sure in the hell wouldn't fuck someone on the day of her funeral.

I turn to Reese who's standing beside me with a look of pure disgust on his face. "What the hell is her problem? Mindy's funeral was today, and she's over there trying to get at him. What do you see in her?" I say, almost hysterically.

Reese looks at me, eyes darkening. "One day, babe, I'll tell you, trust me, I ain't got no choice but to keep her around." He then looks back up and shakes his head at his wife. "If I could, she'd be out on her ass."

I start ask him what the hell he's talking about when the door opens and Kidd and Sarah walk in. I can't believe he brought her here. She's been nothing but a bitch to me for the last three months. I look up to Reese and whisper, "I can't believe that he brought her here after she was such a bitch at the funeral home."

He places his hand on my shoulder and gives it a tight squeeze. "Just ignore her ass. Her expiration date is coming up soon. You won't have to put up with her much longer."

"What do you mean by that?"

He shrugs. "Not my place to tell you, but you'll find out soon enough."

Strong arms circle my waist before pulling me back into a wall of muscle. "What are you two over here whispering about?"

Before I respond, Reese clears his throat and nods his head towards the doorway. I pull away from Timber and turn around. Sarah is walking right towards me. "Shit!"

Timber leans down and whispers in my ear. "Don't let her upset you. That's what she wants."

She stops a few feet in front of me, just looking at me with her hate filled eyes. I swear she stares at me so long, I start to feel like I'm some sort of art piece in a museum. I look around for Kidd, sighing, but only see the back of him, leading Chipper out the door.

Finally, I look back at Sarah. "Can I help you?" I say, doing my best to sound bored.

"Yeah, you can stay the fuck away from my man," she says snottily.

"Excuse me?"

"You heard me, bitch. I've had enough of you strutting your ass in front of him. If he wanted you, he wouldn't be with me."

Her words hit me right in my heart, mostly because I know they're true. He wouldn't be with her if he wanted me, but he doesn't want me. I'm just his little sister. "I don't know what you're talking about. If you have a problem, maybe you should talk to Kidd about it."

"My only problem is you. I want you to take your ass away from here. This is Kidd's brother's house. He shouldn't have to put up with you panting after him every time he comes to visit."

I feel Timber's body tighten behind mine, so I place my hand on his to let him know I got this. "I live here. It's my home, and I'm not leaving."

"You're only here because Chipper feels sorry for you. Do you really think he wants some bit of used goods around all the time?"

"Shut the fuck up," Reese growls out. At the same time as Timber says, "Close your fuckin' mouth before I close it for you."

If her earlier words had been a hit to the heart, these are punches straight to the gut. Not once has anyone brought up what happened to me in Mateland, especially not like that.

Mindy and me talked about it a time or two, but only when I had nightmares, and only to comfort me. The worst part is that I know Kidd had to have told her, because she would've never known about it if he hadn't.

I know I gotta say something, or Reese and Timber are going to go off on her ass. Finally, I choke out. "Whatever, seems to me you're just jealous of this used bit of goods."

With that, I start to walk away. I barely make it a foot before she reaches out and grabs my arm. She swings me around to face her. "Listen here, you little slut."

She doesn't get further before Timber sends the side of his hand into her forearm, causing her to let go. "Hands off. Now!" Timber snaps.

I stumble backwards, landing in Reese's arms. "I got you, Jenna."

Timber gets in her face and starts to yell, "I take it you don't know the fuckin' rules around here, so let me enlighten you. She's the princess of the Renegade Sons. Fuck with her, fuck with all of us. There is not a man in this room that wouldn't lay his life down for her any day. I know you think you're big shit because you're with Kidd, but we don't give a flying fuck whose dick you're riding. You mess with her, and your ass is dead."

Sarah's face pales before responding. "I was just laying

claim to what's mine."

Timber bends closer to her, almost touching her nose with his. "That's bullshit, and you know it. You're time's coming, and you're grasping at strings. But let me tell you, it doesn't matter what you do. You've already lost. Now get the fuck away from me."

At that, Sarah turns around and rushes across the room. I let out a relived breath. "My God, she's a bitch."

Reese chuckles. "You got that right, Jenna." When Reese first came back after being in Mateland with Kidd, he would tell me about Sarah. About how nice she was, sweet, a good person, then she moves here with Kidd, and she turns into a mega bitch. I've never seen a nice Sarah, not once since I've met her.

The words barely leave his mouth, before Roxy storms over, taking Sarah's spot. "What the fuck, Reese? You're always on my ass about what I do, and here you are with your hands all over the kid. I better not find out you're fucking her."

"What I do, bitch, is none of your fuckin' business."

"Everything you do is my business, as long as you want Rosalie to keep calling you Daddy," she shouts.

"Time for us to go," he says, venom dripping from his voice. He grabs her and starts to move through the room, but stops before leaving the room and turns back to me. "We'll talk later, babe," he says to me with a wink, his parting words causing Roxy to freak out yet again.

I shake my head and walk over to Timber. "I think I've had all I can take."

I lean into Timber, wrapping my arms around his waist. He wraps his arms around me, bringing me even closer. "Any other bitches come over here, I'm getting out my gun."

I look up to him and giggle. "You're a wonderful friend. Thank you for being there for me today. I couldn't have made it through the funeral without you."

"Anytime," he says, placing a kiss on the top of my head.

We're quiet for a moment before I pull back and look up to him. "What the hell is going on with Roxy and Reese? They're married, yet she whores around like she doesn't have an old man at all. What in the hell did she mean about Pebbles calling him Daddy?"

"It's not my story to tell. One day, he'll tell you himself. When he does, you'll understand that he's doing the only thing he can," he says, running his hand over my hair.

I nod. "Reese is a good guy. He deserves better."

"So do you."

I cock my brow. "What do you mean?"

"I'll tell you on your birthday," he says, then leans down and places a soft kiss on my lips.

When he does that, the vibe in the room changes. It's so heavy that I can feel it. I jerk back and look across the room. Kidd is standing at the door looking furious. He starts to take a step towards Timber and me, but stops when Sarah walks up to him and wraps her arm around his waist. She reaches up and kisses on his jaw, but he doesn't lose his tense look. When she's done, she looks over and smiles at me. She then grabs his hand and pulls him out the door.

Timber places his chin on the top of my head and mumbles, "Yeah, you deserve better."

CHAPTER Nine

Jenna

It's my birthday, and not a soul remembered. I'm eighteen, eight-fucking-teen, and I'm sitting here at the house all alone. I'm not upset with Chipper. He's had more important things on his mind than my birthday. Mindy's only been gone for two weeks, and Chipper's still in as much pain as he was the day she took her last breath. I am too.

I deal by doing my best to take care of Chipper. I clean and cook, trying to keep everything just like it was when she was still healthy enough to do it herself. So far, Chipper hasn't noticed. If he has, he hasn't mentioned it.

Chipper deals by staying drunk off his ass. In the time that I've lived with him and Mindy, I had never seen him drunk. Sure, he would have a few from time to time. I've even seen him buzzed more than once, but never drunk. Since Mindy's funeral, I haven't seen him sober. He leaves as soon as he gets up and stumbles in after I'm in bed.

Mindy would hate to see him like this. She would also hate seeing me sitting here all alone. She wouldn't want to know that we're all grieving so hard, but she had to know it'd happen. When you lose someone as wonderful as her, there's no way to keep from falling to pieces.

I'm standing in the kitchen frosting a cake. Yes, I'm making my own birthday cake. I don't even want the damn thing. I know Mindy would want me to have one though, so I put on my big girl panties, and made her famous coconut cream cake. I'm just finishing up when I hear the front door open.

I jerk my head towards the living room and see Kidd standing there. "Hey, baby girl."

Shit! I haven't been alone with him since Mindy's funeral. In fact, we haven't even talked. I would have talked to him, but he was with that bitch, and I just can't talk to him when they're together. Being that they're attached at the hip all of the time, I haven't really talked to him much since he got back.

I really did try to like Sarah, but it was impossible. She hates me and makes no bones about it, so it's hard to be friendly with her. Finally, I quit trying. I still wanted to be friends with Kidd, but that all changed after Mindy's funeral. After what he did, turning his back on me again, I don't want anything to do with either of them. I know Sarah is his woman, but I'm his friend. Friends are supposed to be there for each other. He hurt me in a way that I'm not sure I can ever get over.

He walks to me, stopping when his body hits mine. "Still not talking to me? Not even a hello?"

"Hi, Kidd," I whisper, feeling uncomfortable at being so close to him.

He looks at the cake then back to me. "Happy birthday, Jenna."

My eyes go large when I realize that he remembered. Of course, the one person that I don't want to see is the only person that remembers it's my birthday. "Why are you here?"

He steps closer, pushing me against the counter. "I would never forget your birthday. I've been waiting for this day for a long fucking time."

"What do you mean?" I ask, confused by his words.

He lowers his mouth to mine and talks against my lips. "You're legal, baby."

With those words, his lips seal against mine. He kisses me in a way that I've never been kissed before. It's gentle, but all consuming. Finally, I pull back. "What are you doing, Kidd?"

A sexy smile crosses his face. "I'm claiming my girl."

Kidd wraps his arms around me and pulls me against his chest, lifting me off my feet. "You're mine, Jenna. You've been mine since the day you walked in the clubhouse, and I'm about to prove it to you."

I'm still confused. What in the hell is he talking about? He's with Sarah. I'm just his friend, his little sister. "I don't understand," I whisper, my voice sounding strained.

He chuckles before running his hand down to cup my ass. "You're my woman, my old lady. Now, I'm going to claim you."

His words make me feel like someone's doing cart wheels in my stomach. "Your old lady? What about Sarah?"

He shakes his head. "Yes, my old lady. We're not talking about Sarah right now. We're not talking about anything."

He picks me up, barely bringing me off my feet, then places his lips back on mine. He starts to walk backwards, carrying me with him. Before I realize what's happening, he leads me into my bedroom. He stops when he reaches my bed and lays down, pulling me on top of him.

I know I should be scared, but I'm not. In fact, I'm excited. I've only had sex with two people in my life, Timmons and Rig. Mindy said what they did to me was not sex. It was an act of violence. She explained that sex with someone you care about will not hurt, and if I'm lucky, it will feel really good. For some reason, I know having sex with Kidd will not just feel good. It will be life changing.

He rolls me over, placing his body against my side. We continue to kiss while he undresses me. After he rids me of my clothes, he pulls his shirt off. I can't stop myself from touching him. I never wanted to touch Timmons or Rig, but my hands seem to be glued to Kidd's body. When I notice the phoenix tattoo on his shoulder, I lift up and run my tongue over its flames. The taste of his skin sends shockwaves through my body.

He moves down my body and runs his tongue over my nipples. I can feel them tighten to small peaks and let out a throaty moan. My God! I've never felt anything like this in my life. "That feels good," I gasp out.

I feel him chuckle against my breast. "Everything we do will feel good."

While he continues to use his mouth on me, I move my hands down to his pants. I find his pants already unbuttoned and the head of his dick peeking out the top. I lightly run my hand over it, then start to push his pants down. I wrap my hand around his hardness and squeeze. He bucks towards me and mumbles. "Fuck, baby doll."

He pulls away from me and shrugs his pants off before rolling on top of me. The feel of him between my legs is something I can't describe. It gives me a feeling of being home, like my body knows this is where it belongs, where it was meant to be.

Kidd pushes his hands between us, placing it at my core. He gently cups me while kissing the side of my neck. His fingers do things to me that I didn't know was possible. The things that once caused me so much pain are now bringing me pleasure; so much pleasure that my entire body is on fire.

Kidd pulls himself up and looks right into my eyes. "I need to be inside you, but I have to know you want this."

Without even a hint of doubt, I nod. "I want you to make love to me."

A look crosses Kidd's face that I've never seen before, a mixture of tenderness and heat. He places a soft kiss on my lips then gets down on his knees. He grabs his jeans and pulls out a condom. I watch him tear it open and roll it on, my entire body humming with desire.

He comes back to me, kissing me while rubbing his hardness against my wetness. Finally, he starts to push himself in. He doesn't slam into me like the others did. Instead, he moves slowly, filling me inch by inch. There's no pain, just a feeling of amazing fullness. I wrap my legs around him and breathe out, "Ahhh."

He starts to slowly move inside me, causing a knot to form in my stomach. My core starts to tighten, and I know something is coming, but I'm not sure what.

"That's it baby, give it to me," Kidd grunts out as he slides in and out of me. "Feel me, baby. Feel me deep inside that sweet little cunt of yours."

I feel him all right. I feel every inch of him. After nearly two years of feeling next to nothing, having him inside me is almost too much. "Uh huh," I mumble, focused on the pleasure he's giving me.

"God, baby, your pussy feels like silk. It's the best damn feeling in the fucking world. There's nowhere I'd rather than be than sunk deep inside you, claiming you, proving you're mine."

His words send my body into overdrive. My hips start to thrust, meeting his. Suddenly it hits me, and my entire body starts to convulse. My legs lock around him, and I let out a long moan. Nothing, and I mean nothing, has ever felt this good.

I feel his pace start to speed up, and he starts to grunt each time he pushes into me. After only a stroke or two, he buries his face into my neck and growls. He's still for a moment then starts to move in me gently. He brings his face to mine, and starts to kiss me. He kisses me in way that lets me know how precious he thinks I am.

After a moment or two, he rolls onto his side, "Thank you, baby doll."

My sex drunk brain takes a minute to realize what he said. "Why are you thanking me?"

A shit eating grin spreads across his face. "It's your birthday, but you ended up giving me the best present I've ever received."

I can't keep the smile off my face. "You're welcome, I

guess."

He chuckles while getting off the bed. I watch him walk from the room, not even stopping to get dressed. In my mind, I know he's just going to the bathroom, but in my heart, I wish he hadn't left me. I need him now. I need him to tell me that this isn't just a dream. I need him to let me know that he loves me every bit as much as I love him.

My eyes don't leave my bedroom door until he walks back in the room. He comes straight to the bed and crawls in beside me. "Okay, now we can talk."

"Talk?"

He nods, pulling me to him. "You asked about Sarah. I said we'd talk about her later."

"Oh," I whisper, not sure I want to talk about his girlfriend right after we had sex.

"Sarah's a good woman. At least, she was when I first met her. But she was never you, and she knew that I didn't have any real feelings for her. Knowing that she was just keeping me busy, while I waited for you, made her bitter."

I saw them together enough to know that Sarah meant something to him. He can say what he wants, but I'll never believe he doesn't care for her. "Sarah means something to you."

"No, she doesn't. She could have, if it wasn't for you. As soon as I realized you were no longer just a kid, she never had a chance."

I'm about to ask him what he means when his cell starts to ring. He reaches to the floor and pulls it from his pants. "Yo."

I watch as his face instantly loses its color, and he quickly swings his legs off the bed. "Where is she?"

He listens while pulling on his pants. "I'll be there as soon as I can."

Kidd shoves the phone in his pocket and starts to pull on his shoes. I watch him as he continues to get dressed. He stays quiet until he slides his cut over his shoulders. "I gotta go," he barks out, voice sounding cold.

"What?" I ask, shocked at the change in him.

He looks to me with regret in his eyes. "Sarah needs me. We'll talk about this shit later."

With those words, he walks out of the room. Seconds later, I hear the front door slam. I curl into a ball, letting my tears wash away my heartache. I just don't understand how he can say he wants me, but takes off after Sarah right after he we have sex? Maybe that's the issue, he wanted sex and said whatever he had to in order to get it.

The more I think about it, the more angry I get. I know the guys at the club use girls all the time. Shit, the guys at school do too. But Kidd is my friend. At least he's supposed to be. Friends don't treat each other like that. Do they?

After nearly two hours of crying and fuming, I've had enough. I decide to go find out what the hell his problem is. I hop off my bed, grab my clothes, then quickly get dressed. I'm just walking out of my room when Chipper comes in the front door. For once in two weeks, he isn't drunk, but he does look like shit.

"Where're you going?" he asks, as he shrugs off his cut and throws it on the couch.

"I got to talk to Kidd," I say, sounding angry and maybe a little hurt.

"He's not at the clubhouse, darlin'," he says with a shake of his head. "He's with Sarah."

I assumed he was going to Sarah, but hearing Chipper say it still hurts. More than the hurt, it pisses me off. How the hell could he do this to me? "Where are they at?"

His brow rises. "You haven't heard?"

I shake my head in the negative. "Nope."

"Sarah was in a car wreck, a bad one. The doctors doubt she'll make it through the night."

All of my anger vanishes, and I'm filled with a sense of self-loathing. Here I was, worried about what happened between me and Kidd, and she's dying. "I'm going to the hospital."

"I don't think that's a good idea."

"I have to be there for Kidd," I try to explain.

"I'm telling you, Jenna, that's not a good idea."

I know better than to argue with Chipper, so I go to my bed. I sit there silently, waiting for the sound of the TV in his bedroom to turn on. Once I know he's out for the night, I'm going to the hospital. Good idea or not, I won't let Kidd go through this on his own.

Kidd

I run my fingers through my hair, frustration and anger eating away at me. I should have left Sarah in Mateland. If I had, she wouldn't be dead. This is my fault. A good woman is dead because of me. As I walk out of the hospital, our last conversation flashes through my mind.

She was so fucking upset. She didn't want to leave, kept telling me she had nowhere to go. I knew she was telling the truth, but I didn't care. The only thing that mattered to me was getting to Jenna. Hell, I was already on my bike heading to Chippers' before Sarah even pulled out of the parking lot.

The last words she said to me was that she hated me. Well, now I hate myself.

I'm just stepping into the clubhouse when Jenna comes running down the hallway. Shit! I don't need this now. "What the hell are you doing here?"

"I went to the hospital, but you weren't there, so I came here to check on you. I needed to make sure you're okay," she says, stopping in front of me.

"Do I look fucking okay to you?"

She takes a step back. "I was worried about you being here all alone."

My anger is at a boiling point, anger at myself. "Did you ever consider I might have wanted to be alone?"

"I'm sorry. I thought you might need me."

"I don't need you. I don't need anyone. Sarah is fucking dead, and here you are trying to comfort me. Did you ever think that if you hadn't been fucking me earlier, she might still be breathing?"

She shakes her head and tears come to her eyes. "No, no, no... Don't say that. Please, don't say that."

"Did you even once consider that if you had left us the hell alone, I may have claimed her?" I know she doesn't deserve my words, but I'm too keyed up to stop. "If I did, she'd be alive right now. I'd have a woman in my bed instead of a little kid that I could barely even get hard for."

As soon as the words leave my mouth, I want to take them back. Nothing I said was true; far from it. But when I look at her face I know it's too late. I lashed out at her, and I did it in a way that I'll never be able to take back. "I'm sorry," I finally croak out.

She doesn't respond, just shakes her head and turns to run out the door. I can't let her leave like this. I'm just getting outside when I see a few of the brothers roll into the parking lot. Before I can say anything, she climbs on the back of Timber's bike and shouts for him to go. Fuck!

Reese climbs off his bike and walks towards me. He motions towards the tail lights of Timber's bike. "What's going on with Jenna?"

"I'm a dick." I say then turn and wall back into the club. I grab a bottle and head to my room, hoping to drink the pain away.

Jenna

Timber brought me to Merwin to show me some of the abandoned coal mines. The moonlight makes the small amount of coal still in the ground shine like diamonds. I walk around picking off the loose pieces of coal while Timber watches. He hasn't taken his eyes off of me since we got here. I know he wants to talk, and wants me to tell him what happened, but I'm not ready to tell him yet. I'm not sure I'll ever be ready to tell anyone.

I still can't believe what happened at the clubhouse. I thought Kidd would need me to be there for him. I sure in the fuck wasn't expecting whatever the hell that just was. All the things he said to me earlier were lies. We didn't make love; we fucked. Timmons was right. That's all I'm good for.

Today was all just a game to Kidd. He didn't want me for anything other than sex. He's just like every other guy out there. All he wanted was a piece on the side, and I gave it to him. Well, fuck him. That was the last piece he'll ever get from me.

I can't believe I truly thought he wanted me to be his old lady. I swear he could come crawling back to me, and I would never wear his brand. I won't be his old lady. I won't be anyone's old lady. He wants to treat me like a whore. I'll show him. I'll be one.

Finally done with my pity party, I walk over to Timber and lay down. We lay there for what seems like hours, side by side, staring at the stars. I place one of the coal pieces up to the sky, showing Timber how it sparkles. "It's beautiful here."

"Beautiful," he agrees in his gravelly voice.

I look over to him and see that he's staring at me. "You're not even looking," I say, motioning towards my rock.

"Why would I look at a chunk of coal, when I have someone as pretty as you lying beside me?"

His words send a blush to my face. I've been called pretty,

mostly by Chipper and Mindy, but they sure as hell never said it the way he did. I can't stop myself from looking at him, really looking. His light brown hair lays in waves to his shoulders, and he has a mustache that frames his mouth, ending right at his jaw line. I never thought guys with mustaches were hot, but Timber is definitely hot. I can't believe I've never noticed how handsome he is before. I guess I was so caught up in Kidd that I never really paid attention.

I've always liked Timber. He's a great guy. He knows a little of what I went through at the other club. We've never really talked about it, but I can tell by the way he looks at me sometimes. It's a mixture of sadness and anger. I know without a doubt that he would kill Timmons if I ever told him what he did.

While Kidd was away, I met a lot of the guys at the club. I liked most of them, but Timber and I became true friends. When Kidd wasn't there for me at Mindy's funeral, Timber sat by my side. He was there for me the whole time, never letting go of my hand. Why couldn't I just feel the same for Timber what I feel for Kidd? He's a great guy. He could be perfect for me.

"Wanna tell me what's wrong, pretty girl?" Timber asks, bringing my mind back to our conversation.

"Kidd was an asshole."

"I figured that. What'd he do?"

For some reason, the whole story comes flowing out of me. "I've had a crush on him since I first came here. I kept telling myself it would go away, but it never did. Then... Well, you know what happened at Mindy's funeral."

He nods, anger flashing through his eyes. "I know what the motherfucker did. He should've put that bitch in her place."

"You shouldn't talk about a dead person like that."

"Dead or not, that bitch was a bitch."

I ignore his words and continue my story. "My birthday was today. I was at the house all alone when he stopped by. He started telling me all this stuff about how I was his old lady. Then, we... Well, we had sex."

I feel Timber's body grows taut next to mine. "Kidd claimed you?"

"I thought he did, but then he went off after Sarah. When I saw him at the clubhouse, he said it was my fault that she died," I whisper out, afraid that he may agree with Kidd.

"What the fuck?" he shouts. "The bitch was driving too fast. Rum saw her. He said she had to be going eighty."

"But Kidd says that if we hadn't been together, it would've never happened."

"It's not your fault, babe. Kidd's just being a dick right now, because they had just had a fight. He feels guilty, nothing more." He rolls towards me. "He's probably already kicking himself in the ass for saying that shit to you. I know Kidd. He ain't gonna want to let you go."

I shake my head. "No, I waited for him for forever. I would've done anything for him, but now I'm done. Ever since he brought Sarah home, it's been one thing after another. This, well, this was the last straw," I say as I lean my head onto his shoulder.

He shifts slightly and wraps his arm around me, bringing me in closer. "You know there are other brothers that would take you for an old lady."

I shake my head against his chest. "I'm never going to be an old lady."

"Why don't you let me try to change your mind?" He says, placing his lips on mine.

Kidd

"Is she home yet?" I ask.

"I told you I'd let you know when she got here. There's no reason to keep calling me," Chipper growls out.

I don't bother responding, just hit end and stick my phone in my pocket. Calling Chipper and letting him know what happened between me and Jenna wasn't fun. I swear if we'd been face to face, he would've ripped my fucking head off. No doubt, I deserve it.

I lie in bed for a while longer then decide I need another drink if I'm ever gonna get to sleep. I'm walking into the common room just as Timber comes walking through the door. It's nearly four o'clock in the fucking morning, and I have no doubt he's been with Jenna this whole time. "Where the hell have you been?"

He stops and smiles at me, and his smile is anything but friendly. "I was spending some time with my girl."

I take a step closer to him, getting in his face. "She ain't your fucking girl."

"She's not yours either. She could have been, but you threw her away."

"She's mine. I don't give a shit what she told you."

"She's didn't have to tell me shit. Her tears soaking through my shirt did the talking for her," he says in a near shout.

I pull back and wipe my hand over my face. "I fucked up."

"You sure as hell did. You treated her like trash, and she ran away," he says with a nod of his head. "But you know what they say. One man's trash is another man's treasure."

As soon as the words leave his mouth, I have my hand against his chest, pushing him across the room. "You stay the fuck away from Jenna."

"Brother, you can beat my ass all you want. I'll still do everything I can to make her mine." With that, he pulls away from me and walks to his room.

I watch him walk away and realize that I'm gonna be fighting more than just Jenna's anger to get her back. I'll also be fighting at least one of my brothers.

CHAPTER Ten

Jenna

It's finally my graduation day, and I'm so nervous that my knees are knocking together. I'm on stage, getting my diploma; something I thought would never happen; something, both Chipper and Mindy pushed on me; something that would've never happened without them supporting me.

I look out to the crowd and tears start to pool in my eyes. Chipper, my dad, the man that is more of a father to me than anyone ever has been, is sitting in the front. His bright toothy smile hasn't left his face since I walked on stage. He told me this morning that he was as proud as any dad could ever be, and I told him that I was as lucky as any daughter could ever be.

My tears are for my mother. The mother of my heart, that is. Mindy would have been front and center to see this day, this moment. I can almost see the smile on her face, and missing that smile makes my heart ache. I see the time that I had with her for the gift it was, but I'm still angry that it had to end so soon.

Reese, Timber, and most of the other guys from the club are here. In fact, it seems like the front of the auditorium was reserved for the Renegade Sons. But there is one chair empty. The one right next to Chipper. I know that Chipper was saving that seat for Kidd. The fact that he isn't here cuts me to the core.

He was here earlier. I spotted him near the back when I walked in. We stared each other for what seemed like hours, but he never said anything and neither did I. Kidd has tried many times to talk with me since that night. Each time he does, I can tell that he's just doing it because he feels like he has too. I would rather he ignore me than feel like I'm some kind of obligation.

I know he's hurting. His woman is dead, and he was fucking me when she was dying, but it wasn't my fault. I don't care what he says. I didn't cause her death. I never would've let him touch me if I'd known they were still together. At least, that's what I tell myself. To be honest, I'm not sure I could ever tell him no. Even now, knowing he's as much of a jerk as my father is, I'm not sure I could turn him away.

Realizing that, I've been doing my best to stay clear of him. I probably won't be able to avoid him for long, because tomorrow, I have to tell Chipper my choice. I have to leave the club or join it. See, the club has rules. Women can't be members, but they can be property. There's only two ways to become Renegade Sons property. One is by becoming an old lady. The other is to become a whore. What you can't be is unclaimed. Now, I could go out into the world on my own if I wanted to, but I'd no longer be a part of the club. I'd still have Chipper, but my time with the rest of the boys would be cut back. I wouldn't be allowed at the clubhouse, except for family gatherings. There'd be no more poker parties at the clubhouse with Timber, no more bartending lessons with Preach, and no more midnight bonfires in the club yard with Reese and Pebbles.

Chipper doesn't want me to become a club girl. He wants me to get out and get away from all of this, but this is my family. Timber, Chipper, and Reese are three important men in my life that I can't live without. I've made my choice. I'm just not willing to give all that up. Really, I don't have many options. I hate school, so college is out. There's no damn way I'm spending the rest of my life flipping burgers, and that'd be the only job I could get without any kind of education. I could always dance at The Kitty Kat, but those girls end up being club whores before long anyway. So I don't see the reason in putting it off.

I think Chipper knows I'm leaning towards becoming a whore, because he's been talking to me about becoming one of the boys' old lady instead. He says that there are a lot of members that will take me, but I don't want any of them. We fought about that too. Maybe I'm still holding out hope for Kidd? Nah, that can't be it. I need to give up that fantasy. I know what being an old lady entails, and no way in hell am I going to be some housewife while my husband goes out and fucks around on me every night.

I shake off thoughts of Kidd, Sarah, and even Mindy, as I snatch my diploma from the superintendent's hand, and march off the stage. Unlike the rest of the parents that sit in their seats and clap, my family comes running. Before my feet even hit the auditorium floor, I'm tossed over Chipper's shoulders and Timber shouts, "It's time to fucking party!"

They don't even give me time to change, so I end up on the back of Chipper's hog in my gown and cap. We barely make it out of the parking lot before my hats flies off. I watch it sail into the sky, and a big smile crosses my face.

Thirty minutes later, I'm sitting at the club talking to Chipper. I knew we were going to have this conversation, but I didn't realize that it would be so soon. "Can't we talk about it later?"

He shakes his head. "No, darlin'. We need to talk about it now. If you're going to college, we got to get your applications and shit started."

"I know," I whisper, trying to stall. I don't want to disappoint him, but I don't want to leave the only family I've ever known.

"So Jenna, hun, what have you decided?" Chipper says softly.

I sigh and nod. "I've decided to stay."

His face goes hard and turns red. "The fuck you will. I love you girl. You know that, but I want better for you."

"I'm not leaving my family," I say quietly. "I can't leave you."

He grabs my hand and gives it a squeeze. "You don't have to leave forever. Just go to school for a while, and then you can come home."

"I don't want to leave for even a day."

"Then go to community college. It'll be just like it was in high school. You go during the day, but you'll be home every night."

I shake my head. "I hated school. You know that. If it wasn't for you and Mindy, I would've quit a long time ago."

"College will be different," he pushes.

I shake my head again. "No, it won't." I look into his eyes, hoping that he'll see how determined I am. "You said this was my decision, and I've made it. I'm staying."

"So, you want to be a whore. You want to be used by all the guys and tossed to the side when they get what they want."

I shrug. "Been there, done that. At least this time, it'll be for men I respect."

Anger flashes in his eyes. "Think about it a little more, and we'll talk again in a few days."

"I'm sorry if you're disappointed, but a few days will not change my mind."

"Fuck," he yells and stomps away.

Kidd

I walk into The Kitty Kat and hear sounds of *Rag Doll* by Aerosmith pumping through the club. I look over to Preach and Reese who are walking in with me. "Sounds like one of the girls has a new routine. I haven't heard that one in here before."

A smile spreads across Preach's face, and Reese rubs his hands together. "Yeah, let's go see who's shaking their ass."

As I walk further into the room, the stage comes into view. What I see takes my breath away. Jenna has one leg wrapped around a stripper pole, her upper body bent back, and her hair brushing the floor. Her beautiful nipples are covered with red flower pasties, and a silver G-string is the only thing covering her ass.

Anger shoots straight through me. I take a step towards the stage, but Reese grabs my arms. "What the fuck are you doing, man?"

"I'm getting her ass off that stage. I don't know what in the hell she's doing up there, but this shit is gonna stop."

"She's been dancing for a few weeks. You've been on the road, so you didn't know. She's been working here since she graduated."

"Why the fuck did Chipper let her do this?"

Reese shrugs. "Wasn't his choice. You know the rules. Girls are old ladies or whores. The choice of which one she wanted to be was hers."

I jerk away from him. "She could've went to college."

"Jenna wanted to stay part of the club. This is the only life she knows, and she didn't want to walk away from it. Just be happy she's not whoring yet."

I get in his face. "She's not gonna whore, and any brother that touches her will pay. He'll pay with his fuckin' life."

"Unless you plan on eighty-sixing her, then it's not your choice what she does. Long as she follows the rules, she can spread for whoever she wants."

His words send my already bubbling anger to its boiling point. "Like I said, a brother touches her, he dies."

"Until you brand her, she's free game. The boys won't force shit on her, but they will take what she gives them. Jenna's not only beautiful, but she the freaking queen of the Big Clifty crew. Every brother is panting to get a piece of her. You can't fight every one of us."

What the fuck? "Everyone knows she's mine."

Preach steps up and adds in his two cents. "Everyone also knows you did her dirty. Your half ass claim won't stop them."

"Fuck you both!" I shout, as I stomp out the door.

CHAPTER Eleven

Jenna

I walk into the club, my legs shaking with each step. There's a party here tonight, and it's my first night as one of the girls. I've been working at The Kitty Kat for nearly three months now, but I haven't actually slept with any of the guys yet. At least not for money, but I have for pleasure. Believe me, Reese and Timber are all about pleasure. It seems I've got a talent for shaking my naked ass; so much so that some of the guys talked Roxy into letting me work the party.

Most of the girls start working parties as soon as they start working at The Kitty Kat, but Roxy refused to let me come to the clubhouse. In fact, she tried to keep me off the stage. She didn't even want me waitressing. For my first month there, I wasn't allowed out from behind the bar, but Timber put an end to that.

He made sure that Roxy knew that eighteen year old girls did not serve booze. No way, no how. We can take off our clothes all day long, but we are not allowed to do personal dances or touch the liquor. That shit is illegal. He also made sure to tell me that Roxy knew that it was illegal. He said that she's just trying to keep Reese from seeing my naked ass.

Too bad for her; he already has. Yes, I have slept with Reese. Quite a few times, actually. After what my mom went through, I never thought I'd willingly sleep with a married man, but Reese is different. He's married to a bitch. No that's not true; he's married to *the bitch*!

Roxy not only throws attitude his way all the fucking time, but she also spreads her legs for any guy that comes around. In fact, she's been doing that for a while now. Long enough to give him a beautiful red headed daughter; a daughter that he loves more than anything in the world even though he knows that she can't possibly be his. She would and could snatch Pebbles away from him if Reese ever thought about kicking her ass to the curb.

"What the hell are you doing here?" I hear from behind me as I continue to walk into the clubhouse.

I stiffen because I know that voice. It's the voice I've learned to hate. I turn around and glare at him. I motion towards my barely there dress and say, "What's it look like I'm here for?"

His face goes hard. "You are fucking crazy if you think I'm gonna let you be a club whore."

"Sorry, boss. The decision has already been made," I say,

shooting him a saccharine sweet smile.

He shakes his head and leans his head towards mine. "No, fucking way!"

"Your dad already approved it, and last time I looked, he was president," I say, making sure to put just a bit of bitch into my voice. "We can talk about it again when you take up the gavel."

"Aren't you ever going to give me a chance to apologize?" he asks, his voice getting loud.

"There's nothing to apologize for. You didn't do anything that most men don't do on a daily basis. You wanted some pussy and you said what you had to say to get it."

"I'm sorry about Mindy's funeral. I shouldn't have left you. I'm also sorry about the things I said the night Sarah died. They weren't true," he says, his voice strained.

I want to scream and tell him he's right. I want to tell him that he should have been there for me and how much his words hurt me, but I can't. I can't let him see how much pain I'm in.

"You know what? Fuck you." He looks as if I've hit him.

"Don't do this, Jenna. We're friends."

"Here's a news flash for ya, big guy. You and me, we're not even friends anymore. We haven't been in a long damn time, not since you made me your whore. Not since you blamed me for Sarah's death. Now we're not anything. Isn't that awesome?" I say sarcastically and paste on a fake ass smile. "I fuckin' hate you."

And with that, he looks as if he just found out someone died. Good. I want him to feel that pain. I want him to feel the pain that I've been feeling ever since he left me. I only get two steps away from him before he's pulling me back. "I might not be able to stop you, but I ain't going to let you walk in there like that."

I jerk my arm away. "What do you mean?"

"When you go in there tonight, you have no power. They won't hurt you, but you'll have no choice about who you end up with. The only one of the girls that has that power is Roxy. As the lead, she controls what goes on. If she was working the party, she would be able to choose who she hooked up with." He looks me up and down, something important working behind his eyes. "Roxy hasn't been doing her job the way she's supposed to. I've been looking for someone to take over. I know you'll need help, but Mary will lend a hand whenever you want."

"What are you saying?" I ask, knowing he cannot mean what I think he does.

"I want you to take Roxy's place."

I shake my head. "She would shit a brick if I took the girls from her."

147

"I don't give a fuck. If she gives you any trouble, let me know. I'll handle her."

I only take a second to think about it. I know Roxy, and I know the stuff she does to the girls isn't right. "As long as Mary will teach me the ropes, I think I could handle it."

He nods before placing his hand on my cheek. "Are you sure this is what you want?"

"Of course I am. This way I get to choose who I fuck." I pull away and sneer at him. "There are some real assholes out there."

"Yeah, there are," he says, a wealth of meaning behind his words.

"What about tonight?"

He shakes his head. "Nope, you go home. Let me talk to Roxy and let her know she's done. After that, I'll tell the girls you're in charge."

I nod and turn away. Before I reach the door, I hear him shout. "Night, baby girl."

Kidd

I stalk over to the bar where I see Chipper. He looks about as happy as I do. "She's really doing this shit?" I ask him.

Chipper grunts. "Yeah, she's been at The Kitty Kat for a few months now. I was hoping she'd stick to just stripping, but I guess that ain't going to happen."

"She can make good money dancing. She doesn't need to come here."

"I know, brother. Told her that myself. I've done everything I could to talk her outta this shit, but she won't budge." He looks at me, eyes narrowed. "For some reason, she has it in her head that being a whore is all she's good for. Wonder where she got that idea?"

Hearing Chipper say that makes me madder than hell. Knowing that he blames me pisses me way the fuck off. She's not a fuckin' whore, and I never said she was. I may have said shit to make her think that, but I sure in the hell didn't feel like she was anything other than the woman I wanted as my own. I wanted her more than anything in this world. I know I fucked up with Jenna, but I have no damn idea how to fix it. After the night I was an idiot, she hasn't given me the time of day. She won't let me apologize or explain where my head was at. Nothing.

"I'm gonna have her take over the girls," I say after asking the prospect behind the bar for some whiskey.

"Roxy's gonna shit a brick." Chipper says and then grins. "Can't stand that bitch anyway. Not sure what the hell Reese was thinking, tying himself to her."

"Don't know, and at this point, don't care. I just don't want her to turn The Kitty Kat into a free for all," I explain. "This way, Jenna can do what she wants, pick her own partners, and not just get taken like all the rest of the whores."

He nods. "At least it's something."

I toss the whiskey down my throat and look back to Chipper. "Wanna come with me to find Roxy. I might need someone to restrain her," I say chuckling.

"Yeah, I'm down. Grab Reese too. He'll want to hear this shit from us. God knows how Roxy would spin it."

We get up and walk over to where Roxy and Reese are playing pool. Well, Reese is playing pool. Roxy is spending her time trying to get some of the brothers' attention, but most of them have already learned her game and are staying clear. How Reese stands to be around her, I don't know. By the look on his face, he's not a happy man. If I was in his shoes, I'd put a bullet in the bitch's head. I'd raise my daughter on my own. Pebbles would be a hell of a lot better off if he did.

"You two," I say, pointing towards then. "Office. We gotta have a chat."

Roxy stiffens as soon as she hears my tone. The bitch knows her game is over, and she's scared. They both follow us quickly into my office.

"Take a seat."

"Uh, did we do something wrong?" Roxy asks hesitantly.

"Nope, but what we gotta say won't be pretty," I say to her then look towards Reese.

He raises a brow. "What's up?"

"Roxy here is gonna get bent outta shape, so we figured we'd do it with you around." When I say that, Roxy instantly goes on alert, her eyes narrowing.

"I know I gave you control over the women, but that's done now. I have someone to take over. I appreciate the work, but I need someone that's capable to run that shit. I need someone I know I can trust. Sorry to say Roxy, but that's not you."

"I've been doing a good job," She says with a sneer.

I hear Reese mumble under his breath for her to shut up, but I know she's not gonna listen, so I lay it out for her. "You're all kinds of fucked up, and half the girls you've brought into the club are as bad as you. Damn near every one of them is using, and you knew how I felt about drugs in the club from day one. Also, Pop explained the importance of regular check-ups. I know that shit isn't happening, because some of them bitches are a walking petri dish."

Roxy jumps up from her chair. "Fuck you! I've done great things here. I've brought in more girls then you've ever had here!" she yells.

Reese grabs her arm. "Shut the fuck up now, or I'll shut

you up myself."

I don't wait to see if Roxy listens. I'm too fucking pissed off to care. "Yeah, you have. The fact remains, the girls you brought here are shit. They need rules and someone to lead their asses. Jenna will do a better job of that than you ever thought about doing," I say, standing up and getting in her face.

"Jenna? Are you fuckin' kidding me! That bitch can't do shit. She's nothing but a kid." She turns to Reese and looks about ready to kill the guy. "You did this. I knew you were fuckin' that slut!" she yells at him.

"Shut up, Roxy! What Jenna and I do ain't none of your fuckin' business, but I will tell you this. Kidd's right. Jenna does a better job than you ever thought of doing and not just when it comes to running the girls" he says inches from her face.

"What the fuck?" No way, no damn way! Reese can't be fuckin' her. She's mine.

152

CHAPTER Twelve

Jenna

It took me nearly two weeks, but I finally finished hiring the new girls. By the time I was done cleaning up Roxy's mess, there were only two girls left. I need at least ten to work the Kitty Kat, and another ten to work the clubhouse. Needless to say, finding that many girls willing to flash their tits and sell their pussy was not easy. I even have rules in place, and when I showed them to Kidd and Chipper, they were shocked. Monthly check ups and random drug tests whenever I feel the need. Birth control and condoms are a must. No bitches.

Reese's old lady really fucked this shit up. It's hard to believe she's only had control for a year. I can't imagine the mess she would've made if Kidd hadn't removed her. I have no idea what Gun was thinking when he let her run the girls. No, that's not true. We would've had some dead girls and the cops breathing down our necks.

Today is clean-up day. I'm at the apartment that the club

keeps for the girls, trying to get it ready for my new girls. When I decided to tackle this on my own, I had no idea it would be this bad. Looking at the mess I created going through apartments has me pissed. Believe it or not, one of the girls kept records. Everything is here in black and white for me to see. Prostituting in and out of the club, and giving a fifty percent cut over to Roxy. That bitch even had them selling sex out of the private dance rooms. What the fuck?!

That was just the tip of the iceberg. Let's not even get into the fuckin' drugs I found in the dressers. Coke, heroine, meth… you name, and it was here. Some of the bathrooms even have blood splatter on the wall. Being with Timmons, I know what that's from. A needle hitting the vein wrong can send blood everywhere.

I didn't think I'd ever be in this job, especially after working at the Kitty Kat for only three months. Sometimes, I think it's too much for me, but I'm glad I don't have to work for Roxy anymore. That bitch is fuckin' psycho. She turned up a time or two and tried to boss my girls around, but I wasn't having it. We ended up having words, and she tried to come at me. Once I showed her the gun Chipper insisted I carry, she backed up, but not before telling me that this shit wasn't over.

I made sure to tell Chipper about her showing up. I hated to turn to the guys for help, but I had too much to deal with to put up with her shit. I haven't seen her since, and I'm pretty sure

Kidd and Chipper banned her from the club and the clubhouse.

Reese needs to figure out a way to get rid of that bitch and still keep his little girl. I know she holds Pebbles' real dad over his head, but there are more ways than divorce to end a marriage. Even though I don't think a man should take his hand to a woman, I think that bitch deserves a little punishment. God knows, Pebbles would be better off without her around.

I'm brought back from thoughts of murdering the bitch myself when Chipper and Kidd come in. Seeing Kidd sends a wave of heat through my body. When in the hell am I gonna get over him?

"What'd you find?" Chipper asks.

"A bunch of shit." I say as I throw the papers on the coffee table in front of them. "One of the girls was keeping track of what was going on. Looking at the shit she wrote, I don't think she liked it. I'm thinking she was just too scared of Roxy to say no."

"Which one?" Kidd asks, picking the papers up.

"Skittles, the chick with the multicolored hair."

He nods. "I remember her."

"I'm sure you do," I snarl, remembering walking in on him getting his dick sucked by her not too long ago.

He ignores me and shakes the papers in his hands. "What's

all in here?"

"She was keeping track of everything. What the other girls were using, how much they were using," I say, bending towards him and pointing to the yellow sheet of paper in his hand. "This here is proof that Roxy was pimping the girls out to non-club members. It tells when, where, and how much of the money they had to give to her."

"Fuck," Chipper mumbles.

"Like I said, this girl documented everything. She's smart. I'd like to bring her back in."

Kidd opens the papers and looks them over. Every few moments, he looks up at me. I swear every time he does, it makes my knees weak. It's like this every damn time I see him, and that's why I try my hardest to ignore the bastard whenever he's around. He doesn't like it. Kidd is not a man who's used to being ignored, but his reaction to it makes me sort of happy, somewhat. When he realizes I'm not going to talk to him, he gets this sexy jaw clench and muscle tick. So hot!

At first, he did his best to get my attention. I swear every time I turned around he was there, but over the last month, he's stopped talking to me all together. He usually just goes through the boys and gets them to tell me what he wants done with the club girls. I just ignore them too, when they say Kidd wants this or Kidd wants that, I just do whatever in the hell I want.

"I'll let you two sort this. I gotta make a quick run," Chipper says as he walks out the apartment door. My eyes narrow on his back. Before he's fully outside, he turns to me and winks, giving me a knowing grin. Bastard!

Ignoring Kidd's burning glare at my back, I go back to cleaning up the blood from the bathroom walls. I swear I've been scrubbing for hours, and I'm not even half way done.

"You don't need to be doing that. Get the new girls and some prospects in here. They can do that shit for you," Kidd says, walking into the bathroom.

I just ignore him and continue doing my thing. It's not like I really have much else to do today anyways. Plus, I'm used to this. I clean the clubhouse and The Kitty Kat all the time. After Mindy died, I sort of became a bit OCD with the cleaning. As much as I get pissed off at the nasty ass people I work with, there's something about making things clean that seems to take the edge off.

"Jenna!" Kidd snaps.

Again, I ignore him. When's he going to take the hint? I'm not talking to him, because I have nothing to say. At least, nothing nice. I run my sponge behind the toilet and feel something furry. "Oh my God, I think there's a dead rat back there," I say to myself, not to Kidd. Definitely not talking to Kidd.

"Fuck!" I hear, then heavy boots coming towards me. I brace when he wraps a hand around my arm and spins me around to face him.

"I'm tired of you fuckin' ignoring me," he says as he takes a step closer, causing me to take a step back. "I'm tired of your fuckin' ice queen bullshit."

He backs me into the wall, and his hands come up to cage me in. "I miss you, baby girl," he whispers, putting his forehead against mine.

His words slice right through me. Misses me, huh? Well, he must not miss me much when he's fuckin' with a different girl every night. With that thought, I shove him off me.

"Stay away from me, Kidd," I say, trying to keep my emotions at bay. "Miss me all you want. It ain't going to change anything. I miss you too. I miss the friendship we had, but when I think on it, I remember… I remember it was all just a lie. You used me, treated me like shit, then threw me away," I say, moving away from him.

"It wasn't a lie. You mean the world to me," he whispers.

"Everything about you is a lie. If you ever cared anything about me at all, just leave me alone. Just stay the fuck away from me," I shout as I turn and run out of the apartment.

I hear a loud crash and Kidd yelling 'fuck', but I just keep running.

Kidd

I walk into the clubhouse with Preach just as Chipper comes storming towards the door.

He damn near knocks me over, anger coming off him in waves. "Whoa, big bro. What's the problem?"

He doesn't respond, just turns around staring behind him. It's then I notice Jenna standing there, hands planted on her hips. She looks like she's trying to get him to calm down, and he's determined to flip the fuck out. "What the hell's going on with you two?"

"Want me to fill him in on what we're discussin'?" Chipper says and Jenna's face turns hard.

"Do it. Not only will he probably not care, he might even take a few rounds of his own," she says darkly.

"Fuck it!" Chipper yells then jerks his head towards mine. "Some of the girls are sick, can't work the party with the Lords tonight. Jenna's determined to take their place."

"I don't have a choice," she shouts. "Four girls are down with the flu, and two more are on the road with Rum and Timber. That only leaves three for tonight."

Fuck! I don't want Jenna part of this shit. She's been working the girls for a few months now, and I know she's been with a few of the brothers. So far, I'm pretty sure only Reese and Timber have taken her to bed. That's two too many for me, but it's a hell of a lot better than her being shared amongst all the brothers. With the Lords being here tonight, there'll be over a hundred bikers looking for a piece of ass in the club. I don't want that for Jenna. "You have no idea what tonight will be like. Believe me, you don't want no part of it."

Her eyes hone in on me. "I don't have a choice. I can't make three girls deal with all those boys. I'm not saying I'm gonna let them pull a train on me, but I can be here to watch out for my girls."

"You better change your mind girl! If one of those, hell all of those, boys want you, there won't be a damn thing you can do about it. The party will be out of control. It always is when another crew comes to town," Chipper yells. "I don't want you doin' that shit. It'll kill you. I don't know why the hell you just don't become Timber's old lady!"

When the words leave his mouth, I turn to him scowling. "Shut the fuck up about that shit."

The fucker knows how I feel about Jenna. Hell, I've talked to him a million times about it. I finally broke down and told him everything that happened between us, even took the ass whooping for it. He probably knows what he's saying right now is pissing me off, but he doesn't seem to care.

"I told you a million times that I love Timber. He's my

friend, a better friend than anyone else. But I'm not going to be an Old Lady. I've tried that once, and it didn't work out too great," Jenna says, sending me a fuck you look.

"Don't go there, Jenna. I already told you, I'm tired of the ice queen act."

"Fuck you, Kidd." she says walking past me. She rushes out the door with Chipper on her ass.

I run my hand down my face, frustrated as fuck.

"Give her time, man. She just needs a little time to work through her shit. You laid her low. It's gonna take a while for her to forgive you," Preach says, walking towards the bar.

I follow and tell the prospect tending bar to bring me a beer. "It's been months, damn near a year. How much fuckin' time is she gonna need?"

He shrugs. "You treated her like a kid, called her your little sister. When she becomes legal, you fuck her and claim her without explaining shit to her. Then you tell her it was her fault your piece on the side died. Not sure, man, but I'm thinking it might take a while to get over all that shit."

I give him a look that says fuck off. "Thanks for laying it out for me, brother."

"Not a problem," he says with a smirk, but then his face goes serious. "You need to back the fuck off. If you keep getting in her face, she ain't ever gonna have a chance to get over this shit. She needs space to come to terms with her own feelings. If you don't give her that space, you're gonna lose her forever."

"I'll give her space, all the fuckin' space she needs. But one way or another, she'll be mine someday."

Part Two

Six Years Later

CHAPTER Thirteen

Jenna

Reese rolls to his back, pulling me into his side. "God, baby! Every fucking time I sink my dick into you, it's better than the last."

"If it gets any better, you just might kill me." I say, throwing my leg over his.

He chuckles then starts to run his hands through my hair. "That is true."

We lay there quietly for a few minutes until I feel my eyes start to get heavy. I may want to sleep, but I don't have time right now. I shake off my sleepiness, sit up, and then crawl off the bed. I've just about made it when Reese tags me and pulls me on top of him. "Where the hell do you think you're going?"

For a minute, I just stare at him. Other than Kidd, Reese is the sexiest man I have ever laid eyes on. He stands a good five inches over six feet, and his body is pure muscle. His eyes are so dark that they're nearly black, and his hair is the color of dark chocolate, hanging low on his back. He's half Polynesian and half Native American. The combination is pure beauty.

Finally, I place my hands on his cheeks and give him a soft kiss. Reese and Timber are the only two guys that I kiss. The others may get a quick peck every now and then, but my guys get anything they want. Reese and Timber are definitely my guys. "You know I got to go. I told you before you pulled me to your room that I had to dance tonight."

His eyes search my face, and he says the same thing that he says every time we make love. "I wish I could make you mine."

I close my eyes, trying to hide the pain I feel. Being a whore isn't so bad, but falling in love with one of the guys you service is, especially when that guy is married. I know I'm falling in love with Reese. Shit, I've loved him for years. It's different than the love I feel for Kidd, but it's love all the same.

I look into his dark chocolate eyes and smile. "I know you would, but you got to think of Pebbles."

He squeezes me tight and smiles sadly. "Yeah, baby. I got to take care of my girl, but I can still wish that you were mine."

Pebbles' bright green eyes and sweet smile flash through my mind. She's nearly grown now, but she's still just a kid to her dad. Blood or not, Pebbles is his baby girl, and he has to be there to protect her from her bitch of a mother. Soon he'll able to cut his ties with Roxy, but until then, he's gotta do what he's gotta do.

I bury my face into his neck and sigh. "We can both wish."

We cuddle for a few minutes more before we get up and get dressed. As soon as we step into the hallway, I hear one of the club hanger-ons screaming. "You think you can just use me, because you're a Renegade Son. You need to think again. I'm not just some piece of trash, and I won't be used."

I look to Reese and roll my eyes. "When are these girls ever going to learn?"

A hanger-on is nothing in the club. Shit! They're less than nothing. A hanger-on is a chick that only comes in to get her rocks off every once in a while. The members don't hurt them, but they don't respect them either. For the guys, these women are nothing more than cum buckets.

If a woman wants to be treated with respect, she has to earn it. There are only two ways to do that; become a club girl or become and old lady. Granted, old ladies and club whores are considered property of the club, but everyone knows that the Renegade Sons take care of what they consider their property.

How much respect an old lady is given depends on her old man. Most of the members treat their old ladies like they're gold. Roxy and Lula are the only ones that I've seen that aren't respected. Believe me, those two deserve any shit that is thrown at them.

Reese grabs my arm just before we step into the common room. I look towards him, but he's not looking at me. He looks almost afraid, but not for himself. What the hell? I turn to look into the common room, and see that it's one of the girls that's been coming around here for years, totally bitchin' out Chipper. What the hell did he do? He doesn't touch the bitches here; mainly, because I'm here and he doesn't want his little girl to see that shit, or so he says.

But, I know the truth. He hasn't gotten over Mindy yet. She's been dead nearly six years, but she's still on his mind every day. I'm sure he uses women when he has an itch that needs to be scratched, but I figure he doesn't scratch that itch very often.

I pull my arm from Reese and take a step into the room just as Cary sticks her finger into Chipper's face. "I don't come to this club to give blow jobs, I come to get laid. If you knew that you couldn't keep your dick up long enough to fuck me, you should have gone to one of the club skanks to get blown."

Chipper doesn't respond. He just keeps looking at her like she's crazy as shit. I can tell he wants to knock her on her ass, but he would never lay a hand on a woman. Well, he may not believe in hitting women, but I sure as hell do. I take a step towards him when Reese grabs my arm. "Let Chipper take care of this."

I shake my head. "Hell no. I'm not letting that slut talk to him like that."

"He's a man, Ice. He won't want you stepping into his shit. What would his brothers say if you did?"

I take a second to think about his words before nodding. I know Reese is right. Chipper would kick my ass if I got into the middle of this shit. Even worse, he'd have to listen to the rest of the guys calling him a pussy for letting his little girl take care of him. Then, he'd kick my ass for that. Finally, I nod. I'm just about to turn away when the bitch rears back and slaps him. All thoughts of letting Chipper deal with it fly out of my head, and I totally fuckin' lose it as I rush towards them.

Reese tries to hold me back again by grabbing my arm. "I said, let him handle it."

"Fuck that shit!" I scream as I swing my body and dislodge his grip on my arm. I race forward and tackle the whore. She starts to use her nails and gets on top of me, but Timmons taught me a few things and every one of them is going to come in handy now.

I grab the side of her face, placing my thumbs in her eyes

and push. As I do my best to push her eyeballs through her fuckin' brain, I roll her over and straddle her. Then, I start punching. "You crazy ass bitch. You don't come in here and pull this shit."

I continue to punch and scream, until someone jerks me off of the bitch. I'm so damn mad that I start to fight whoever's holding me.

"Damn it, Ice. Quit this shit."

As soon as I hear the gravelly voice, my body goes rock solid. "Let go of me, Kidd."

This is the first time he's touched me in years; nearly six to be exact. Even though I'm angry as hell, I have to fight from melting into him. After all this time, my body still knows where it belongs.

He gives my midsection a squeeze. "I will, if you promise to walk out of here."

"She slapped Chipper." I shout, wanting to pummel the bitch a little more.

"I know she did, and she'll pay for that, but you gotta let me take care of it."

I want to argue. My heart is aching to defend the man that saved me, but my brain is telling me to let the guys do what they need to do. I take a deep breath and nod my head. "Fine, but make sure the bitch gets what's coming to her."

I can feel his body vibrate as he chuckles. "Didn't know you were such a blood thirsty bitch."

I pull away from him and turn around. "I am, and don't you forget it."

Without looking back, I start to walk towards the door. I'm only a few steps away, when I hear a shout. "Grab her."

I turn around and see Cary running towards me with a fuckin' knife in her hand. Without taking the time to think about it, I run towards Reese, pull the gun from his hip, and then turn to her. A second later, she's lying in a pool of blood at my feet.

I can't seem to take my eyes off of her frozen, crumpled body. The sight of her makes my stomach roll and my heart hurt. What did I just do? Did I really just take another's life? Oh my God! I drop the gun and sink to the floor.

I feel arms around me and hear murmured voices telling me that it's okay. It's ok? How can that be true? How the fuck is this okay? I just killed someone. I just took someone's life. Nothing will ever be okay again.

I feel tears running down my face. I reach up and try to wipe them away before pulling my shaking hands back and looking at them. For the first time, I notice the vibrant red blood that they're covered in; blood of the woman I just killed. My already rolling stomach starts to churn, and I know I'm gonna be sick. Oh my God.

"I've got Jenna. You take care of this shit. Make sure that her body is never found." I hear shouted as I start dry heaving. I can't believe I killed someone.

I'm jerked up into Kidd's arms. He pushes my face into his neck. "Shh, baby girl. It's ok. I've got you," he whispers into my hair.

I shake my head and whisper, "No, no, it's not ok. Nothing will ever be okay again."

He walks me to his room and crawls on the bed, still cradling me in his arms. He holds me close as my tears drench his shirt. I can feel him rubbing slow circles on my back, doing his best to soothe me. Neither of us says a thing as I lay there crying. Slowly, the sobs fade away and sleep over takes me.

I wake up still sprawled across Kidd. He used to touch me all the time, but that changed after my birthday. Being in his arms again feels good -- too good. I carefully pull my head back to look up at him, hoping that he's sleeping, but he's not. He's wide awake, and his eyes are glued on my face.

I know I need to say something, but I'm not sure where to begin. I end up blurting out, "I'm sorry I killed her."

He gives my waist a squeeze and smiles. "It happens to the best of us."

I know he's trying to tease me, and trying to make me feel better, but I'm not in the mood for that. I know a shit storm is heading my way, and I need to be prepared. "She was coming at me with a knife, so it was self-defense."

He nods. "Yeah, baby doll. It was."

"Do you think I'll have to go to prison?" I whisper out.

He shakes his head, squeezing me tight. "Hell no."

"The police might not believe it was self-defense. Look at Timber. The guy he cut was trying to rape one of the girls at the strip club, and they still sent him to prison."

"Yeah, baby, but Timber sliced him in The Kitty Kat parking lot. There were people there, and they only saw Timber shooting the guy. They didn't see the bastard trying to rape Skittles. Plus, Timber had a record." He takes a deep breath and continues. "Skittles was his only witness. Even though it's not right, truth is that a stripper who whores herself on the side doesn't look that great up on the stand."

What he says is true, but the only people that saw Cary with a knife was Chipper, Kidd, and Reese. All three of which have seen the inside of jail cell more than once. Plus, Chipper is like a dad to me, Reese is my lover, and Kidd... well Kidd is something that I can't quite put a label on. "The cops might not believe you guys about the knife."

"Cops?" he asks, confusion lacing through his voice. "The cops ain't ever gonna know shit about this."

"You're not going to tell the police? What about her? You

know, her body and stuff?" I ask, the word 'body' making my stomach ache.

"It's been taken care of. Everything has. All you gotta do is keep your mouth shut," he says, looking determined. "Just forget this day ever happened."

I lay my head back on his chest and close my eyes, but the sight of her bleeding out on the floor at my feet flashes through my mind. "How do you forget something like that? How do you forget that you killed someone?"

He starts to run his hands through my hair as he answers. "I'm not sure if you'll ever forget it, but that pain you got coursing through you will go away. It just takes time. I want you to remember, though, that she would've taken your life if you hadn't pulled that trigger. Believe me, I'm glad that you took the bitch down. I'm just sorry that I didn't do it for you."

We lay there quietly before he says something that rocks my world. "I miss you, Jenna. I know I fucked up, but that was a long damn time ago. Can't you at least give me a chance to make up for it?"

Before I have an opportunity to respond, someone knocks on the door. A second later, Chipper sticks his head in. "How's my girl?"

I jump from the bed and run to Chipper, wrapping my arms around him. I'm happy that he's here, but even happier that I didn't have to tell Kidd how much I missed him too; how all it would take is one kiss and I'd fall right back into his arms. "I'm going to be okay, but I want to go home with you. I don't want to stay at the clubhouse tonight."

He looks towards the bed and lifts his chin to Kidd before leading me out of the club. I never look back at Kidd, and do my best to forget his words. He may miss me, but he doesn't love me. I can never forget that.

Kidd

Watching Jenna leave my room with Chipper pisses me way the fuck off. I hate that she has to go through this shit. I know what it's like to take someone's life. It's not something you can just get over. That shit doesn't hurt; it kills. I know it's going to eat at her for a long time, maybe forever. I knew she needed someone to be there for her, and I jumped on the chance to be that someone.

It felt nice holding her, even though every one of her tears cut right through me. Holding her in my arms and having her talk to me without bitchin' reminded me of what it used to be like between us. I felt like I was finally getting somewhere with her, finally breaking through that wall that she built around her heart after I royally fucked up. Then, Chipper walked in. I'm not stupid. I know she took him showing up as a chance to run, and she did. She ran as fast as she could.

Now, I feel like we're back at square fucking one. How did I let shit get this bad between us? I know that what I said to her after Sarah's death cut her to the core, but it's hard to apologize when the person you wronged hasn't spoken to you in over six fucking years.

There's no way she thinks that I really meant the things I said to her after Sarah's death. She had to know that Sarah was only her stand in. Everyone knew that I was just waiting for her to get older, to be able to make her mine. I know now, I should have sent Sarah packing as soon as I laid eyes on Jenna. I most definitely should have told her to hit the road after Mindy's funeral. Shit! I should have never brought her down here in the first place.

If I hadn't made those mistakes, I would have my Jenna. Instead, what I got is a cold hearted bitch that barely talks to me, let alone acknowledges I even fuckin' exist. Hell, that's not true. I don't even have the cold hearted bitch either. Truth be told, I'd take the new Jenna, Ice, in a heartbeat and just pray I could thaw her out.

For now, I'll give Jenna this play. I'll let her pretend that she doesn't want me. Hell, I'll let her pretend I don't even exist. She can play at being as cold as she wants, but when I see she finally has her shit together, she's mine, and I won't be taking no for an answer. I just hope it won't take too long for her to see the light, because I'm not sure I can hold off much longer.

I shake off my thoughts of Jenna when my phone rings. I pick it up and see a number that's from one of the throwaway cells that we sneak into the boys in prison. "Hello."

"What the fuck, man? How the hell could you let that happen?" Timber growls into the phone.

I take a breath to control my temper. "How did you find out?"

"I talked to Reese. He's pissed as fuck! I can't believe you let that shit go down."

Again, I have to fight to control my temper. Not only is my brother screaming at me, but he's also doing his best to claim my woman. Seeing Jenna with the guys around the club makes me mad as hell. A few times, Chipper's had to lock me in my room to keep me from beating the piss outta whichever bastard is touching her. Yeah, seeing my Jenna with other guys hurts, but it's nothing compared to her relationship with Timber. He loves Jenna. Sometimes, I wonder if he may love her as much I do. What's even worse is that she loves him too.

"If you talked to Reese, you know what happened. There's no reason for me to tell you again, and if Reese is pissed, he should be pissed at himself. He was standing right beside her. It's his piece she used."

Reese is another problem that I don't even want to think

about. He and Jenna are tight, too fucking tight. Brother is so pussy whipped when it comes to her that I'm surprised he can even function on his own. He's been asking me to let him cut his old lady loose and claim Jenna, but there's no fucking way I'm going to let that shit happen.

"I know, he told me, but he's not the president of the fucking club. You are."

"I can't control everything."

"Well, brother, that's the job you took on when Gun died. If you can't handle it, maybe you should step aside."

"Fuck you, man."

"No, fuck you. I'm not stupid. I know what happened. You were too busy watching Ice's ass to notice the bitch had a blade."

His words make me angry, but the truth behind them makes me furious. "I don't want to talk about this shit any longer, so if you got something important to say, you better get it said."

"Have you been giving Ice my letters?" he asks, sounding sure that he already knows the answer.

Shit! When I first started getting letters at the clubhouse for Jenna, I just couldn't stop myself from opening them. When I saw what was inside of them, I knew I'd never let one make it to her. Timber, my best fucking friend, wants to make my girl his old lady. Just like with Reese, I'm not letting that happen.

"Yeah man, I am. Ice doesn't need that shit right now. You get out, then you can talk to her. Until then, keep your fucking feelings to yourself."

He laughs again, but this time it sounds genuine. "Sure, man. I'll do that. As soon as I'm home, I'll have her on the back of my bike. Oh, and just so you know, my parole was approved two days ago. I should be home in a few weeks."

I have to grind my teeth together to keep from shouting that she would never be his. "Is that all?"

"Yeah, brother, that's all."

I hear the line go dead, and my frustration gets the best of me. I fling the phone across the room and watch it shatter against the wall. Fuck!

CHAPTER Fourteen

Kidd

I hear someone stomping into my office, and I know without looking up that it's Chipper. I'm sure he's about to rip into me about Jenna again. She's been in a downward spiral since that shit went down with Cary. We may not talk much, but I see her every damn day, and every day for two fucking weeks she's been drunk as hell and crying into her bottle of Jack.

Not many people throw shit my way, but I allow Chipper to say what he wants, as long as he doesn't take it too far. Not only is he my vice-president, he's had a hard fuckin' six years. When he lost Mindy, he fell apart. I wasn't sure I'd ever get my brother back, but when Pop died, he stepped up somewhat. Without him, I'm not sure I could've run the club.

Pop passed away a few years ago. He had a heart attack in his sleep, but even before that, he'd already stepped down, and I was acting Pres. Once I took the gavel, I had Chipper take his place as my VP. He should have taken the reins, but he was still being a stubborn fuck and refused. Even as my VP, he ends up passing most of his shit on to other brothers to do. I hate to even think it, but I might have to replace him if he doesn't straighten his ass up soon.

"You got to do something, brother. I've had enough of this shit. If you can't stop it, I will," he growls out as he takes a seat across from me.

I finally look at him just in time to see him run his shaking fingers through his hair. "What has she done this time?"

"Same old shit. It's nine thirty in the damn morning, and she is so fuckin' drunk she can't even walk straight. The shit with that bitch is tearing her to pieces." He jerks his eyes towards me. "I'm telling you, man. If you don't do something, she's going to kill herself."

I shake my head in frustration. We've had this discussion a hundred times over the last few days. He wants me to claim Jenna as mine. He thinks that'll help her get her shit together, but he doesn't understand how bad I fucked up. Mom always told me to be careful with what you say, because your words will come back to haunt you. She was never more right.

"I don't know what you want me to do about Ice. She's a grown ass woman. If she wants to kill herself at the bottom of a bottle, there's nothing I can do about it." Even saying the words sends bile up into my throat. I would do anything to protect my girl, if only she would let me.

"She's your woman. You're the only one that can put a stop to it."

I shake my head again. "She ain't my woman. I haven't touched her in years." Not that I haven't wanted to every damn day. As the President, I could have made Jenna come to my bed. Believe me, I've been tempted to more than once, but I just couldn't. She may play the role of a whore, but she will never be one to me.

"No, man, you haven't. When you want pussy, you want easy pussy, and you know getting Jenna back will be anything but easy." A sarcastic smile spreads across Chipper's face. "But, not having your dick in her doesn't make her any less yours."

"Ice is not mine," I say again, hoping he'll shut the fuck up about it. Every time he pulls this shit with me, a spark of hope is lit somewhere deep inside me, but when I try to talk to her, that hope is doused with her hatred. It hurts too fuckin' much to keep trying.

His smile turns into a smirk. "If she's not yours, then let Reese have her."

"No!" I say in near shout. No one is getting Jenna. "Reese has a damn woman. He doesn't need Ice too."

Chipper laughs out loud. "Reese has a she-bitch from hell, and he'd be willing to kick her to the curb if you even hinted that he could have Jenna."

That isn't exactly true. He wouldn't be kicking Roxy anywhere. He'd be burying her ass out back. I slap my hand onto my desk, causing everything on it to shake. "I said no."

"Fine," he snaps. "Don't give her to Reese, but you need to step the fuck up before something happens to her."

"I'm not ready, brother. I'm just not ready to take on an old lady yet," I say the words, even though they're not entirely true. I would take Jenna in a heartbeat. It's just easier to lie than to admit that the one woman I want to spend the rest of my life with doesn't want shit to do with me, even though I know it's all my fault.

"Kidd, you've been ready since the day you laid eyes on her. You're just too fucking afraid." He looks at me. "Jenna is not Sarah, man. She's not gonna turn into a raving bitch. She's strong as hell. She won't break under the pressure of being the Pres' old lady. She'll be good for you and good for the club. She'll be by your side every step of the way."

I hate to even hear Sarah's name. The guilt from her death is finally starting to fade, but the guilt for the things I said after she died is still fresh in my mind. "That ain't what this is about."

"You can't lie to me, man. I know what happened after Sarah died. It damn near tore your ass to pieces, but Jenna needs you by her side. She's been part of this club for years. She's had control of the girls for nearly six. She can handle being your old lady. You'll just have to give her a little time to get used to it."

His words bring back memories of Sarah begging me to claim her as mine, but I couldn't do it. Everyone knew Sarah was just there to keep my bitch seat warm until Jenna got old enough to take her place; everyone but Jenna that is. "Things change when a bitch becomes an old lady. Ice is used to making her own calls. Once I claim her, she won't have the freedom she does now. It could break her."

I keep trying to make excuses, hoping to shut him up, before my mind starts imagining Jenna being mine.

He chuckles. "Ain't shit that could break Jenna, and you know it. My girl is hard as nails. Ain't never met anyone like her. Strongest person I know."

I have to nod at that, because he's right. No one here has been through what Jenna has. Losing her mother, being raped, then losing the woman that was the mother of her heart. Most people would have given up a long time ago if they had to put up with half the shit she has. I finally blow out a frustrated breath then stand up. "Fine, I'll talk to her."

I don't wait for him to respond before walking out of my office. I head straight to the club's bar. Jenna's sitting on a stool, talking to the prospect tending bar. Her head is tilted, and her long midnight black hair is covering her face from view. She has her hands wrapped around a fifth of Jack. It only takes a glance to see that she's fucked up. "Yo, Ice."

Her bloodshot, coffee colored eyes narrow as she jerks her head towards me. The fast movement nearly causes her to lose her seat. "Yeah. What the hell do you want?"

My brows go up at her bitchy tone. I should be used to it by now. She's been given me the same shit for years. None of the other girls would even consider talking to me like that. Only she has balls big enough to go head to head with a member, especially me. "Just saying hi, baby girl'."

"Yeah, which is something we don't do. We don't talk, remember? Like I said, what the hell do you want?" She says, turning back to her whiskey and chugging it back. "Say what you gotta say, then leave me the fuck alone.",

Looking at her sends fear through me. Chipper's right; she's killing herself. There're dark circles under each of her beautiful eyes. Her cheek bones are sharp, proving that she hasn't been eating. Even the hair I love so much has lost its shine. No matter what, no matter how pissed off she's gets -- it's time I step in.

"I've decided that I've left you alone long enough. I'll be telling you all about that soon, but right now I wanted to tell you that you're done with the whiskey," I say firmly, grabbing the bottle from the bar.

"What the fuck?" She screams, trying to take the bottle from my hand.

"I don't want you drinking all the fuckin' time."

"I don't give a fuck what you want. You can't tell me what to do."

I step closer to her. "That's where you're wrong. You're mine now, and you can't do shit without my permission."

"I'm not yours!" she yells, her voice full of panic.

"Yeah, you are. From this moment on, you are mine and mine only. Don't fuckin' fight me on this, or you'll be done with the Renegade Sons. Do you get what I'm saying?" I growl out, letting her hear my anger. I would never hurt her, but she doesn't need to know that.

She swallows nervously. "What am I supposed to do now?"

"Just sit around and look pretty, but you're going to lay off the booze from now on," I say, pasting a fake ass smile on my face. "I've decided it's time that I claim you, and I don't want an old lady that's plastered all the fuckin' time."

"Hell no! I'll never be your old lady. I'll never be anyone's old lady. We tried that once, and it only worked until you busted your nut. Plus, I don't even fucking like you," she shouts, her words slurred.

I hate to hear her say shit like that. It's hard to believe that after all this time, she still thinks I just used her for her pussy. "Don't have to fuckin' like me, baby girl, just gotta be there for me and only me. You step out, you're done."

I'm not sure why I added those last words. I know Jenna, and she would never fuck around on her old man. Club girl or not, she's loyal to the bone. The only thing is making sure that she accepts me as her old man.

Jenna keeps shouting, but I ignore her and look around the room. "Listen up, boys. Ice is mine. You touch her, you deal with me."

I spot Preach lounging on the couch with one of the club whores grinding on his lap. I point towards him. "You, take Ice to her room. She's to stay there until I say different."

I start to walk away, but turn back to Preach. "Do what you have to do to keep her in her room, but don't hurt her. She's my old lady now, so make sure you show her the respect she deserves."

As soon as the words leave my mouth, I hear Jenna screech at the top of her lungs. I can't help but chuckle. She's gonna take me on one hell of a ride, but making her mine is going to be worth it.

Jenna

I watch Kidd walk away and have to fight the urge to wiggle in my seat. Even through my alcohol induced haze, he's the sexiest man I've ever seen. His hair is the color of melted butterscotch and his eyes remind me of a cloudless sky. His face isn't what most women would consider classically handsome; it's too rugged, and too harsh. He always sports a five o'clock shadow, and I've often thought back to what it felt like against my skin.

His body, well I don't think a person could find the right words to do it justice. He's temptation walking around in a pair of faded Levi's. He's not as big as some of the other brothers, barely reaching six foot and probably weighing around 200 pounds, but he carries himself in a way that makes him appear to be the biggest and baddest of them all. Kidd is one of those men that makes you wet just by looking at him. Too bad he's such a self-righteous prick.

He is such a damn tool. We haven't talked in nearly six years, and now he says I'm going to be his old lady. What the fuck is he thinking? Me as his old lady? No damn way. Been there, done that, and not going there again. If he thinks he can just walk in here and tell me what to do, he's got another thing coming. I'm not going to be his old lady. I'll never be anyone's old lady. I'm not going down that path again, especially not with Kidd.

Chipper keeps telling me to get over my issues with Kidd, but I can't forget everything that happened between us. I opened myself up to him, only to get ground under his boot heel. I don't care what he's saying now, he doesn't really want me. He didn't want me six years ago, and nothing has changed.

"Another," I shout to Rum, the prospect manning the bar.

Rum shakes his head. "I can't give you anymore, Ice. You heard the Pres. Preach has got to take you to your room."

"I'm not going any-fucking-where!" I shout, banging my empty glass onto the bar.

"You got to do what Kidd says, and so do I. I have no choice but to take you to your room and you know it, so make this easy on both of us and don't fight me," Preach says as he walks towards me.

I shoot him a glare. "If you ever want to get your dick sucked again, you better not touch me. You know my girls listen to me. I'll tell every single one of them to cut your ass off."

Preach's face goes pale, because he knows what I say is true. I run the girls, and they listen to me. If I say so, his ass will never get another piece of club pussy again. "Oh shit! Come on, Ice. That's not fair. You know this shit isn't my fault. I have to do what the Pres says, or I'll catch seven kinds of hell."

I start to respond, but I'm cut off by the sound of people walking into the room. I turn and see Reese walking towards me with a sexy smile beaming on his gorgeous face.

Thank God it's him; my best friend and occasional fuck buddy. He's the only man I'm close to other than Timber. That's not really true. I'm close to Chipper too. I'm only alive today because of him, but Chipper and I have been on the outs for a while. He wants me to clean up my act, yet he refuses to understand that I'm as clean as I am ever going to be.

"Tough mornin', sweetheart?" he says, leaning down and placing a soft kiss on my neck.

"Yeah, you could say that. You'll never believe what Kidd just did," I say in a near shout.

He chuckles at me. "I wouldn't put much past him, especially where you're concerned."

"He came in here and took my whiskey away," I say, showing him my empty glass. "He said I couldn't have any more."

"Well, that's not such a bad thing. You have been spending a lot of time at the bottom of a bottle lately."

"Whatever, that's not even the worst of it."

He cocks a brow. "What else?"

"He said I'm gonna be his old lady. He didn't even ask. He just told me I was his, but I'm never going to be anyone's old lady, especially not his. You know how he treated me. How the hell can he even think I'd take him as my old man after all that shit?" I finish with a shout.

A flash of pain crosses Reese's face. "Old Lady? Are you sure he said that?"

"Hell yeah, I'm sure. I may be half drunk, but I'm not

deaf."

Reese places his hand on my arm and gives it a tight squeeze. "What did you say to him?"

"I told him hell no!"

"You know you should accept it. Either that or leave the club," he says quietly. "You know if it wasn't for Roxy, I would've made you my old lady a long fucking time ago, but it's too late now," he says, mumbling something under his breath about Kidd and not wanting to give his girl to anyone.

I snort. "Leaving the club will never happen. This is my home."

He shrugs. "Then you're going to have to be his old lady."

"Right, you know my thoughts on that, Reese. I'm not gonna be anyone's old lady. I'm not going to have an old man that'll be telling me what to do while he's out fucking around. Kidd is the fucking Pres. He already thinks he's God. Plus, he has a different woman in his bed every damn night, so monogamy would never happen with him. You know how much it bothers me to share."

"I think Kidd will be true to you. Not all of the brothers fuck around. You're the only woman I touch. Shit! I haven't even fucked my old lady in years," he says in a quiet voice.

If I didn't know Reese as well as I do, I wouldn't believe that shit, but it's true. Reese is loyal, very loyal, just not to his old lady. Roxy doesn't deserve his loyalty, though. She's a raving bitch; a fucking loon through and through.

"You know that I'm not old lady material. I just can't do it."

His eyes go soft. "Don't do this, Ice. I don't want to lose your friendship. If you fight Kidd, you'll be tossed out."

I decide it's time to change the subject, so I stand up and wrap my arms around Reese's waist.
"Let's go to my room," I whisper, putting my mouth to his.

He doesn't say anything, just pulls from my grasp and grabs my hand. We barely reach the hall before Preach steps in front of us. "Sorry, Reese. Pres told me to take Ice to her room. I can't let her go anywhere alone with you, man."

"Fine, walk with us," Reese says, pushing past him and leading me down the hall.

I'm the only woman with a room at the club. All the other unclaimed girls have apartments in town. The building is owned by the club, of course. I have an apartment there too, although I've never even spent the night in it. Chipper wanted me to stay with him, but his house just hasn't felt the same since Mindy died. It's still my home, and always will be, but it's just different without her there. It's been years since I slept anywhere but the club. I feel safe here, and here is where I plan to stay.

As soon as Reese and I step into my room, I reach for the bottom of my shirt and pull it over my head. I look back and see him standing in the doorway, looking sad. "What's wrong, baby?"

"I can't fuck you tonight, Jenna."

His words feel like a direct hit to the gut. Not that I care if I get fucked or not, but I hate knowing that he's already accepting Kidd's claim on me. Timber would've never given up so easily. "Why not?" I ask, even though I already know the answer.

"My *Wahine*," he says gently, speaking in Polynesian, "you know as well as I do that Kidd has laid a claim. As far as the club is concerned, you're his old lady. Whether you've accepted him or not doesn't matter. If I fucked you, it'd be a betrayal to the brotherhood."

"Your *Wahine,* I don't think so. Roxy is your woman. She's your *wahine.* I'm not your woman. I never have been, and now I never will be."

Anger flashes in his eyes. "Don't do that shit, Jenna. If you keep on talking your shit, you'll have me going after Kidd. Do you want that?"

I look into his eyes and shake my head. I know if I push it, he'll do anything I want, but I won't be the reason that Reese gets hurt, and he'd be more than hurt if he fucked another brother's old lady. "Can you just hold me then? I really need someone to just hold me right now."

He shoots me a sad smile. "I can do that."

I pull off the rest of my clothes and crawl into my bed. As soon as I get settled in, I feel him lay down beside me. He immediately pulls me into his arms. "If Kidd wants you, you're gonna have to accept it. If not, you won't have a place here anymore."

"I know, but I don't want to talk about it anymore right now. I just want to go to sleep," I say as I close my eyes.

"You know I love you, Jenna."

"I love you too, Reese."

He arms grow tighter around my waist. "I know you do, but not the way I want you to."

I don't respond, because he's right. I love him with my entire soul, but I don't love him the way he loves me. To me, he's more a friend than a lover. Sure, we have great sex, but the sex isn't what holds us together. It's the fact that I know he would lay his life down for mine without any hesitation. I hope he knows that I'd do the same for him.

As much as I love Reese, he's not what I need right now. He's just too easy going. Who I need is Timber. He'd kick me in ass and tell me to stand up for myself. He wouldn't just say to go with the flow. Timber would back my decision, no matter what it was. He'd put me on the back of his bike, and we'd ride away from this shit.

I haven't seen him in over two years, not since he went inside. I want to visit him in prison, but he doesn't want me there. He says that he doesn't want me to see him behind bars, especially when it's a place he shouldn't have to be in the first place. Just because he's a biker and the bastard he cut is a doctor, Timber got screwed. Well it doesn't matter now, because Timber will be home soon, and the fucker that got him put away will pay.

I lay quietly, continuing to think of Timber, until sleep finally claims me.

CHAPTER Fifteen

Kidd

I'm sitting in my office, looking over the papers for The Kitty Kat, when Chipper comes in. "Where's Jenna? The girls called and said she hasn't come in yet?"

"What's their issue? It's only three o'clock, and Ice doesn't usually go in until five," I say, still focused on the papers on my desk. Why the hell didn't Pop tell me that running this club meant I had to do fucking paperwork?

He shakes his head and chuckles. "One of the girls over at The Kitty Kat called. Daisy was practicing some new routine. Seems one of her props got stuck."

I jerk my head up. "Got stuck?"

"Yeah, I guess she watched some porno where a woman was able to shoot grapes from her pussy," he says through a smile. "Well, Daisy figured if that woman could do it with grapes, then she could do it with something bigger."

I shake my head and look back down towards my desk, trying to hide my own smile. "What in the hell did that idiot push up her twat?"

"An orange," he says with a laugh.

"What the fuck? Why the hell would she do that for?"

"Well, it seems that Preach is real fond of oranges. She figured if her pussy smelled like his favorite fruit, then he might spend some time down there later on tonight."

I can't wait to rib Preach's ass about this. "Well, find Ice, and tell her to pick up Daisy and get her ass to the hospital to make sure she's ok. Also, have her tell Daisy's stupid ass not to do that shit anymore. I'm sure if Daisy had just told Preach that she wanted him to eat her snatch, he would've jumped on it."

"What the hell do you think I'm doing here? I would've already told her ass this shit if I could find her. No one has seen her around, and she isn't answering her phone."

"Have you checked her room?" I say without looking up.

"Hell no. The last time I went in her room was more than three years ago, and she was fucking Reese and Timber at the same damn time, a show I do not want to walk in on again. I think of her as my own daughter, and seeing her like that damn near blinded me."

The image of her with them flashes through my brain, and I growl out. "Get Reese to check it out."

"I was gonna do that, but he's not in his room. I called his house, but his old lady said he didn't come home last night. In fact, she says he hasn't spent the night there in over a year. He stops by to see Pebbles every day, but that's it." With that last comment, I stand up, my chair toppling over.

"Motherfucker!!!" I shout then storm out of my office.

I make my way to Jenna's room in less than a minute and push the door open without knocking, sending it banging straight into the wall with a deep thud. My eyes immediately land on Reese, who is laying on the bed, glaring daggers at me. Jenna is beside him, wrapped up in his arms.

For the last six years, I've watched him and Timber be all up in Jenna's shit. Whenever either motherfucker is near her, they have her in their arms. I didn't like it before, and I sure in the hell don't like it now, especially since I've staked my claim on her. This shit ends now.

Sometimes a part of me thinks that she went to them just to make me jealous. She would catch me watching them all together and shoot a vicious smirk my way. I tried to pay her back by fooling around with Skittles, but that shit didn't go over well at all.

A few months back, I'd had enough of thinking about my brothers' having their hands all over my girl, so I sent Jenna a text message telling her that I needed to talk to her about one of the club girls. After confirming that she was on her way to my office, I called Skittles in and got down to business while I waited for Jenna to show up. Jenna walked in just as Skittles was taking me down her throat.

I knew she was jealous as she took in Skittles going to town on my dick, but she put up that damn wall and acted as if she couldn't give two shits. So there I sat, with my dick being worshiped by a rainbow headed trick, while I tried to pull some bullshit out of my ass for having Jenna there in the first place. It wasn't my finest moment, and I may or may not have nutted only after seeing Jenna bounce her fine ass out my office door; an ass that I wanted to be buried deep inside of oh-so-fucking bad.

After that, she refused to even talk to me about the girls. I ended up having to send her texts or relay messages through my brothers. It was a total dick move, but I wanted her to feel a little of the hurt that I've been nursing while watching her love on men that ain't me. I'm just the dumbass that forgot that Jenna isn't called Ice for shits and giggles. She's a cold blooded Ice Queen, and once you're on her shit list, you stay there. Bitches, man.

"We need to talk, brother." I growl out, snapping out of my memories and focusing back on the scene before me.

Reese nods his head and gently untangles his arms from Jenna. Before he gets up, he places his lips on her temple and gives her a soft kiss. It takes every bit of self-control I have not to rush over to the bed and knock him on his ass. "Get the fuck away from her," I seethe out through my painfully clenched teeth.

He looks back towards me and shrugs. "That's the last kiss I'll get to give her. I think you owe me that much," he says, standing up.

"I don't owe you shit," I say, turning around and heading back toward my office.

As soon as I walk into the office, I turn back and look at Reese. "Shut the fuckin' door."

I walk over to the fridge and grab two beers. I toss one to Reese and sit down. "You need to stay away from Ice. I mean it, brother."

He shrugs. "Why should I stay clear of Ice, brother? We're close, and always have been. I'm not real sure if I'm willing to walk away from her." His emphasis on 'brother' doesn't have me fooled. He wants to push my buttons. Fucker.

"I'm not saying you can't talk to her, but you better keep your fucking hands off her."

A slow smile spreads across his face. "Man, have you seen her ass? How the hell is a man supposed to keep his hands off something so damn fine?"

I have to fight the urge to punch him in his smart ass mouth. Instead, I just give it to him straight. "She's my old lady now, and I don't share."

"She won't either," he says before opening his beer.

"She won't what?"

A slow smile spreads across his face. "She ain't gonna share you either, Kidd."

"She'll do what I tell her to do," I reply, even though I have no intentions of sinking my dick into anyone but her. I've spent the last six years pretending every woman I've touched was Jenna. Why the fuck would I stray when I have the real thing at home?

Reese chuckles. "Obviously, you don't know Ice as well as you think you do. She does what she wants."

I shake my head. "Not anymore."

"Jenna isn't like the rest of the bitches here. She isn't going to take your shit lying down. She's not gonna do something just cause you told her to. "

Hearing him use Jenna's real name kills me. It proves that they're a lot closer than I ever realized. She doesn't let anyone but Chipper call her Jenna anymore, and that's my fucking fault too. I made the mistake of calling her the Ice Queen and it stuck. "She'll learn."

This time Reese barks out a full laugh. "She'll learn? Do you really believe that?"

"Yeah, she's an intelligent woman. She knows what's expected of her. Ice will fall in line. It'll just take a little time." I can only pray that what I'm saying is true; pray that someday she'll let me back into her heart.

"Pres, I thought you were smarter than that."

"What the hell is that supposed to mean?" I ask in a near growl.

He shakes his head. "She's not gonna just fall in line like other women. She's going to fight you tooth and nail every step of the way."

"I'll win," I say, determination filling my voice. I have to. If not, I'll lose her for good this time.

He nods. "Yeah, but do you want Ice or some half-ass broken version of her."

I push my hands through my hair. "I don't know what the fuck I want." That's not true. I want Jenna, the Jenna that looked at me like I was the only man in the world for her, but I'm not sure that Jenna exists anymore.

Reese stands up and walks towards the door. "You better figure it out. You can make her be your old lady, but you can't make her give a shit about you. If you want Ice to be by your side, you're going to have treat her like she belongs there. Bossing her ass around isn't the way to go. There's a reason why she never wanted to be an old lady."

She never wanted to be an old lady? What the fuck did he mean by that? All the girls in the club would fight to the death to become an old lady. I knew she didn't want to be mine, but I figured she'd jump at the chance of being claimed by Timber or Reese. Shaking off the thoughts of what Reese just said, I get up and walk back to Jenna's room.

She's still curled up on the bed sleeping. I go over to her and kick the bed hard enough to make it shake. "Wake the fuck up," I shout.

She bolts upright. "What the hell is wrong with you?" she sneers, then looks around, then back to me, eyes narrowed. "What did you do to Reese?"

"What I should have done was put a bullet in his fucking head. He knew he shouldn't be in here with you, but he was in your damn bed anyway. He got off with a warning this time, because he's my brother. Next time, he won't be so lucky. Don't make me have to pull the fuckin' trigger, Ice."

"Bullshit! I'm not stupid, Kidd. I know you wouldn't kill Reese. Bloody him up a bit, yeah, but he'd be breathing when it was over. He's a brother, and I'm just a club whore. If anyone in this situation ends up dead, it'll be me and you know it. Even though my life sucks right now, I still want to keep on breathing," she says like a snotty teenager. She throws back the blankets, and I notice she's naked underneath. I told her last night that she was mine. She better pray that nothing happened between her and Reese.

"Did you fuck him?" I growl out.

She turns towards me with her hands on her hips and doesn't even attempt to cover herself. The woman feels no shame when it comes to her body. She has no reason to feel any. Even with the weight loss over the last few weeks, her body is still fucking perfection. It's the sexiest damn thing I've ever seen. She's long and lean, standing near five foot nine, and so damn gorgeous.

"I wish, but he wouldn't give me any. He said you laid claim, and he couldn't do that shit to the brotherhood. You know, you guys don't fuck each other's old ladies. You only fuck every other piece of pussy you can lay your hands on." She walks to her dresser and pulls out a Buck Cherry tee and a pair of faded blue skinny jeans. "Plus, like I told you before, I'm not ready to die."

"I wouldn't have killed you, but I would've made you pay," I state in a voice that lets her know I'm not bullshitting her one bit. I've watched her with too many guys over the years, and that shit stopped this morning.

Her deep brown eyes fill with anger. "I can't believe you're trying to pull this shit now. My life was finally coming together. I had so many plans, but you push your way in and ruin every damn thing."

I don't respond. Instead, I watch her pull the shirt over her beautiful breasts and it causes me to have to hold in a groan. Her tits aren't as big as a lot of the other girls, but they're real and so fucking perky that they make my dick ache. She notices me staring and a sarcastic smile crosses her face. "Damn, you can't take your eyes off me. Can you? Why not just take a picture? It's better than the real thing anyway. Pictures don't fight you when you use them to get off."

"No, baby. I don't need a damn picture. The sight of your sweet ass and even sweeter tits is already burned into my brain."

She shrugs her shoulder. "It's nothing you haven't seen on stage at The Kitty Kat dozens of times."

I nod. "That's true. I've seen your naked ass more times than I can count, but it was never mine before, at least not for long. Now, when I look at your beautiful body, I know it belongs to me. That alone makes my dick hard."

"I'm not yours," she denies in a voice slightly lower than a shout. "Just 'cause I'm a woman now, and not a little girl that can't make your dick hard, doesn't mean you should claim me."

"Ice," I grind out, not wanting to remember the things I said to her in the past.

"Why don't you go pick someone that wants to be an old lady? One that wouldn't give a flying fuck about you turning to the whores when you need a quick nut at the club or on the road?"

"That's why I chose you. With you, I don't need anyone else," I say, staring at her ass as she bends over to put her heels on.

She lets out a throaty laugh. "Right. I didn't satisfy you last time. What makes you think this time will be different?"

"That's not fucking true, and you know it. I don't want different. I just want what we used to have back."

She ignores my words. "I would never hack it as an old lady, especially not yours. You should know that about me already. But no, why would you know any damn thing about me, huh?"

"You can tell me anything you want to, Ice. I want to know everything about you." And I do. This girl means the world to me.

"That's new. As far as you were concerned, I wasn't anything but a gullible piece of pussy. What happened to make you see me in this new light?" She's quiet for a moment, but then her eyes narrow. "This is Chipper's idea isn't it? He talked you into this shit. Well, you can just tell him to stay out of my business and fuck off."

I start to reply, but she places her hands up stopping me. "No, don't worry about it. I'll tell the nosey bastard to kiss my ass myself."

She starts to walk towards the door, but I grab her arm and pull her to me. I place a hand across her mouth. "For six years, you've been throwing shit my way. I wouldn't have taken it from anyone else, and I'm done taking it from you. I am the president of this fucking club, and my word is law. You'll either do what I say from now on, or you'll hit the road."

Her eyes narrow at me even further before a quick look of defeat shines in her eyes, and she slowly nods her head in compliance. I gently pull my hand away from her mouth as her body begins to go slack in my arms. "You will never talk to me like you have been today again. If you do, I will beat your ass."

"You don't believe in hitting women."

"You're right about that, but I don't see a damn thing wrong with laying you across my lap and smacking that sexy ass of yours a few times," I say while squeezing her tight little ass. "Who knows? Maybe you'll like it."

That flares her temper again, and she tries to pull away from me, but I pull her in closer. "You need to make up your mind up. You can either walk now, or you can be my old lady."

She looks up at me with the most beautiful brown eyes I've ever seen. "Kidd, I don't think I can do this. I don't want to leave the club. It's my whole life, but I don't think I can be your old lady."

I lean my head down and place my forehead against hers.

"You can do it, Jenna. Please, give us a chance."

I feel her take a deep breath before replying. "Fine, I'll be your old lady, but if you pull the same shit as last time, I'll walk away. I don't want to leave the club, but I will if I have to. You also need to know that if I catch you fucking any of the other girls around here, I will cut your dick off. I'm not like the other old ladies. I won't be able to watch you fuckin' around with the club girls. I don't share, Kidd. If I'm yours, then you're mine."

I know I should be pissed. Hell, I should tell her that it isn't any of her damn business what I do with my cock, but I kind of like the idea of her claiming my dick as hers. Plus, there's no fuckin' way I'm sharing her with anyone else. I've done enough of that already. "Same here, baby girl. If I hear about you spreading for anyone other than me, I will kill the bastard. That includes Reese and Timber. I won't hurt you. I would never hurt you, but I will make you pay."

"Fine," she says as she pulls her head back from mine. "I get it. I'm your old lady, but that doesn't change the fact that I have shit to do. I gotta get to The Kitty Kat before those stupid bitches tear the place down."

I know she's lying. She's still got an hour before she's supposed to be there, but I don't call her on it. "Speaking of the club, there was an issue with Daisy this morning. Seems she decided to start sticking produce up her snatch, and something got stuck."

She looks at me as if I've lost my mind, and then repeats my words from earlier. "Something got stuck?"

"Yeah, an orange," I say, letting out a chuckle. "Chipper said Kandy called looking for you. She wanted to know what to do with Daisy."

"What the hell did she think I could do, reach up there and pull it out? They need to get her ass to the hospital. I gotta go," she says and starts towards the door.

I step in front of the door, blocking her path. "I'm going to try to make this easy on you. After that shit went down with Roxy, the brothers and I decided there would be no more old ladies running the girls, but I'm gonna make an exception for you. You do too good of a job to take them away from you."

Anger flashes across her face. "Anything else I need to know before I can leave?"

I reach out and grab the back of her head then pull her face towards mine. "Yes." I say before slamming my mouth down on hers. "Tonight, you're in my bed."

Jenna

I watch Kidd walk out of my room after he kisses me, and as soon as my door slams shut, I have the sudden urge to scream. In fact, I would like nothing better than to lay down on my bed and have a screaming fit, but I don't have time for that shit. I've got a life to live, even if it's not the life I'd originally planned for myself. As soon as that thought passes through my brain, another rolls in, and I realize I just told Kidd that I'd be his old lady. SHIT! What the hell is wrong with me?

Not only did he hurt me, he's also the biggest horn dog in the whole fucking club. I don't want my mother's life. She was nothing but weak and stupid when it came to men. Did I love her? Hell yes, I did. She was my mom and all I had. But really, that woman needed to grow a pair, dig her head out of her ass, and put my father in his place, or better yet, kick his ass to the curb. If she had, maybe she'd still be alive, and Timmons would've never gotten his hands on me.

I shake the bad thoughts away, grab my keys, and head over to The Kitty Kat. I barely make it two steps out of my room before Rum stops me to tell me about the situation with Daisy. He thinks it's funny as hell, and I know it's just a matter of time before he starts calling her something stupid like 'produce stand' or 'fruit salad'. When you do something idiotic, the club never lets you forget it.

He also fills me in on some shit that's been going down at The Kitty Kat that I need take care of. Sounds like I need to go over some rules with those bitches--again. Apparently, someone was passing out drugs at the strip club last night, and it's a known fact that selling drugs at The Kitty Kat is a big time violation. Even doing drugs is against the rules. They can smoke a little weed, but anything else isn't allowed. They all know the rules, and the girls that broke them will have to hit the road over it. Then, the one that brought the drugs inside of the club will be feeling the bite of my hand before she follows them out the door.

I pull out my phone and text Skittles to let her know that she needs to take Daisy to the hospital, and that I'll straighten that chick's head out later. I love Daisy to death. She's one of my best friends, but she can't keep doing stupid shit.

Then, I decide to go to the apartment complex that houses the club whores and the strippers that work at The Kitty Kat. I'll take care of my business there, because there's no reason to bring that shit to the clubhouse.

Head down, I walk out to my car, a shiny silver-blue BMW Z4 Roadster. I bought my baby just last month with the money that I've been saving. Chipper got pissed as soon as he laid eyes on her and told me that we're badasses. We drive Harley's, not BMW's. I guess he forgot, as a woman, my only spot on a Harley is in the bitch seat. That's a club rule; one of many that I don't agree with.

I'm sure he'd been okay if I'd have bought a Ford or a Chevy, but that's not what I wanted. I wanted something classy. I haven't had a lot of classy in my life, but my baby is pure class. Chipper may be the closest thing I have to a father, but I worked my ass off to get this car, so he can just fuck off. I smile at my baby one last time as I run my hand along her hood and make my way to the driver's side door.

"Jenna!" I hear shouted from behind me. Jesus fucking Christ, am I ever going to get out of this place? I feel the urge to run as soon as it registers in my brain whose voice is calling for me. Shit! It's Chipper. Only he calls me Jenna in front of the other guys. In fact, only a few people here even know my real name anymore. Kidd christened me Ice a few weeks after I stopped talking to him. Since then, I've done my best to bury the name Jenna, along with the rest of my secrets.

"You keep your ass right where it is. We need to talk, and I mean for us to talk right now," he says as he stalks towards me.

I turn around and look at him square in the eye. I have to fight the smile that normally crosses my lips whenever I see him. I'm madder than hell at Chipper, and I plan to let him know it, but I'm just not ready to have the 'Kidd' conversation yet. I know he wants what's best for me, but that doesn't mean he can try to run my life. I am, damn near, twenty-four years old. It's time he learns how to step back and let me make my own decisions.

As much as I hate to admit it, sometimes it's hard being around Chipper. He reminds me too much of Mindy. Losing her was one of the hardest things that I've ever been through. Mindy was just like a mother to me. Shit, she was more of a mom than my mother even thought about being. I would spend the rest of my life back at the Mateland charter, and let Timmons do anything he wanted to me, if it meant I could get just one more day with her.

Chipper makes out like he's a badass, not to be fucked with, but around Mindy and me, he was always loveable and friendly. Hell, Mindy used to call him her big teddy bear, and I used to tease him all the damn time about it. Now, I only mention it when I'm drunk, and that's not to tease him. Instead, it's to remind him how much Mindy loved him and how good he was to her.

When Mindy finally passed away, there was a change in Chipper. He still treats me the same as always, but there's a sadness in his eyes. Sometimes, I think watching him wallow away in his grief is worse than losing her.

I know Chipper didn't want me to be a part of the club. We fought about it, but nothing he said could change my mind. Finally, Chipper gave in to what I chose, and I started working at The Kitty Kat. Of course, him giving in doesn't stop us from having a full out war whenever he feels the need to remind me that my life is too fucked up and he wants me to change it.

Trying to ignore him, I open my door and attempt to get in before he can get to me. I don't even get my ass halfway in the seat before his hand wraps around my upper arm and he pulls me out and slams my door. "When I call you, you stop," Chipper growls out.

"Sorry, oh great master," I say sarcastically.

His hand slightly tightens on my arm and he growls out, "Don't test me, Jenna."

I yank my arm out of his grip and fold my arms across my chest. "What do you want?" I say sounding bored, even though my heart feels like it's pounding out of my chest.

"Heard Kidd finally laid claim to you. I gotta say, it's about fuckin' time. Now, you need to smarten up a bit."

"What the hell does that mean?"

"Leave the past in the past, Jenna girl."

I shake my head. "He can claim me all he wants. That doesn't mean I'm going to let him run my life. I do what I want, when I want."

He shakes his head at me. "If you think he's gonna put up with your shit, you'd be mistaken."

"Oh fuck off, *Daddy*. If he doesn't want to put up with my shit, he can go choose another whore to claim. It's not like there's a shortage of bitches that would give their left arm to wear his brand."

He leans closes and whispers, "You better not forget who you're talking to. I won't hesitate to lay your ass out."

I roll my eyes at his words. If there is one thing I know for sure, it's that Chipper would never raise a hand to me. "I've told you over and over again that I never wanted to be an Old Lady, but you never listened. Something tells me you put him up to this shit, so now you have to talk some sense into him. You need to make him see that I'm not the woman he wants."

He shakes his head. "Not gonna happen. Kidd claimed you, and now you're his. You need to get used to the idea, and you need to get used to it quick. Just to put your mind to rest, you've always been the only woman he ever wanted."

I scoff at his words and blow out a frustrated breath, then look into his eyes. "Yeah? That's funny. I thought he wanted Sarah. The real woman that could make his dick hard."

"Jenna, enough!" He shouts then runs a hand through his hair. "I helped you out. Shit, me and Mindy did everything we could to give you a real home. You know I love you more than anything, and she did too. How do you think Mindy would feel about the way you've turned out?" he says, shouting at me.

How dare he say that! No one, and I mean no one, throws Mindy in my face. Before I can fully think my shit through, my fist is raised, and I clock him right in the jaw and split his lip. "Fuck you! Never bring her up to me again. I loved her more than life itself!" I scream into his face, then get into my car and speed away.

Only one thought crosses my mind as I head down the road; I wonder what my punishment is going to be when I get home.

CHAPTER Sixteen

Kidd

I take a swig of my whiskey and stare at the financial reports littering my desk. Something's not lining up. There's money missing, but I can't figure out where it went. It's only a few thousand, not enough to make me think someone is skimming, but it's enough to make me take notice, enough to make me realize that I am not a fucking accountant. I'm a biker, damn it. I try to run the numbers again, but finally toss the papers onto my desk. I need to hire someone to do this shit. If not, I'm going to go crazy.

I'm about to head out when my office door crashes open. I look up to see Chipper walking in, sporting a split lip. He also has a small bruise on his jaw. No doubt he's been fighting again. Not that him fighting is unusual, but him getting marked is. Usually, my brothers' are the ones leaving with the bruises. My eyes narrow as I take it in.

"Who the fuck did that to you?"

"Jenna," he grumbles as he walks towards my desk and grabs my bottle of Jack.

I chuckle as I ask, "What'd you say to piss her off this time?"

"I brought up Mindy. Asked her how Mindy would feel about the way she's been living her life." He sits on the couch and sighs. "Dick move. I shouldn't have done that shit."

I flinch as soon as his words sink in. Jenna loved Mindy in a way that was so pure, so true, that even someone that didn't know them would be able to see the way she felt about the woman. Even though Jenna only knew her for a little over a year, she still considered Mindy her mom. Some people might have thought it was strange, but I thought it was fuckin' beautiful.

Chipper throwing her up in Jenna's face the way he did would tear her to pieces. Most women would cry over it, but not Jenna, at least not the Ice Queen that Jenna's became. When she gets hurt, she fights back. She'll fight twice as hard when it comes to Mindy. Anytime someone in the club brought her up, she would turn almost homicidal. Hell, she even shot one of the brothers, Brakes, in the leg, about a year after Mindy's death.

I had just taken up the gavel when it happened. I was sweating bullets when the boys brought Jenna to me. I knew it was my place as president to punish her, and there's only one punishment for using a weapon on a member. She would have to die, and I would have to be the one pulling the trigger, but when she explained what Brakes did, there was no fucking way I was going to make her pay. In fact, I wanted to put another bullet in him myself.

The douche was trying to get her to fuck him, but club girl or not, Jenna's selective. She knew Brakes was a piece of shit and wasn't about to spread for him. When he realized he didn't have a chance, he told her that her pussy probably would have sucked anyway. He said that he had a taste of Mindy back in the day, and she was a dead fuck. Considering Mindy helped raise Jenna, he figured she would be too.

Needless to say, Jenna flipped her wig. Not only was Mindy dead, and half the club was still mourning her, but every member knows that you don't talk shit about a brother's old lady. Yeah, Mindy was a whore before she wore Chippers brand, but whore or not, when a woman is claimed, she's treated with same respect that you give her old man.

I shake the memory away, and then smile towards Chipper. "So, what are you gonna do about it? I know you better than to think you'd let her get away with that shit."

A month or two after Mindy died, Jenna decided she had had enough of Chipper's drinking every fuckin' day and decided to do something about it. She waited until he left the house one night and called a lock smith. When Chipper came home, he couldn't get into the house. Needless to say, he didn't like it one fuckin' bit. He ended up breaking a window and crawling in.

The next morning, Chipper went off on Jenna, but she played it off like she didn't know what he was talking about. She even told him that he was so drunk, he couldn't figure out how to use a key. When he got up to show her the keys didn't work, the door opened. The sneaky bitch had changed his keys while he was passed out.

This happened three more times before Chipper decided he needed to straighten his ass up. A year later, she finally told him what she'd done. He was pissed at first, but when she told him that she was tired of watching her dad kill himself, he got over his anger really damn quick. He still had to pay her back, and he did that by having her car painted cotton candy pink. My baby girl doesn't do pink, so she was pissed as hell. It took her nearly three months to earn enough money to have it repainted back to its original color. A few weeks back, she ended up getting her new car, and I thought Chipper was gonna blow.

"This was my own fault. I shouldn't have said that anything about Mindy to her. You can deal with Jenna anyway you want. You can just pretend that she never laid her hands on me, or you can remind her of the rules." He grins at me. "If I was you, I'd punish her, and I'd be creative about it when I did it."

At that thought, my dick begins to swell. "Fuckin' hell, bro!" I yell and try to think of something else, anything but being creative with Jenna; the financial forms, baseball, cats. No, not cats. Not shit that reminds me of the The Kitty Kat and Jenna's fine ass shaking across the stage. Now my hardening dick is rock solid. I hear Chipper laughing and open my eyes, mumbling a short, "Fucker," at him.

He stops laughing and looks at me seriously. "Just watch over my girl for me. I know she's grown now, but she will always be that scared little kid to me. I'm worried about her. I know shit is bothering her. It's more than just shooting Cary, even though that alone would fuck most people up. There are still things she keeps from me, shit she just won't talk about. I watch her walking that edge and I feel like she could step over to the dark side at any moment."

I nod, trying my best to ignore the pain swelling up in my chest. "We need to talk to Reese and see if there's something he knows that we don't."

Chipper shakes his head. "She may be best friends with him, but he doesn't even know half the shit that she has buried deep inside of her. I don't think anyone does. As close as she was to Mindy, she never even opened up to her."

I get up and walk to Chipper. I grab the bottle of Jack from him and take a long pull then look towards my brother. "I'll do my best to take care of her," I say, hoping like hell she will let me.

He nods. "I know you will."

Jenna

Within minutes of getting to the apartment complex, I'm fuming. How could these bitches be so stupid? Half the damn stable is showing signs of drug use. I've been around this shit long enough to know the difference between a hangover and coming down from a drug high. I look around at all the ashen faces and decide it's time to scare these bitches straight. "Who brought drugs into the club?"

Everyone stays quiet, so I decide that fear is the way to go. "Do you know what happens to club girls that break the rules?"

I look around and watch a few heads shake. Seems like I need to give my girls a refresher course on club rules.

"Of course, it depends on what the girl did. If it's something small, you'll be punished, but you'll also be allowed to stick around. If it's something big, I'll kick your ass to the curb and you're eighty sixed from The Kitty Kat and the Club for life. No club member will even acknowledge you." I make sure to meet each girl's gaze before going on. "Now, if it's something huge, that's a whole new ballgame. The bitch that fucked up will be lucky if she leaves Big Clifty breathing."

I hear a few gasps and smile. I may be bluffing a bit, but that's the only way to get things done with these chicks. "We all know that bringing drugs into the club is huge offense, and since none of you will tell me who did it, I guess I'll have to assume that all of you played a part in this."

A chorus of 'nos' echo through the room. "Well, someone better be telling me which one of you brought the shit in The Kitty Kat then."

As soon as the words leave my mouth, I hone in on Cheyanne. She's looking around, doing her best to intimidate the rest of the women into keeping their mouths shut, but that bitch isn't as strong as she thinks she is. She's been Kidd's go to girl for a while, so she thinks she's got a little power, but that shit's fixing to change. Not only will she not be visiting Kidd anymore, she'll also be getting an attitude adjustment.

I know she tries to play Head Bitch when I'm not around. Guess it's time to show her who the true leader is. Without a moment's hesitation, I walk up and grab Cheyanne by the back of her hair. I pull her across the room and push her into the wall. "You like to play mama to my girls, so I figure you know who brought the shit in. You better start talking now, or I'm gonna assume it was you."

A look of pure contempt crosses her face before she responds. "I don't know shit, and you can't treat me like this! I'll tell Kidd."

"Oh, you mean my old man?" I ask, almost choking on my own words.

"What?"

I smile at her. "Yeah, he claimed me this morning. I don't figure he'll care what I do to the bitch that used to suck his dick."

Her face loses all of its color before she responds. "I don't know anything about the drugs."

I let out a soft chuckle. "Oh, really. Then why the hell do you have black circles under your eyes and dried blood caked on your nose."

The last part isn't true, but I know that I'm on the right track as soon as she wipes her hand under her nose. "Still want to tell me you don't know anything?"

She starts to shake her head, cringing when it causes me to pull her hair. "I didn't bring it in. I just did a few lines."

"You gonna tell me which one these bitches broke the golden rule?"

She looks towards the girls then back towards me. She answers, her voice full of contempt, "Kandy."

Hearing her name is a shock. Kandy's a bitch, but I thought she was loyal to me. She's one of the girls I brought into the club after I found her eating out of a garbage can in Kansas City, nearly a year ago. She was just a kid, barely eighteen, and as soon as I saw her, I knew I had to help her. She's one of the few girls that don't work at the clubhouse, but she does dance at The

Kitty Kat. She might not make as much money as some of the other girls that get paid for pussy do, but she is making enough to avoid the need to sell drugs.

I toss Cheyanne to the floor and head straight for Kandy. "What the fuck?"

Her eyes grow as big as saucers as she watches me stalk over to her. "It wasn't that big of a deal."

A cruel smile crosses my face as I send my fist flying into Kandy's face. "You knew the rules."

"I'm sorry, Ice," she says, doing her best to cover her face.

I turn to the rest of my girls and look until I find the newest addition to our stable. "What's the rule about drugs, Tonya?"

Her eyes grow large when she realizes I've singled her out. "Nothing but weed, Ice. I swear I didn't do anything. You can test me. You won't find that shit in my system."

I look back to Kandy. "See there? Even Tonya knows the rules and she's only been here for three weeks. How is it that your ass didn't know, when you've been here for almost a year?"

"It was just a little blow. I didn't think you would mind."

"No, you didn't think at all." I send my fist flying back into her face, which sprawls her skank ass on the floor. "No, that isn't true. You were thinking about the extra money the blow would make you."

She starts to shake her head in denial. "No, no, no," she chants.

"Now, you're going to tell me who supplied you the coke, or shit is about to get worse for you." Her body starts to shake in fear, and I know that she's more afraid of her supplier than she is of me. Guess it's time to put the fear of God in her. I grab my purse, dig out my Smith and Wesson 380, and point it right between her eyes. "You're going to tell me, one way or another."

"I can't tell you. If I do, he'll kill me. Please, don't make me tell you his name," she begs, tears streaming down her face.

"Maybe, maybe not." I say with a nod. "But, I can guarantee you that I'll kill you if you don't tell me who he is right now."

"Please, Ice. Please don't make me tell you."

I don't respond. I just cock my gun and shove it against the center of her forehead. There's no damn way I would ever pull the trigger, but she doesn't know that. The reality of her situation finally hits and her head drops to her chest. "Timmons," she says in a voice so low that I have to strain to hear what she said.

It takes a second for the name to register, but when it does, I feel my body go rigid. *No.* Without thinking, I slam the butt of my gun into the side of her head. "Take care of the bitch," I say without looking at anyone in particular. I rush out to the car and head back to the club as fast as I can.

I make the fifteen minute drive in less than ten, and as soon as I pull into the parking lot, I rush inside the club. I can't believe he's finally come for me.

CHAPTER Seventeen

Kidd

I'm sitting at the bar, nursing a Jack on ice, when the door flies open and Jenna comes running through it. As soon as I see her face, my body tenses. There's something wrong, and whatever it is has got her spooked. She's looking around the room with wild eyes, searching for something. Her eyes lock onto Chipper and she rushes towards him. Hell no! She is my old lady now. She needs to learn that she brings shit to me first.

I jump from the bar stool and head towards them. I'm about a foot away when I hear Chipper shout, "What the fuck are they doing here?"

"Who?" I ask, joining them.

"Looks like the boys from Mateland have come for a visit," Chipper growls out.

Oh shit! That is definitely something I didn't want to hear today. The Mateland chapter of the Renegade Sons have been a thorn in my side for years. If it was up to me alone, they would have lost their charter years ago, but my Pop made me promise not to cut them out before he died. As fucked up as they are, I can't break that promise. Things are tight now that Brew is holding the power. I thought that they finally got their shit together, and I could depend on them to do what they're told, but I still hear shit I don't like. Word on the street is the Mateland Renegades take what they want, even if it's not willingly given. Rape is not something I want the Renegade Sons known for.

Chipper draws me away from my thoughts. "We need to call church tonight."

I shake my head. "I need to know what's going on first. Why they came to Big Clifty without giving us a heads up? Let me talk to Brew before we call the boys in."

I hear Jenna's indrawn breath and look down to her. She has tears in her eyes. I've known her for nearly ten years, and the only times I've ever seen her cry were at Mindy's funeral, when she shot that bitch, and... the night that I broke her heart to pieces. "There's more to this than just the Mateland boys coming for a visit, isn't there?"

"There sure in the fuck is!" Chipper shouts, and then look towards Jenna. "I gotta tell him."

"I know, but I don't want to be here when you do," she says with a nod, then looks up to Chipper. "Before you start sharing all my deep dark secrets, you need to remember the promise you made Gun. He's dead, but the promise still stands."

With those words, she walks away. I watch her head towards her room and I have a feeling this conversation is going somewhere that I won't like at all. "What the fuck is going on, man? What the hell is she talking about?"

Chipper motions towards my office and walks that way. I follow him, barely getting into the room before he slams the door shut. "I didn't tell you everything that happened when I found Jenna."

I lift my chin for him to go on while I walk to the fridge and grab a beer. "Well, tell me now."

He shakes his head. "I can't. Jenna's right. I made a promise to the old man. I plan to keep it."

"That shit ain't right, brother. Not only am I the president of this fucking club, but Ice is my old lady now. I need to know it all. If not, how the hell can I protect her? How the fuck can I protect the club if trouble is coming and I don't know what the hell it is?"

"Talk to Jenna," is his only response.

"She ain't going to tell me shit, and you know it, so you've got to give me something."

"You're right, and you're also right that you need to know what's coming," he continues with a nod. "but I can't break my word to Pop."

I run a hand over my face, trying to control my temper. "Fine, but you gotta give me a heads up."

He nods. "Keep an eye out for Timmons. Don't let that fucker anywhere near my girl. Hell, don't let him near any of the girls."

"I thought you said that you caught Rig raping her? What the hell did Timmons do?"

"Rig did rape her, and he paid the price for doing it," Chipper says in a near shout.

"Then what the hell does Timmons have to do with it?" I ask, frustration making my voice sound strained.

"Dad loved Killer like a brother. They were more than just club brothers. They fought side by side, putting their asses on the line to keep the others safe in that fucking jungle."

"I've heard Pop's war stories, just like you. What the fuck do they have to do with this shit?" I ask, my frustration turning into anger.

"Timmons is Killer's son," he states matter-of-factly.

"And?"

Chipper walks towards me, stopping only a few inches from my face. "What do you think Pop would have done to make Killer happy? What would he have done if he thought Jenna was going to cause problems for Killer or his son?"

I shake my head in denial. My first instinct is to defend my old man. Of course, he wouldn't protect a grown man over a young kid, but memories of him calling Jenna a stray pop into my head, and I know I can't. To my dad, their friendship meant everything. If he thought Jenna might cause trouble between him and Killer, he would have sent her back. "Are you telling me that Timmons had something to do with Ice being at the Mateland MC, and Dad knew about it?"

"I'm not saying shit. Like I told you, I made a promise and I plan to keep it, but I will tell you that Timmons is a sick motherfucker. If he's here, he's here for Jenna."

"Fuck!" I shout. "I need to know everything."

Chipper backs up a step and nods. "Yeah you do, but you're gonna have to hear it from Jenna."

"That's exactly what I'm going to do now," I say as I start towards the door. "Either she tells me, or you do. One way or another, I'm going to know the truth."

I don't wait for Chipper's response. I just walk out of my office and head towards Jenna's room. As I push open her door, I realize that I'm gonna have to talk to her about moving her shit into my room, but now isn't the time. When I step inside, I see Jenna standing by the window with a bottle of Jose' Cuervo in her hand. "We need to talk."

She doesn't even look towards me when she responds.

"What did Chipper tell you?"

"Enough," I say, doing my best to bluff her. "Now, it's your turn."

"If he told you, there's no need in me repeating it."

"Ice," I growl out. "You need to tell me what's got you so fucking scared."

She jerks her head to me, her eyes shooting daggers my way. "I'm not scared."

I run a hand through my hair in frustration. "Fine, let's start with something easy. Why were you even at Mateland clubhouse in the first place?"

She looks back towards the window and takes a moment to respond. "My sperm donor was affiliated with the club. I pissed him off, and he thought that giving me to them as a toy would be a good punishment."

"What the fuck?" I ask, anger filling my voice. "Who's your dad?"

She turns back towards me. "My dad is Chipper; my mother was Mindy."

"Ice, you know what I mean."

She shakes her head. "I can't tell you."

"Hell yeah, you can."

She walks to me and wraps her arms around my waist.

"You know there are a lot of other things we could be doing instead of talking about this shit."

Damn! Just having her near makes my dick twitch. "We need to talk."

"We can talk later," she says as she molds her body to mine, rubbing against my hardening cock.

I have to fist my hands to keep from tossing her onto the bed. I've wanted her under me for so fucking long that it takes every bit of willpower I have to resist her. "Quit using your body to distract me. You know I want you, and I will fuck you if you really want me to, but first, we're going to talk."

She jerks away from me and mumbles something under her breath before walking back towards the window and grabbing her bottle. After taking a swig, she lets me have it. "My father was a stupid fuck who didn't give a shit about me. To him, I was nothing but a result of a misplaced load of jizz. I'm not telling you his name, so you can just give up on that shit now."

I can tell by her voice that she's not gonna give in, so I know trying to change her mind will be useless. "Fine, but you'll have to tell me someday."

She lets out a mocking laugh. "Sure, I will. You made me your old lady. I'm sure you can make me tell you all my darkest secrets too."

I shake off the sting of her words and walk to her. "I gave

you a choice. You could have left."

Her eyes cut to me, anger vibrating throughout her body. "Not much of a choice there, was it?"

I grab her arm and pull her into me. "Nope, but at least I gave you a choice, and you chose me."

At first her body is tense, but within seconds, she melts into me. "Yeah, I chose you."

As soon as the words leave her mouth, I drop my head and place my lips on hers. She tastes of tequila, cinnamon, and something that is purely Jenna; something I haven't tasted in six fuckin' long years. The combination has me aching to get inside her.

I'm just about to lead her to the bed when I hear a knock at the door. Fuck! I jerk my head away and roar. "This better be fucking good."

"Some chick named Krista is here. She needs to talk to you, and she says it's important," Preach responds from the hallway.

I feel Jenna's body tighten before she pulls away. "Who's Krista?"

"Just a chick I know," I say, doing my best to avoid the truth. No way in hell am I telling Jenna that Krista is a piece of my past that I would rather forget; a reminder of the good woman that died because of me.

"I'm sorry, babe, but I gotta go. We can finish this later."

"Sure, run off to Krista." Her eyes narrow before she responds with a sharp edge to her voice. "I'll be right here waiting for you when you get back."

I know she's drawing her line in the sand. If I walk out of this room, I'll lose whatever ground I gained with her today, but I don't really have a choice. "Sorry, Ice. I gotta deal with this."

Jenna

I watch Kidd walk out of my room and grab my purse. I walk out the door and make my way out of the club, doing my best to avoid Kidd and his guest. I can't believe that he claims me as his old lady and then walks out on me to see some other chick not long after, but it isn't the first time it's happened, and it sure as hell won't be the last. I should have known it was coming. Well, he can just kiss my ass. Fuck him!

Ten minutes later, I pull into Daisy's parents' driveway. Daisy is one of the few girls who works at The Kitty Kat and doesn't live at the apartment complex. She's the only one that still lives with her parents, although the term 'parents' is stretching it when it comes to the two people that Daisy calls mom and dad. As far as I'm concerned, they should be called the Fuckwad and the Cunt.

Daisy's dad, Maker, is a member of the club. He was around when Chipper and Kidd's dad started the Renegade Sons, but he was never more than a worker bee. To be honest, he's a pretty good guy, but he's dumber than shit and lets Lula run him around by the hair on his balls.

Lula, Daisy's mom, is one of the biggest bitches I've ever met. I swear her and Roxy are fighting for the title of bitch numero uno. Not only does she control every aspect of Maker and Daisy's life, but she does her best to make Daisy feel like shit every time she talks to her.

I get out of the car and look towards the fancy ass house that Lula and Maker live in, and then look towards the tiny garage that Daisy calls home. Every time I come here, it pisses me off just seeing it. She tells everyone that the garage has been converted into an apartment, but that's bullshit. It's nothing more than an old garage with a few pieces of ratty furniture stuck in it. When she first moved into it, the damn thing didn't even have any insulation or sheetrock. It was so damn cold in the winter that I'm not sure how in the hell she didn't freeze to death.

The first time I saw how she was living, I got mad as hell and made sure everyone at the club knew what her place was like. At the time, I didn't have much money set back, but I still offered to pay to get the place fixed up a bit for her. In the end, I didn't have to spend a single penny. Preach came in and did all of the work for free. He even bought all of the supplies too. He tries to pretend that Daisy doesn't mean shit to him, but anyone with eyes can see right through all of his bullshit bravado. As much as I hate to admit it, Preach looks at Daisy like I look at Kidd.

I walk towards the garage, trying to plan out what I'm going to say to Daisy. I know I need to talk to her about the shit she pulled this morning, but I don't really know how the hell I'm supposed to tell a twenty year old not to be shoving food up her twat. Shit. That's just something she should know without having to be told. Common sense is not strong with this one if she really did think that she could stick an orange in her vag and get away with it.

I don't even get a chance to knock before Daisy is jerking the door open. "I knew you'd show up sooner or later."

I try to hide my smile before I respond. "Well, someone had to come over here and straighten you out."

Her eyes narrow before she steps out of the doorway and motions for me to come inside. "Don't tell me that you believed Kandy's bullshit too?"

"What do you mean, her bullshit?" I ask as I make my way to her sofa.

"Preach came over here earlier, giving me seven kinds of hell." She blows out a frustrated breath before sitting beside me.

"Can you believe he honestly thinks that I shoved an orange up my hoo-hah just to get his attention?"

I nearly laugh at her words. She's the only chick I know that takes off her clothes for a living, but still calls her pussy a hoo-hah. "You didn't?"

A blush crosses her face as she starts to shake her head. "No way. I'm not an idiot, no matter what everyone else thinks."

"Well, then what the hell happened? I know Skittles took you to the hospital."

She nods. "Yes, because I had an allergic reaction to the new body glitter you bought last week."

"Where the hell did the orange story come from?"

She jerks her purse from the coffee table and pulls out a jar full of orange glitter gel. "The glitter is orange."

"You stuck the glitter up your pussy?" I ask, confused at the directions that this conversation is going.

"No!" she shouts. "I would never do something as stupid as that. I just rubbed the glitter around my G-string. I thought it would look cool on the stage."

"Then why the hell did Skittles have to take you the hospital?"

Daisy stands up and jerks down her shorts. There is a deep

red rash running from mid-thigh to her lower stomach. "The doctor said there's something in the new glitter that I'm allergic too."

Ouch! "So why the hell was I told that you stuck an orange up your snatch?"

She pulls her shorts up and plops back down on the couch. "Leah," she says with a hiss. "She walked in when I was showing the rash to some of the other girls. Next thing I know, she's telling everyone that stupid story. You know how the girls are, anything for a laugh, especially that bitch."

Oh, I should have seen that one coming. Leah and Daisy used to be pretty good friends, but ever since Leah and Preach started hooking up, they haven't gotten along. "She's jealous of you."

She looks at me as if I'm an idiot. "There's not one damn thing about me that anyone would be jealous of."

I shake my head at her stupidity. She's a tiny thing, barely reaching five foot. I doubt she weighs much over a hundred pounds. She has blonde hair that's so light, it almost looks white. It's cut in a cute pixie style and shows off her high cheekbones and the two sweetest deep dimples that you've ever seen. The girl is knockout. "You're a beautiful girl, Daisy."

She shrugs then shoots me a smug smile. "Enough about me, let's talk about you. What's this I hear about you and Kidd?

Did he really make you his old lady?"

I shrug back at her. "You know how the boys work. When they want something, they take it. For some reason, Kidd wants me now. I'm sure he'll get tired of me before too long."

Even saying that shit out loud kills me. After all these years of trying to avoid him, one kiss was all it took and I was his again. I'm fighting it, but I can feel my heart melting for him. The Ice Queen is finally starting to thaw out.

"I don't know, Ice. I don't think Kidd will ever get tired of you. He loves you too much."

I cut my eyes to her. "He doesn't love me. He just likes playing games with me."

I have never told Daisy about all the shit that happened between me and Kidd, but she knows. Everyone does. It's practically club lore.

Daisy shakes her head. "I don't know Kidd all that well, and you know Mom kept me away from the guys in the club when I was growing up, but I know that he loves you something fierce. Shit, girl, everyone knows he loves you. He's never tried to hide it."

"What are you talking about? If he loves me, then why is he with a different girl every night? Why did he treat me like shit when he got his chance with me?"

Her eyes go sad before she replies, "I can't answer that for you. No one but Kidd can. I will say that I think you should give the two of you a second chance. Not for Kidd, but for yourself."

I snort. "For myself? Why the hell would I do that?"

"Because you love him. If you don't give it a chance, then you'll spend the rest of your life wondering what if..."

Shit! Why does she have to be so smart and say the things that I've been thinking about out loud? I know she's right. I need to give it a chance. I've been running from him so long, and I'm not sure I know how to make this thing between us work, but I love him too much just to walk away without trying.

"I'm not talking about that shit anymore."

She rolls her eyes. "Fine, then what do you want to do?"

A smile spreads across my face, and I say, "Let's go get drunk."

A half hour later, Daisy and I are sitting at the clubhouse bar, downing shots of tequila, when I hear a commotion in the front of the club. I turn to look just in time to watch Timber walk into the common room, and a big smile spreads across my face. "Finally home, huh?"

His head jerks towards mine and he shoots me one of his panty dropping smiles. He doesn't respond, but instead rushes towards me and pulls me into his body. Before I realize what's happening, he crushes his lips onto mine. Shit! I know I should be pulling away, but Timber is so aggressive, so powerful, that I forget myself for a moment and get lost in the feeling of his lips on mine.

I've really missed Timber. If Kidd hadn't have claimed me, I'd be hauling him to my bedroom right about now and showing him how much. He's sexy as hell, great in the sack, and fun to be around. When he went away, Reese and I got closer, but I never forgot Timber. Timber is the only man I would have ever considered becoming an old lady for. He's asked me a million times, and I was right on the verge of giving in to him before he went to prison.

Ever so slowly, he pulls back. "It's good to be home, pretty girl."

"Be a damn shame for you die as soon as you get here, and that's exactly what's going to happen if you don't take your hands off my old lady."

I turn my head just in time to see Kidd walking into the room. "He didn't know that you claimed me, so you better not lay a damn hand on him, Kidd. I mean it!"

Kidd ignores my words and walks straight towards us. Within seconds, he has me tossed over his shoulder and is walking towards his room, my face directly in front of his ass. Without a second thought, I bite down. He doesn't even miss a step, but instead, just smacks my ass and keeps on walking.

As soon as we make it back into his room, he tosses me

onto the bed. "It's time."

"Time for what?" I ask.

"Time to go see Greg over at Ink Kings. We need to get you branded, before I have to kill some asshole for trying get near you. I know Timber's been inside for over two years, so he doesn't know that I claimed you, but once my name is on your arm, everyone will know that you're mine. Then, and only then, will they know to keep their hands to their fucking selves."

I roll to the side of the bed and sit up. "Nuh huh, no way. It's bad enough that everyone in the club thinks you own me. There's no way in hell I'm putting your name on my body-- permanently."

"You're not stupid. You had to know this was coming. You've been around here long enough to know that old ladies wear their man's brand."

Brand! I hate that freaking word. "You brand a damn cow, not a woman."

Kidd crosses his arms over his chest. "What the fuck ever. Call it what you want, but my name is going on your arm."

"Nope, not happening. Once you pull your head out of your ass, this charade will end, and then I'll be stuck wearing your name for the rest of my damn life." I shoot him a sarcastic smile. "Maybe that Krista chick will take my place."

Even thinking about another woman wearing his brand

makes my stomach knot up. I'm not even sure why I said it. Maybe I just need him to reassure me and tell me that this isn't going to end the same way as it did last time.

"Baby girl, you need to get this straight in that thick head of yours. This is not gonna end. You're mine, you'll be mine tomorrow, and you'll still be mine twenty years from now," he says as he leans closer to me.

"Fine, but if you're branding me, then I'm branding you. You don't have any more room on your arms, so you can just get a big ole 'property of Ice' tattoo on that sexy ass of yours," I say, pasting on a saccharine sweet smile.

"Not funny, Ice."

I shrug. "Do you see me laughing? If you want me to get your name on me, then you're getting mine on you."

He shakes his head. "I don't fucking think so."

"Well then, looks like I'll be the first old lady that doesn't get branded," I say as I climb from the bed and try to walk past him.

He grabs my arm before I even take a step. "Fuck yeah, you are."

"Unless you're getting one too, then you'll have to pull me kicking and screaming into Ink Kings. I promise you that I'll throw such a damn fit that Greg won't even be able to tattoo a straight line," I say, determination lacing through my voice.

He stares at me like I have a second head. "You're serious, aren't you?"

"Hell yeah, I am."

He blows out a frustrated breath before replying. "Fine, I'll get your name, but I ain't getting shit on my ass. I'll have your name where everybody can fuckin' see it, but there is no way in hell I'm getting a 'property of' tat, so your name will have to do."

I start to argue some more, but stop when it hits me. Kidd is giving me more than any other old lady has ever gotten. Sure, a few of the brothers have their woman's name on them, but I doubt they got it for the same reason that Kidd is getting mine. A true smile finally crosses my lips. "Set it up. I'll wear your brand, baby."

As soon as the words leave my mouth, Kidd's lips cover mine. His kisses are so different than any other ones I've ever had. It's slow and soft, as if he's taking the time to memorize the feel of my lips. It sends shivers down my spine, and within seconds, my whole body is on fire. I'm about to lose myself to it, but one name keeps popping into my brain.

I slowly pull back and look into his eyes. "Who exactly is Krista?"

Kidd

Shit! I knew she'd want to talk about Krista, but I'd rather be doing other things right now. I pause a second to get the words straight. "She's Sarah's sister."

"Sarah?" she asks in a whispered voice.

I nod. "Yep. I only met her once, but they were real close."

"I can't believe your old lady's sister would come here after all this time."

"Sarah was never my old lady," I say, trying to figure out the best way to tell her everything. "She was someone that I was with for a while, but nothing more."

"Come on, Kidd. Be real. She would've been if she hadn't gotten in that accident. Everyone knew you were eventually going to brand her."

I shake my head. "No, that's not true."

I'm not sure how in the hell to tell her the truth. How do you tell someone that you had just kicked another girl to curb because you wanted to be with them instead? Then, minutes later, that girl dies in a car accident. I know the kind of pain and guilt that causes, and I don't want Jenna feeling it. "She and I had already ended our shit before she died."

A confused look crosses her face. "When?"

"Right before she left the clubhouse."

I watch as the words sink in, and she realizes I had just got shot of the chick minutes before she was killed. "Yeah, right before she died."

She places her hand on my shoulder and takes a step towards me, placing her body flush with mine. "My God, Kidd. I'm so sorry."

"Nothing for you to be sorry about."

An angry look crosses her face, and she pulls away from me. "That's not what you said the night she died."

Fuck! I knew having Krista here was going to lead to this shit. "I was pissed off that night. Not at you, at myself. Sarah was a good woman. I enjoyed my time with her when we were in Mateland, but that all changed when I got back here."

"Why?"

"I saw you."

Her body goes tight before she responds. "I don't understand."

If I had been honest with her six years ago, she would. I guess it's time to lay it all out for her. "When I went to Mateland, I left a kid behind. A kid that had me thinking things that didn't sit well with me, because she was so damn young. But when I got back, that kid had become a woman. A woman that I knew I wanted to spend the rest of my life with."

I take a step closer and give it all to her. "I wanted you so damn bad, but you were only seventeen. You can't imagine how hard it was to keep my hands off you. For some fucked up reason, I thought I could use Sarah until you got old enough for me to claim. Sarah knew it, and that's why she hated you so much. It's also why she turned into a raging bitch when we got here. That Sarah, the woman that you knew, was a Sarah I'd never seen before. What I did to her was shitty, but I told her before we ever left Mateland that I didn't know how long we would last."

She watches me closely as I continue laying it out for her. "The truth is, she had no reason to blame our shit on you. Yes, I had feelings for you, but that's not the only reason I got rid of her. Even if it wasn't for you, Jenna, just her acting the way she did, I would have scraped her off."

"Maybe she wouldn't have acted that way if she hadn't been jealous," Jenna says quietly.

"Maybe, but I'm not sure. There was always something missing about her. She was really sweet, but she had no fire, never even had an opinion of her own. I swear she just went with whatever I wanted without question. It was just fuckin' weird." I take a second to consider how to explain it the best way, and then I go on. "When we were in Mateland, Krista came down to visit her. She was just a kid then, so Sarah didn't want her around the clubhouse. They got a hotel room in St. Louis and had a ton of shit planned to do. Sarah was so excited to get to spend time with her sister, and she wanted me to be part of it. I drove her down, and we picked Krista up from the airport. We barely made it to the hotel before I got a call about some shit going down at Mateland."

I shake my head at the memory. "I had no choice but to get back to the clubhouse. Sarah could have stayed with Krista, but instead of spending time with her sister like she had planned on doing, she put the kid on a plane and followed me back to Mateland. It fuckin' crushed Krista. She'd only been there for less than an hour. I felt so damn sorry for the kid, even tried to talk Sarah into staying, but she wouldn't even consider it."

"She loved you, Kidd."

I look to Jenna and shake my head. "I don't think she loved me. Looking back on our time together, I think she was obsessed with becoming an old lady, especially an old lady to a man that would be president someday."

"I got in her way. That's why she hated me so much."

"No, my feelings for you got in the way, but that wasn't all of it. I would've realized the game she was playing sooner or later."

She nods. "You would have, but she still would've hated me."

"I'm not sure if that's true. I wasn't faithful to her when we were in Mateland. I didn't rub it in her face, but I didn't try to hide it either. She had no claim on me, and I didn't make any promises to her. She never seemed to have a problem with it. In fact, she was real good friends with one of the girls I used to hook up with. She had an issue with you because of some shit I did."

"What?" She asks.

"I told her the first night here that it wasn't gonna work between us, but that didn't mean I turned away from her completely. I couldn't have you at the time, so I used her. I was with her only once after we got back, but once was too much. I ended up calling out your name when I came. She flipped the fuck out. The sweet girl I knew disappeared, and she became a complete bitch."

"I can't say I blame her. If you called out another woman's name while you were inside me, I'd cut your fuckin' balls off."

I smile at her. "Baby girl, when I'm inside you, the only thing I can think of is staying there. No damn way another bitch's name would even flash through my mind."

She smiles. "It better stay that way."

I continue on after shooting Jenna a quick wink. "After all that happened, she became someone I didn't know and kept doing stupid shit. She even tried making me jealous. I walked in on her having a threesome with a couple of the boys. At that point, I didn't really give a shit who she was fuckin', but I was disgusted that she was doing it just to try to piss me off. No matter how hard she tried, and believe me, she tried really fuckin' hard, I never touched her again. I wouldn't even let her ass in my room. That's when she threatened to kill herself."

"My God," she whispers out.

"At first, I was scared as shit. That's why you kept seeing her at my side. It wasn't that I wanted her there. It was because I was afraid to leave her ass alone. But it didn't take me long to figure out that she was running a game on me, doing anything she could to keep me by her side. That's when I told her I was done and took one of the club girls to my bed. I made sure Sarah saw me taking her there, did my best to let her know that what we had was dead. Instead of making her go away like I wanted it to, she just got worse. She became my shadow, always on my ass. She stayed that way until the day I told her to leave on her own or I'd have some of the boys take her ass to Mateland and dump her in the middle of their clubhouse. That was the day she died."

"My God," she says again.

"Yeah. I was a bastard, and because of that, she's dead."

She shakes her head. "You made a lot of mistakes, but not one of them is the reason she died. You didn't make her drive so fast. You didn't cause her to crash her car. That was all on her."

I start to deny her words, but she cuts me off. "No, you listen to me. How you treated her was shitty, but her death is still not your fault."

I wrap my arms around her waist, pulling her even closer. "It happened a long time ago. Nothing we say about it now matters, but you got to understand that I can't just turn my back on Krista. I owe it to Sarah to look out for her little sister."

She nods. "I do understand. I don't like it, but I understand. What's this girl want?"

"Her old man kicked her out, and her parents won't let her move back home. She came here because she needs a place to stay and a job. I figured you could work her into the rotation over at The Kitty Kat. She told me that she's been waitressing since she was sixteen. Maybe she can sling drinks for you. Can you do that for her?"

"Not for her, but I can do that for you."

I lean down and kiss the top of her head. "Thank you, baby girl."

"Don't thank me yet. If I hate the bitch, I will place her right back in your lap again," she says, and then looks up to me. "Well, maybe not in your lap. Actually, she better not ever be anywhere near your lap."

As soon as the words leave her mouth, I throw my head back and laugh. "God, I love you."

I don't even register my own words until I feel her body go tense and her breaths become labored. I look down to her eyes and see them shining bright with tears. "You can't love me. There's nothing about me to love."

I lean my face down to hers, nearly touching her lips. "I love everything about you. I have since you were just a kid. Even when you were too young for me to love you, I still did. I'll keep on loving you until the day I die."

I gently place my mouth onto hers, nipping her bottom lip. I run my tongue across her mouth and slowly push it in. I take my time kissing her, savoring the taste of her, and loving the feel of her tongue against mine. I'm so fucking hard that it feels like my dick could burst at any moment, but I know I have to be gentle. Jenna has been fucked enough. I'm going to make love to her tonight.

I slowly walk towards the bed, not letting go of her. I gently push her back, lying down beside her as I continue to kiss her, while my hand makes its way under her shirt. As soon as I reach her breast, her body bucks. "God, Kidd. That feels so good."

I don't respond. I just smile against her mouth and keep kissing her. I slowly push her shirt up, raising my head to pull it off of her. After it's gone, I try to go back to kissing her beautiful body, trying my damnedest to be patient, but she isn't feeling the need to go slow. She pushes me away and shakes her head before she reaches for the bottom of my tee and pulls it up.

"I think you can handle the rest," she says with a smile. She then leans back and jerks off her jeans, tossing her shoes off at the same time.

When I see her lying on the bed with nothing but her black lace bra and tiny black panties on, I lose all of the control that I had. I jump up and kick off my boots, toss off my jeans, and jerk my boxers down. While I'm doing this, she takes off her bra and slings it in my direction. Before she can get her panties off, I grab the sides of them and tear them down her legs, then crawl onto the bed and cover her body with mine.

I start to kiss her neck, grinding my hardness into her core. "I want you, Jenna. I want you more than I've ever wanted anything else in my life."

"I want you too," she says, sounding desperate.

I slowly make my way down her body, only stopping when I reach her nipples. I run my tongue over a stiff pink peak and pull it into my mouth. I lightly bite her nipple, using just enough pressure to cause a little pain, and when she sucks in a sharp breath, I know that she likes this just as much as I do. Hearing her contented sigh, I move on to the other breast and do the same, worshipping her with every lick, bite, and suck that I place on her plump breast.

While I'm enjoying her beautiful tits, I move my hand to the dampness that's pooling between her legs. I stop when I reach her clit and give it a gentle pinch, causing her hips to jerk. I smile against her skin before I pull my head back and look up at her. "Do you like that, baby doll?"

"Um hum," she moans out while fisting the sheets.

My mouth goes back to work on her nipples, and I move my fingers from her clit to her core. I slide one finger inside of her and then another. The feeling of her tight heat surrounding them feels amazing. I swear just touching her is better than having my dick inside any other woman.

"I need to be inside you," I say as I reach to the floor and grab a condom from my jeans. Before I have a chance to open it, Jenna grabs it from my hand and rips it open with her teeth. She places her hand between our bodies and rolls it on. The feeling of her hand on my cock has me ready to explode.

I settle myself between her legs and grab my rigid cock, rubbing it up and down her sweet little slit. "I planned on taking this slow and savoring every inch of you." I rumble out to her as the head of my cock teases her most sensitive parts.

She wraps her legs around me, pulling me even closer to the entrance of her core. "I don't want you to go slow. I just want you inside me. NOW."

With those words, I lose my ability to be patient and slam

myself into her. As soon as I'm buried deep inside her, I go still and enjoy the feeling of having her wrapped around me. "Fuck, you feel so damn good."

"It would feel even better if you'd move," she says as she lifts her hips.

I smile at her and pull out, only to push myself back into her. "Is that better?"

"Oh, yeah," she drawls out, scraping her fingernails down my back.

After only a few strokes, I feel my balls start to tighten. I reach between our bodies and tweak her clit. "Give it to me, baby. I want to feel your pussy squeeze me."

The words barely leave my mouth before she starts to moan and her pussy starts to convulse around my cock. I speed up my pace and slam into her, giving her everything I've got. Within minutes, I'm exploding inside of her. I bury my face into her neck and shout out my release.

Afterwards, I lay there for a moment, trying to catch my breath, before I pull out of her and give her a soft kiss on her swollen lips. "I gotta take care of the condom. Don't move."

I crawl from the bed and walk to the bathroom. I do what I have to, and then walk back to the bed, cutting the light switch off on the way. I crawl in beside her and feel that her body is tight. I know she's trying to think of a way to get out of this, trying to think of a way to get me out of her bed, but that shit isn't happening.

I throw my arm over her and pull her body tightly against mine. "Go to sleep, baby doll. We'll talk about whatever you got on your mind in the morning."

She stays quiet and her body stays alert as I lay beside her, keeping her in my arms. After what seems like hours, I feel her body go slack and her breathing even out. I place my lips against the top of her head and give her a kiss, and then close my eyes and let sleep takeover.

Jenna

I wake up with a warm tingle blooming between my legs. I try to press them together, hoping to relieve a little of the pressure, but am blocked by Kidd's broad shoulders. I slowly run my hands down to his hair and grab a handful. "What'cha doing?"

He gives my clit a quick lick then raises his head, a cocky smile spread across his face. "I'm eating breakfast. Best damn meal I've had in a long damn time."

I don't have time to respond before he gets back down to business. I've had more men than I can count with their heads between my legs, but not one of them has ever come close to Kidd. Having him between my legs makes me feel things that I didn't even realize were possible. With each lick, each suck, and each nip of his teeth, I get closer to the edge.

Within minutes, I'm exploding, and I can't hold back a shout of pure pleasure that erupts from my body before I go slack. Closing my eyes, I try to hold on to my afterglow for as long as I can.

After a few seconds pass, and Kidd has licked me clean, I can feel him slowly make his way up my body, kissing me the entire way. "Damn, baby doll. You taste so fucking good. I'll never get enough of you."

I open my eyes and look up to him. "Don't worry, you can do that any time you want."

He chuckles and rolls to his side, pulling me with him. I reach up and lick his lips, tasting myself on them. "I do taste pretty good, don't I?"

I hear him chuckle as I make my way down his body. Doing my best not to miss an inch of his chest, the saltiness of his skin makes my tongue tingle. I run the tip of my tongue around his belly button, causing goose bumps to prickle across his skin.

"I don't think I can take much more of this, baby," he says, sounding pained.

I get up on my knees, between his legs, and smile. "You'll take all I got to give."

"I'll tell you what I'd like you to give. I'd like you to give me your lips," he says while holding his beautiful cock in his hand.

For some reason, I almost have the urge to do just what he says, but in the end, I can't do it. I haven't done that shit in a long time, and I won't be starting now. "I don't give head. Haven't done it since…" I trail off. "Ain't going to start that shit again now."

"What?" he asks, sounding truly shocked.

"I don't want anyone's dick in my mouth. I've had enough cocks shoved down my throat to last a life time."

He shakes his head in frustration. "Baby girl, don't talk about that shit. It's in the past. You got an old man now, so things are different."

"Nope, nothing's different. Like I said, I don't give head. If you want your dick sucked off, then you should've picked someone else to call your old lady."

The look on his face turns from frustration to bewilderment. "What the fuck, Jenna? I just spent the last twenty minutes with my head between your legs, and now you're telling me I don't get anything in return for all my hard work?"

I shrug, trying to act like it's not a big deal. "You can have all the pussy you want, and if you ask nicely, I may even let you have my ass, but you're not getting my mouth."

"Tell me what happened," he says in a near shout.

"What are you talking about?"

He places his hands on my cheeks and brings his face to mine. "Tell me what happened. I'm not stupid. It's more than you just sucked your fill of cocks. Tell me why you don't give head."

I shake my head, preparing to deny him, but he cuts me off. "Nope, you're gonna tell me. You're gonna tell your man what happened."

I start to tell him no again, but then I decide to give it to him. If he wants me, he's gonna have to take all of the fucked up baggage that comes along with me. This is just the tip of the iceberg, but it'll give him an idea of the shit that I have going on inside of my head. "One of the guys in Mateland used to force me to blow him all the time."

Kidd lowers his hands to my shoulders and gives them a squeeze. "It's more than that. Don't get me wrong, that's bad enough, but I know you. There's more to the story than you being forced to suck his cock."

I take a deep breath and lay it out for him. "He would shove his dick so far down my throat that I thought I was going die. He'd hold my head there until I'd start to pass out, and then he'd finally give me a little air. He'd do that for what felt like hours."

"Fuck," Kidd mutters.

I can feel my body shaking. Fear courses through me as the memories of being Timmons' plaything play on loop in my brain. "I swear, I thought I was going to die with his dick shoved down my throat."

"Shit, baby girl. I'm sorry," he whispers as he pulls me closer to him.

His sympathy is the last thing I want. "You don't have to be sorry. You just gotta keep your cock out of my mouth," I say, letting my inner bitch shine through.

He chuckles, but somehow it comes out sounding sad. "I can do that."

We're both quiet for a few minutes before he breaks the silence. "What about when you worked for the club? The guys here didn't make you do it, did they?"

I shake my head. "No, none of the brothers ever made me do anything. I never slept with anyone that I didn't trust. Some of the brothers had me blow them a time or two, but you know the boys. They catch on to that kinda shit quickly. They knew that I hated doing it, so after the first couple of months I was working here, they quit asking for it. They're different than most of the guys I've come across. They ain't into forcing anyone, even club whores, to do what they don't want to do, so I haven't done it for almost five years."

A confused look crosses his face. "Five years?"

"Yeah."

"But, you also said the guys quit asking for it a few months after you started working the club. You've been working for the club for almost six years. Those numbers don't add up, babe," he says, explaining his confusion.

I shrug. "Well, sometimes the club girls have to service guys that aren't part of this charter. You know, when outsiders are here for parties or club business."

"Yeah, others do, but you ran the girls. You got to choose who you were with," he says, but it comes out sounding more like a question.

I shrug again. "One of boys from the Lords didn't think it was right that a whore got to pick and choose. He also didn't like the idea of a whore that didn't give head. I tried to fight him off, but he was bigger than me, so he won."

I do my best to make it sound like it didn't bother me, but that's not true. When he forced himself on me, it brought back all of my memories with Timmons and Rig. The worst part was that Chipper had begged me not to come to that party. He knew something would happen. God, how I wish I had listened to him.

Kidd's eyes flash with anger. "What the fuck? Who?"

"I don't know his name, but it wouldn't matter anyway. Reese took care of him. I figure he's pushing up daisies in some field between here and Kansas City, or he's rotting at the bottom of the Marais De Cygnes River by now."

When Reese found me trying to fight the man off, he flipped the fuck out. The gentle guy I'd known turned into a stone cold killer. He pulled the bastard off me and used his hands to snap the guy's neck. I've seen a lot of things in my life, but there's nothing like seeing the light in a man's eyes ceasing to exist in an instant.

"Why didn't I know about this shit? I'm president of the club. I need to know everything. You should've told me. Reese should've told me."

"You weren't president then."

His eyes narrow. "That don't fuckin' matter. I was VP! I should have known."

I shake my head. "I wouldn't have told anyone, if Reese hadn't walked in on it. I even begged him not to tell anyone else, and he gave me his word that he wouldn't."

"Why the hell would you do that? You know that nothing goes on in the club that I don't know about. I don't care if it happens to a member, a prospect, or a club whore. If something goes down here, I need to know about it."

I bury my head into his chest, trying to hide from his penetrating stare. "Yeah, I knew that I was supposed to tell you, but I also knew that whatever business you had going down with the Lords was important. Shit, the whole club had been on edge for weeks before they came. I knew there was something big going down, and I wasn't going to let what happened get in the way of what you had planned."

"That wasn't your choice," he says, giving me a tight squeeze.

"No, it wasn't, but in the long run, I was right. A lot of shit happened that weekend that helped both clubs. The Lords and the Renegade Sons have been working together ever since," I say, finally looking up. "I knew they were a good club. Most of the Lord members are as solid as our boys. I wasn't going to start a war with good men just because one of their brothers was a bastard."

"It wouldn't have started a war," he says with a shake of his head.

I nod. "It would have, and you know it. There is no way Chipper would've kept quiet about what happened. He would have raised all kinds of hell until you made sure every Lord paid for what their brother had done. I doubt it would've took too much convincing."

Even after all we've been through, I've always known that Kidd cared about me. If he knew someone had hurt me, he would have wanted revenge.

He stays quiet for a few minutes, running his hands slowly over my back. Finally, he starts to talk in a quiet voice. "You got anymore secrets?"

"Tons," I state matter of factly.

He gives me another squeeze. "You feel like sharing?"

"Not right now," I say, hoping he'll drop it.

Kidd pulls back and looks down to me. "I'll let you keep your secrets for now, but someday you're gonna have to open up to me."

I nod, praying that he won't make me say I agree. "You know, there are still things I can do with my mouth, even if they don't include your dick."

A slow, but sexy smile crosses his face. "And what would that be?"

I place my hands on his chest and give him a little push. "Roll over, Kidd. Let me show you."

Kidd and I spend the next hour in bed. By the time he walks out of my room, I'm ready to go back to sleep. I know I need to get to the strip club to check on things, though, so I roll out of bed and get dressed. Less than thirty minutes later, I pull into my spot by the backdoor of The Kitty Kat. I knife outta the car and make my way inside.

Walking past the bar area, I head right back to the changing rooms. Krista's starting tonight, and I need to make sure she knows how things go here before customers start rolling in. Maybe I should've had this talk with her before I let Kidd talk me into taking her on, but I had other things on my mind at the time. Just thinking about those other things sends a smile onto my face.

I'm still scared that he'll hurt me again, but his words last night have helped alleviate some of that fear. No matter what, I love him. I always have. I'm still not sure if I trust him, but I'm willing to give it a chance. If he screws up again, I'll do the one thing I've always thought I wouldn't do; I'll leave Big Clifty and my family behind.

I knock on the door before entering. "Coming in, girls," I shout as I open the door.

As soon as I walk in, I see her. She's young, somewhere around twenty. She's got a body that will drive the guys crazy. When she turns to look at me, I see the resemblance to Sarah. She has the same blonde hair and blue eyes. The only difference that's truly noticeable is the coldness that shines brightly in her eyes. Sarah's eyes always shot daggers at me, but this chick's eyes are dead. Something about it sends a shiver through my body.

"New Girl!" I shout.

She rolls her eyes at me and replies, "My name is Krista."

I roll my eyes right back at her. "Until you earn your spot, you're New Girl."

She shrugs. "Whatever."

Her tone has the other girls backing away. They know I don't take shit. I've only had to use my fists a time or two here, but I'm not scared to use them when necessary. "We need to talk."

"Yeah? So, talk," she says, looking back to her mirror and finishing up her makeup.

"I want to talk in private, so get your ass up and follow me."

I hear her let out a frustrated sigh as she stands up. Daisy and Ginger gasp. This bitch has an attitude, an attitude I'm more than happy to break.

I narrow my eyes at her and put on my Ice persona. "You best not have sighed 'cause I told you it's time to chat, bitch."

Her eyes go wide, but my warning tone doesn't stop the attitude from coming out in her. "Who the fuck do you think you are? You can't talk to me like that."

The girls that haven't been here very long let out another shocked gasp, but the girls that have been around for a while start to laugh. They know I'll never let her get away with this shit.

"I can talk to you however the fuck I want to. I'm the one in charge of the club girls, the strippers, and this fucking club," I say, walking up close to her, grabbing her by her blonde hair, and pulling her face towards mine. "And you should know that girls who piss me off have a bad habit of ending up dead."

She gulps and shrinks back, leaving me with a handful of her skanky ass hair. "Now let's go."

With that, I turn around and lead her to my office.

"Sit," I say, motioning towards the chair before taking a seat on the ugly ass beige couch that's been in this office for more years than I can count. I really need to replace this piece of shit. I shake off my thoughts of my crappy ass furniture and look towards Krista, who decided to sit beside me. I can't figure out if she's brave or just stupid. "Now, New Girl. Have you ever been a part of an MC?"

She shakes her head no, but the way her eyes flash tells me that she's lying. Something isn't right here, and I know it. I have the urge to toss her out and let Kidd handle her, but I don't like the idea of her being around Kidd. I decide to keep her here and see what I can find out.

"Well, looks like I'll need to fill you in. Around here, I'm the boss. I control who I let into the clubhouse to be club girls, and I control who gets on the stage here. I even control who goes behind the counter."

"Kidd told me I could work here," she states, looking pleased with herself.

"He may have, but if I decide I don't want you, he'll back me. He told me so last night in bed," I say, embellishing the truth just a bit.

I watch her gulp then nod. "I understand."

I shake my head. "No, I don't think you do. You follow my rules, or I will fire you, but not before I kick your ass."

She nods again, so I continue. "The rules are simple. I catch you doing drugs, you're out. If I catch you selling drugs in my club, even to the other girls, you're dead. You don't sell your pussy inside or outside of this club to anyone but a member or a friend of the MC. You only do that when you get my go ahead. Now, do you understand?"

She nods, but looks anything but sure. I take a minute to let my words settle in, and then say, "You wanna be a club girl, then you need to get tested regularly. You also need to get on the pill, if you're not already on one. The most important thing is that you always make the guys wear condoms, but you also need to take the pill just in case one breaks. We don't need you to get knocked up and having some Old Lady whack ya. Even if the guy doesn't have an Old Lady, he may not step up and take care of you and the kid. You need to protect yourself; respect yourself."

I look at her, and she looks scared now; almost as if she's re-thinking her position here? I can only hope so. This lifestyle isn't meant to be lived by pussies. "I also don't tolerate back talk. Which means that if I say jump, you say 'yes ma'am, how high?' and if you ever talk to me the way you did this morning, you better believe that you'll find yourself pounding pavement."

"I won't," she replies, but her tone tells me that what she doesn't say to my face, she will be saying behind my back. "Can I go now?"

"One more thing. I catch you anywhere near Kidd, I'll bury you alive," I say, meaning every damn word. I may not have wanted to be his Old Lady, but that's exactly what I am, and I ain't sharing.

She gulps. "Kidd's like family."

I have to roll my eyes at that. "I know Kidd dated your sister, but he's not your family, so you need to keep your ass away from him. Do you get what I'm saying?"

She nods and her eyes go to the floor. "Yeah."

"Stay behind the bar until I decide you're ready for the stage. No going off with guys until you've been tested and I have the results. Now get out of here. You're on soon. "

CHAPTER Eighteen

Kidd

I'm sitting in my office when Reese and Chipper walk in. I can tell right away that something is wrong. "What's up?"

"Let him tell you." Reese shakes his head before tilting it towards Chipper and walking to fridge to grab a beer.

I look in Chipper's direction and shrug, letting him know that I'm not going to ask twice.

"None of the boys I've talked to have seen Timmons around, but three of the club girls have." He lets out on a frustrated breath and sits down. "There's a reason why he's laying low with the club, but making sure the girls know he's around."

I hear Reese snort and look towards him. "You got any theories?"

He looks towards Chipper then back to me. "Sure do, but I can't tell you a fuckin' one of them."

"What the hell do you mean by that?"

He tilts his head towards my brother again. "Like I said, let him tell you."

I jerk my head back to Chipper and growl out, "I'm tired of this shit. One of you is going to tell me what's going on, and you're going to tell me right fuckin' now."

He shakes his head. "I made a promise to Pop."

Reese walks across the room and gets in Chipper's face. "Gun is dead. Jenna's not, at least not yet. What's more important? Keeping your word to a dead man, or protecting the woman you think of as a daughter?"

I've had enough of this bullshit, so I don't wait for my brother to respond. I reach to my side, pull out my gun, and then aim it straight at Reese. "I can't kill Chipper. He's blood. I love you, man, but if you don't tell me what's going on with my woman, then I will put a bullet right through your skull."

Just as I expected, Reese doesn't even flinch. Instead, he just shrugs. "Gotta die sometime, but I have a feeling you're going to need me soon, so you may want to put down that gun."

"What I need is to know what in the hell is going on," I say without lowering my arm.

"Put the fucking gun down, and I'll tell you everything," Chipper says, sounding defeated.

I lower my gun and nod to Reese, letting him know this was my plan all along. "Tell me."

"Timmons wants Jenna, and he'll do whatever he has to do to get her."

Since Chipper opened the flood gates, Reese decides to add his two cents. "He's hurt her before, so I don't doubt he'll hurt her again."

"What the fuck?" I shout. "What the hell did Timmons do to her?"

"I don't know everything," Chipper says in a voice filled with pain. "He was there right along with Rig. From what I hear, Rig just went along with whatever Timmons told him to do."

I don't respond. I don't even take time to let the words sink in. Instead, I pick up the phone and call Brew. As soon as he answers the phone, I start to yell. "You get your ass down here, right now."

"Kidd?" he asks.

"Yes," I ground out. "I want you and Killer in Big Clifty this weekend. That gives you four days. If y'all ain't here by then, you both can step down. I'll be placing my own boys in your spots."

I slam the phone down without giving him time to ask questions. I then look towards Chipper and Reese. "Spread the word. I want Timmons taken out. I don't care how it's done, but I do want to see the body."

A slow smile spreads across Reese's face. "I think I can do that for you."

I shrug. "I don't care who does it. I just want it done quickly."

I look to Chipper and say, "Step down."

"What?" Reese and Chipper say at the same time.

"I want the VP patch off your cut. You don't deserve it."

Taking Chipper's patch is something I should've done years ago, but I wanted my family by my side. Before, he was just slacking off and tossing his duties at the other brothers. Now that I know he put my woman in danger, I can't keep calling him my VP.

"I should've told you," he says, starting to see the light. Brother or not, it's too fucking late.

"Yes, you should have, but you didn't, and now I want you to step down."

Reese steps towards me and places his hand on my arm. "You can't do that, Kidd. He was just keeping his word to your Pop."

I jerk away and turn towards Reese. "He was keeping his word to a dead man, when the woman that I love is in danger.

That is not the action of a man that I want watching my back."

He's quiet for a second then raises his hand to his Sargent at Arms patch; the same patch I gave him the day Timber went inside. "You want my patch, you got it."

I nod. "I sure in the hell do, but you're going to be putting that VP patch on as a replacement."

I see shock work its way through his eyes before he responds. "But, man. I knew the same shit he did, and I didn't tell you."

I take a deep breath in an attempt to try and let out some of my anger. "You didn't tell me, because your VP told you not to. It was his job to come to me, not yours. From now on, you'll be VP. It will be your job to tell me shit."

I look back to Chipper. "You're my brother, and I love you, but you will never hold office in this club again. I want you here and I don't want you to leave. You'll always be a member of Renegade Sons, but a member is all you'll ever be."

He nods, taking the news better than I expected. "If that's how you feel, I understand."

"Let everyone know that you're stepping down. Don't tell them why. As far as anyone is concerned, it was your decision. Everyone knows you never wanted to hold office, and that's why you're not president. They'll understand."

With those words, I walk away. I grab a bottle of Jack from

my desk and head straight to the common room. I see Timber sitting at the bar and sit my ass on the stool next to his. "You feel like wearing the Sergeant at Arms patch that you gave up when you went inside?"

He shoots me a smile. "Hell yeah, brother."

Jenna

It's just after midnight when I walk into the clubhouse. I see Kidd, Reese, and Timber sitting at a table and throwing back shots of Jack. Timber has a girl on each leg, one of which is leaning against Reese's chair. Kidd is alone, but I know for a fact that every chick in this place has tried to get with him tonight. After what I experienced last night and this morning, I can't blame them.

I know how this club works. When you become an old lady, you're supposed to turn a blind eye to their fucking around, so I'm on a mission to find a suitable whore just for Kidd. One that won't make me jealous or lose my shit. One that I know he wouldn't touch, even if his life depended on it.

I walk further into the room and look around, needing to find Mary. Mary is one of the sweetest women I have ever met and she's also one of the funniest. She loves a good joke, so I'm sure she'll be perfect for what I have in mind. I spot her in the back, talking to a few of the boys. It's hard to tell the older ladies here apart, but she's the only one not wearing a cut.

I make my way over and wrap my arm around her waist, leaning my head against her chest. Even at five foot nine, I barely reach her chin. I look up at her wrinkled face, wrinkles that show nearly sixty years of laughter. "You want to help me out?"

"What'cha got planned?"

I get on my tiptoes and whisper in her ear. A slow smile spreads across her face, and she starts to laugh. "I don't know. I'm not as young as I used to be. I'm not sure I can handle the Pres."

"Trust me, he'll treat you right," I say with a wink.

Her eyes sparkle and she starts to laugh even harder. "All right, sweet pea. Take me to my man meat for the night."

"Follow me."

We make our way to where Kidd is still talking with Timber and Reese. I grab Mary's arm to bring her close to my side, and swing my arm around her waist.

"Well, hey there, boys. Kidd, I got you a little something," I say smiling. His eyes narrow as he tries to work out what the fuck I'm up too. "Mary here is just the woman for you, baby. I figure I'll start a new trend around here where Old Ladies get to hand pick a girl to be her man's side piece."

The whole room goes quiet for a second, then Reese and Timber start to chuckle. I shoot them a wink then look back to Kidd. "You see, since I'm your Old Lady, I figured it's only right that I get to help you choose your mistress."

I hear a chuckle behind me, so I turn and see that it's Chipper. Raising my eyebrows at him, I ask, "What's so funny, Daddio?" He always hates when I call him that.

The grin he has plastered on his face remains as he gets close to me and whispers, "You are gonna get your ass spanked."

I smile then whisper, "Why do you think I'm doing this?"

My candid response makes him turn around and let out a belly laugh.

"What the fuck, Ice?" Kidd yells from behind me. I look back to him just as he stands up. He grabs me by the waist, throwing me over his shoulder, and then storms towards the hall. As he walks me out of the main room, I look up and blow kisses to Mary. I can hear her cackle as he carries me down the hallway.

Kidd

Storming through the clubhouse with Jenna hanging over my shoulder, I'm getting more pissed off with each step I take. What the fuck is she thinking? Does she really think I will fuck around on her, and with Mary of all people? I love Mary, everyone does, but she's old as dirt. She's a part of the originals and has been here since the club was originally founded.

Digger, Timber's dad, brought Mary in when he started the club. She was one of the first whores. She even ran the girls until Roxy took over. She was never the prettiest in the bunch, but she was loyal as hell. She earned her spot. Even when she got too old to be passed around, she still had a place here. Now, she just helps around the clubhouse, cleaning and shit. Mostly, she just sits around and tells stories of the glory days.

Holt and Wayne are the only ones who still take her to bed. They're two of the original members too. They don't do much anymore either, but they'll have a spot here until they're no longer breathing. They are also the only two people around here that can fuck with Mary. She says that they just love her pussy, but we all know that's a damn lie. Both of the old men would die for her. They look at her the same way I look at Jenna.

Thinking of Mary being sixty and still being a club piece has me thinking about Jenna's future. If it wasn't for me, would Mary's life have been hers? Will Jenna still be here thirty years from now, spreading for the senior members? Would she be the one telling stories of the past?

Mary has been asked by both of the men in her life to be their old lady, but she's turned them down every single time. I know they've asked her more the once over the years. At some point, they got tired of asking. Now, after forty years, she's alone and so are they. Well, they're not really alone. They share five kids. She has three from Holt and two from Wayne. Hell, they now have a slew of grandkids. I doubt it won't be long before they have a great-grandkid or two.

Jenna's friend Daisy is Wayne and Mary's granddaughter. Their daughter Lula had Daisy when she was just sixteen. Neither Wayne nor Mary claim Daisy's bitch of a mom, but they both love Daisy to death. She's their baby girl, and they don't like the life she's living. Every so often, I see her getting reamed out by one of the two. Sometimes, Holt will even step in and add his two cents.

None of them want her living this life. They want better for her, just like Chipper wanted for Jenna. All of them tried like hell to get Daisy to go to college, but just like Jenna, Daisy wouldn't budge. She ain't leaving her family. Only good thing that came out of it is that she isn't one of the club girls. She only dances. In fact, none of the guys touch her, and believe me, it ain't from not wanting her, because that girl is hot as hell.

No, they stay away because of Preach. He's had a thing for Daisy since he was just a prospect. Just like me, he held off for her to get old enough to claim. We were all sure it was going to happen as soon as Daisy turned eighteen, but when the time came, it was like a switch flipped inside of his head, and he didn't want jack shit to do with her. That doesn't mean she's free game either, because he won't let any of the guys within a mile of her.

As soon as I open the door to my room, I shake off thoughts of Mary and Daisy and toss Jenna on the bed. "What the fuck was that?" I ask, clenching my jaw.

She just looks up at me with her sexy grin beaming on her face, one that never fails to send sparks right to my balls. "What? You don't want my help? I just thought I'd give you a few options for who you're gonna fuck around with."

My eyes narrow, even though her tone is playful. "First, I wouldn't fuck Mary. Second, if you haven't figured this shit out by now, then you're a fuckin' idiot! I wouldn't fuck around on you, Jenna. Your pussy has me worn the hell out. If I tried to spread the joy of my dick around, it'd fall the fuck off."

She looks towards my crotch and licks her lips. "Joy, really? You think you're that good, huh?"

I raise my brows, finally figuring out the game she's playing. "I know I'm that good. Keep talking, Ice, and I'll show you."

"Ohhh, is that supposed to scare me?" she mumbles out, a shit eating grin covering her face.

"That's it!" I shout, pretending to be angry. I reach for her, flip her over, and lift her dress up. I rip off her fuckin' barely there panties and toss them across the room. My dick twitches at the sight of her beautiful ass. There are a lot of things about Jenna that gets my dick hard, but if I had to pick a favorite, it would be her ass. Damn, what a sight.

I reach down and rub my hand over her globes, and then run my finger over her pucker. I play for a minute or two, before dipping my finger inside. I lean down and whisper, "I'm having this tonight."

"Oh, God," she moans, throwing her head back.

"Do you like that, baby?" I ask as I start to unbutton my pants.

She moans again and says, "I like everything you do to me."

I crawl onto the bed, taking time to nip her ass cheeks. With each touch of my mouth, her body bucks with pleasure. I slowly make my way up to my knees and line my cock up with her pussy. I rub it up and down her slit, thankful that she's already wet.

Reaching in my pocket, I pull out a condom and tear it open quickly before rolling it on. All the while, I continue to glide my finger in and out of her glorious ass. As soon as the condom is in place, my dick is back between the folds of her slit. Finally, I rear back before sinking balls deeps into her heat. "Fuck!"

She gasps and lets out a throaty laugh then throws my words back at me. "Do you like that, baby?"

"Hell yeah," I say as I continue to pound into her.

Each stroke sets me on fire, sending me closer and closer to the edge. Never, and I mean never, has it been like this. When I'm inside Jenna, I'm like a kid whose just getting his first piece of ass. I'm already on the verge of coming, and I've only been in her for a minute. "God, baby. Your pussy's too good, and it's all mine."

She rears back, impaling herself even further. "It's all for you, Kidd. It's your pussy, all yours."

"Fuck!" I shout as I start to pick up my rhythm. There is nothing smooth about this. It's pure fucking.

I know I'm not gonna last long. Even after getting off this morning and last night, I'm ready to explode, so I reach around and pinch her clit. I then start to rub fast circles around it with the tip of my finger. "Come on, baby. Let me have it. Milk me."

With that, I feel her pussy contract on my dick as she throws her head back and screams. I've never seen anything sexier in my life. It's more than enough to push me over the edge. I slam into her once more and moan out my own release.

I'm so fucking weak that I have to stop myself from falling right on top of her. Instead, I roll to the side, pulling her with me. "Damn, baby doll. That was good."

She takes a deep breath and gasps out, "It always is."

I touch my lips to her cheek before I crawl out of the bed. I take care of the condom first, and then lay down beside her, pulling her into my arms again. "You gonna tell me what all that shit with Mary was about?"

"I was just teasing you, Kidd." she says in a sleepy voice.

"I don't like to be teased."

She rolls towards me and smiles a lazy smile. "But you like what comes after the teasing."

Damn, this woman will be the death of me. "You don't have to tease me to get my dick. All you got to do is ask."

She throws her leg over mine and reaches up to kiss me. "I never ask. I just take what I want."

With those words, she crawls on top of me and goes about taking what she wants, and she does it in a way that blows my mind. Never in my fucking life have I felt anything like I do when I'm with Jenna. I've had some good sex in my life; hell, I've had more than my share of great sex, but nothing's ever been as great as it is with my girl.

She passes out after round two, but I'm not done. I feel like a fucking teenager. I could go all night. I lay there and watch her sleep, loving the satisfied look on her face. Problem is that the longer I watch, the harder my dick gets. I know that I should let her sleep. She definitely earned it. If I was a good man, I'd let her be, but I never said there was even an ounce of good in me.

I told her I wanted her ass tonight, and I am gonna have it.

I carefully move my body from hers and climb from bed. I'll give her a break, a small one, while I go look for some lube and more condoms. I really need to talk to her about birth control and soon. I'm done with this condom shit. I don't want anything between us.

"Wake up, beautiful," I demand when I slide back into bed. "I ain't done."

Her eyes flutter open and she smiles lazily up at me. "I don't think I can go again, Kidd. I may be used to being fucked, but I have never been fucked like that," she says as she closes her eyes again.

A spark of jealousy shoots through me when she mentions being with other men, but I know I've got to get passed it. If I hadn't fucked up so bad, she would have never been a club whore. That's on me, and I'll have to learn how to deal with it. Sooner or later, we're going to have to have a talk about her bringing that shit up all the time though. I can learn to deal with her past, if she can learn to forgive me, but I don't need that shit shoved in my face constantly.

I run my hands over her ass and bend down to whisper in her ear. "Told you what I wanted earlier, but I still haven't had that sweet ass of yours yet." Her eyes flash open, and fuck, she looks like a wet dream. "You can sleep later, but right now, I'm gonna tap that ass."

Bringing my mouth down to hers, I kiss her hungrily. The

sleep fades from her as she answers my kiss. Breaking away from her mouth, I grab the lube and a condom that I placed on the nightstand. "Turn over, baby doll. I want you up on your knees."

She does as I ask while looking over her shoulder at me. Damn, she's sexy. Just looking at her has me rock hard again. I crawl behind her and cup her pussy. She's fucking drenched. I'm not sure if she's turned on or just wet from our earlier sessions. At this point, I don't even care. I just need to get inside of her.

I grab the lube and pour it between her cheeks. Then, I move my hand from her pussy to her ass, slowly sliding it up and down while circling her rosebud with my thumb. "You done this before, babe?"

"Yeah," she says breathily.

I smile, knowing I don't have to take this shit slowly. I'm not sure if I'm capable of going slow right now. I gently push a finger inside her and growl out, "Play with that pussy for me, baby."

I watch her move her hand between her legs and seconds later her hips begin to rock. I lean over and kiss her back in approval. My kisses quickly turn into nips, each one causing her to moan. I glide my fingers in and out of her for a few more seconds, and then pull back to put a condom on.

After making sure the condom is in place, I line myself up with her and start to push in. I try to be gentle, going as slow as I can, because there's a little resistance at first, but Jenna is as impatient as ever. Before I can break the suction from her tight little hole, she rears back and impales herself on my dick. "Fuck me," I moan out before pulling out a little and slamming back in.

As soon as my balls hit her pussy, she throws back her head and groans. Her ass convulses so hard, it feels like I have a vise on my cock. "Fuck, baby. You're going too fast."

She doesn't respond, just continues to rock her hips. I start to thrust in and out of her, each stroke sending shockwaves through my dick. I know I'm close, so I reach around and pinch her nipple. "Squeeze your clit, baby."

Within minutes, she's coming again. When I feel her start to quiver around my cock, I begin to pound into her hard, exploding seconds later.

CHAPTER Nineteen

Jenna

I wake up smiling from last night's fun. I'm so sore I can barely move, but it was so worth it. I think Kidd and I had sex in every way possible, and I know I'm going to pay for it today.

Having anal sex with Kidd was something new. It wasn't about pain. It wasn't even truly about pleasure. It was all about trust, and him proving to me that he would never hurt me. I've done it before. It was either forced on me or something I did to keep one of the guys happy, but I never enjoyed it. Last night, I loved it. Kidd made me sing the fuckin' National Anthem. It wasn't just good, it was fan-fucking-tastic.

I stretch out and realize I'm alone in bed. I look towards the clock and see that it's still early, so I start to wonder where Kidd went to. I take a second to shake off my sleep before I get up and get ready for the day. I start to head to my room when I notice some of my stuff on Kidd's dresser. I look around a bit and realize that everything I own is in here now. Shit! When did he do this?

I rush through getting dressed then head out to give Kidd an ass chewing for moving my stuff without asking me first. It took me three years to earn my room in the clubhouse, and I'm not giving it up without a fight. I go straight to his office and open the door without knocking. I'm about to start bitching, but I stop when I see Kidd, Chipper, Reese, Timber, and Preach sitting around Kidd's desk talking. Rum and Wayne are standing a few feet away, watching the rest of the room. I can tell by their vibe that they're standing guard, making sure no one gets too close. Something's going on, but I have no idea what.

I start to walk towards them, but stop when Rum rushes towards me. "Sorry, Ice. The meeting is private."

I'm about to ask what's up when Kidd motions towards us. "Let her in. This involves her too."

His words send chills down my spine, because I just know that shit is about to hit the fan. I walk slowly towards Kidd's desk and ask, "What's going on?"

Kidd looks towards the guys then back to me. "The crew from Mateland are coming for a visit."

My heart starts to pound, and I have to struggle to take a breath. I knew this was coming. I knew it the moment I heard Timmons was in town, but a desperate part of me had had hoped that he'd just go away. "When?"

"They'll be here this weekend," he says, watching closely for my reaction.

"Who's coming?"

He shrugs. "I'm not sure about everyone. I doubt they'll travel light, but I know at least Killer and Brew will be here."

As soon as I hear my dad's name, I turn around and start to run. I rush past Rum and Wayne before they even realize what's going on. I go straight to Kidd's room and start tossing my stuff onto the bed.

"What the hell are you doing?" Kidd asks as he walks in the room behind me and slams the door shut.

"I'm getting the hell out of here," I say, digging in the closet for a suitcase.

"You ain't fuckin' going nowhere."

I dig out an old duffle bag and rush to the bed. "I have to get out of here. I have to be gone before they get here." I'm about five seconds from completely losing it.

He walks to the bed and leans over to face me, placing his fists on the mattress. "I said, you're not leaving."

"You don't understand!" I shout, fighting desperately to hold my fear back.

"I understand more than you think. I understand that your Dad gave you to Timmons, and you're scared out of your fuckin' mind that he's gonna get his hands on you again, but you need to understand that I would never let that happen. Never, Jenna. You are mine."

No, no, no.... He can't know about Timmons. That was my secret to tell, no one else's. "Who told you that?"

"Chipper finally broke down and told me the truth, a truth that should have been told many years ago. I don't give a fuck what Pop said. I should've known. If I had, the bastard would be dead now and you wouldn't be standing there scared out of your fuckin' mind."

My heart starts to pound, and my fear crashes through me in waves; waves that are so strong that I just know at any given minute, they're going to take me under. "What are you talking about?" I whisper, hoping that I misheard.

"I'm telling you I finally know everything, and I'm gonna deal with it from this point on. All you need to do is step back and let me take care of this shit for you. I'm your man. It's my job to protect you."

No! I don't want Kidd involved in this. I don't want anyone to deal with Timmons. That man is evil, and I refuse to allow him around the people I care about. "You don't get it. Chipper might have told you what he knows, but you still don't know shit about my past."

He steps back and stalks around the bed. "And whose

fucking fault is that? I've known you since you were sixteen years old, and not once in those years have you let me in. I've tried to get you to open up to me, but every time I crack the door open to Jenna's world, you slam it right back in my face. Shit, Ice. What the hell can I do to get you to let me in?"

He reaches out and places his hands on my face and gently rubs my tears away with his thumb, tears that I didn't even realize had started to flow. "I know I screwed up before. I should've been by your side since the day you turned eighteen, but I was angry with myself. I was too angry to see the pain I was causing you, but I got my shit together. I'm here for you now, and I'll never let anything hurt you again."

His words crash straight through the layer of ice that I've been living in, and the words come tumbling out. "My father's name is Peter David Brewster. You know him as Brew."

"Brew's your dad?" His words come out in a shocked whisper. If he thinks that's all that I've been holding inside of my head all of these years, then he's fixing to be rudely awakened. Now that the ice wall has been broken, nothing will stay inside.

"I grew up in trailer park a few miles outside of Mateland, Missouri. It was just my mom and me most of the time. Dad would show up every now again, mostly when he needed somewhere to lay low for a while." I wrap my arms around myself, trying to fight off the chill that my memories always bring. "I swear my mom lived for the times Dad was there. It's like her life was put on hold when he wasn't around. She barely even noticed me. Sometimes, I think she forgot she even had a daughter. To her, I was just part of the scenery."

I look up and see the confusion on Kidd's face, but I don't stop. "Every time he came home, she'd work her ass off to make him want to stay. The house would be so clean, it would shine. She'd make these amazing dinners, stuff we couldn't afford. She'd make prime rib and all this other shit that cost out the ass, even knowing me and her would probably go hungry until the next round of food stamps came in. She'd dress up, do her make-up and hair, just to get his attention, and she'd get it, but only for a day or two. It didn't matter what she did, nothing was taking Dad away from the club. A wife and a kid was nothing compared to the freedom he got from being with his brothers."

"Baby girl," Kidd breathes out, still catching my tears with his thumb.

"When I was little, I'd listen to Dad talk about the Renegade Sons. Shit, I'd even dream of someday being a part of it. I wanted to be someone's old lady, wear their brand. I wanted it all." I step back and walk towards the window. "That was until I figured out why he loved the club so much. It wasn't the brotherhood that kept him at the clubhouse so much. No, it was all the easy pussy. My dad was addicted to that shit."

I see Kidd walking towards me, and make a beeline for

other side of the room. I know I can't stand him touching me right now. "Half the club didn't even know that dad had an old lady, and less than that knew about me. Dad had a different girl on the back of his bike every damn day. It killed my mom, and I grew up watching her slowly fade away to nothing. The pain of knowing he was out there with other women, night after night, literally killed her. It wasn't the damn pills that took her away. It was him. It was his betrayal."

"What pills? What are you talking about?"

"When I was sixteen, I came home from school to find my mother had OD'd on the kitchen floor." I close my eyes to hide my pain from him. "She left a note to Dad, but she never even mentioned me in it. Not one 'I love our daughter' or 'take care of Jenna.' Nothing. All she said was how much she loved him and how she couldn't live knowing he was with all those other woman."

"Shit, baby. I'm so sorry," Kidd says as he starts towards me again.

I place my hands out in front of me, letting him know that I don't want to be touched. "Don't you see, Kidd? I can't let you in. I can't give you my heart again, because I know if I do, you'll end up shattering it. You did last time. If it happens again, I'll end up just like my mom."

As soon as the words leave my mouth, Kidd grabs my hands and pulls me flush against his body. "No fucking way, baby. If you give me your heart, lay it right in my hands. I promise I will protect it until the day I die."

Kidd

Hearing Jenna tell me about her father put together all of the pieces of why she was so against becoming an Old Lady. It's not just my fuck up that I'm fighting against; it's her past as well. Still holding her close to my body, I whisper into her hair, "I would never stray, baby. What we have now, we'll have until the day we die, and it will be fucking amazing. I would never hurt you in that way."

"I love you," she whispers out.

My body goes taut, and I pull her even closer to me. "What did you say?" I ask, wanting to hear the words again.

"I love you, Kidd. I do, but I'm scared. You hurt me so bad, and not just with the words you said. It was how you just walked out on me after. That was the first time I had ever willingly given myself to anyone. I may have had my body's virginity stolen from me, but I gave you the virginity of my heart. I know that doesn't make sense, but that's how it felt."

"It does make sense. That's why I told you thank you that night. I was thanking you for giving me that part of you. You may not have had that little piece of skin, but you were a virgin all the same." I place my hand on her cheek. "I'm sorry I walked out on you without telling you how I felt. Just so you know, I felt same way then as I do now. I love you, Jenna. I love you with everything I am."

She reaches up and kisses me. When she pulls back, she smiles up at me. "If you love me, and I love you, then why in the hell aren't you making love to me?"

I smile and pull my shirt over my head. Then my hands go under her shirt and start to pull it off. I reach down and wrap my arms under her ass. Lifting her up, I walk us over to the bed and lay her down. I take my time removing her clothes, getting off on every inch of skin I expose before I take my own clothes off and crawl over her.

I spend time making love to her with my tongue before venturing down her body. I make sure to kiss every inch of her, starting with those gorgeous tits I love so much. I make my way to that sweet pussy of hers, and as soon I get a taste, my balls start to tighten.

When I feel her first release against my tongue, I crawl back up her body. Looking into her eyes, I say, "Baby, no more condoms. I want nothing between you and me anymore."

She nods yes, and I slide into her. She feels like fuckin' heaven. I watch her face as she takes me, her love for me shining bright. This is the same face I stared into when I had her on her eighteenth birthday; the same face I fell in love with six years ago. I lean into her, my face tucked into her neck, thrusting hard towards our release. "I love you, baby girl. Love you more than anything in the whole fucking world."

A few minutes later, we lay quietly beside each other. I have her held tight to my side, and she's holding onto my hand like there's no tomorrow. Finally, she breaks the silence. "This isn't a game, is it?"

"What do you mean?"

"You and me. You're for real, aren't you? It isn't just some game. This time you mean it. I'm really your old lady."

I lean my forehead against the top of her head. "No, baby girl. This isn't a game. You're my old lady, and you will be until the day I die."

She doesn't respond, just rolls over and throws her leg on mine. She then burrows her face into my neck. Within minutes, her body goes lax and her breathing evens out. I relax and try to join her in sleep, but my mind keeps wandering back to her words from earlier. I still can't believe that Brew's her dad. I remember him asking about her. Shit, he was asking about his own daughter. The bastard denied even knowing her. Well, he won't be able to deny it much longer. When he gets here, he's gonna pay for the shit he put her through. Brew's sorry ass is going to die, and the motherfucker is going to die in pain.

CHAPTER Twenty

Kidd

I slide into my normal table at The Kitty Kat and motion for a waitress to bring me and the boys a round of drinks. As soon as my beer's in front of me, I turn to Reese. "Any news?"

He shakes his head. "Nah, man. It's like the motherfucker disappeared overnight. Not one brother or any of the girls has seen him. Timmons is a ghost, man."

Timber leans into the table, placing his palms on top of it. "I got an idea. Don't know if it'll work, but it's worth a try."

I lift my chin. "Tell me."

"I think we should consider sending Preach to Mateland." Timber motions towards Preach. "You all know that he's got a talent for getting information. He's got a way of getting a guy to talk, and you never even realize you're telling him all your fuckin' secrets until it's too late. If they know where Timmons is, he'll find out."

Preach nods. "I don't know if it'll work, but I'm willing do anything to keep Ice safe."

I nod my head. "Sounds like a plan to me, but I don't want him going out on his own."

"I'll ride with him," Reese offers.

"As much as I'd like to get your ass away from Jenna, I think it'd be better if you stayed here. I'll need all the help I can get if Timmons goes after my old lady."

"I think you should send Maker with me," Preach says. "He's a good brother, but he's dumb as fuck. You send him with me, it'll help get their guard down. There's no way the Mateland crew will think I'm searching for information with Maker around."

Chipper clears his throat. "That's a good plan. The only hitch is that Kidd already called Brew. They know we're on the war path, but they don't why. It doesn't matter though. They'll be keeping shit tight until they find out."

"If that's true, why don't you just ask Brew? He hates Timmons. If he knows anything, he'll give it up," Preach says.

Timber's right: Preach is good at getting information. He learned a lot of shit when we were in Mateland, including that Timmons and Brew didn't see eye to eye.

Reese shakes his head. "No he won't. He's protecting Timmons, so that Timmons will keep protecting him. Brew doesn't want his secret getting out."

I cut my eyes towards Reese. "You know about Brew and Ice?"

He nods. "I've known since the day Chipper took her out of that shithole."

"What in the hell are you two talking about?" Chipper asks, looking between Reese and me.

I hate to tell my brother this shit, but it's all gonna come out anyway as soon as Brew's sorry ass steps foot in Big Clifty. It's gonna kill him that Jenna didn't trust him more. I hope he can understand that she was too scared to tell anyone. "Brew is Jenna's father."

His body goes rigid. "No, he's fucking not. Her father's name is David."

"Her father's name is Peter David Brewster," I say, watching for his reaction.

He looks at me for a while, as if he's searching for truth in my words, and then slams his fist onto the table. "She fuckin' lied to me. I took care of her ass for years, and she fuckin' lied to me."

He starts to get up, but Reese grabs his arm and pushes him back down. "She was a scared kid. All she knew about the club was what her dad and Timmons told her. Timmons had her convinced that no one could take her away from him. She was afraid that you'd be forced to take her back to him."

"Why the fuck would I do that?" Chipper asks, clenching his teeth together.

Reese looks towards me then back towards Chipper. He reluctantly says, "He claimed her, made her his old lady. Her dad and Timmons told Jenna that no one can take an old lady away."

"What?" Chipper and I ask at the same time.

Reese shrugs. "I'm not sure of everything that happened when she was there. She refuses to talk about it, but I do know he claimed her. I also knew she was Brew's daughter the moment she told me her name was Jenna. I wasn't in Mateland long before I came here, but long enough to know that Timmons had claimed Brew's daughter, Jenna. I was also told that she didn't get a choice in the claiming."

"Why didn't you tell me?" Chipper shouts out. At the same time, I ask. "Why the hell didn't you help her?"

Reese ignores Chipper and looks at me, fury flashing in his eyes. "I never saw her. I didn't know she was just a kid. Didn't have no fuckin' idea what he was doing to her, or that she was being abused either. Do you honestly think I would just stand around and let her be hurt?"

I take a deep breath, trying to bury my anger. "No, I don't. I know you better than that. I shouldn't have even asked that shit."

Reese cuts his eyes to Chipper. "As for you, I didn't know you well enough at first. By the time I did, you and your father had made me swear not to tell anyone about Timmons. If I remember correctly, your father threatened to cut my fuckin' balls off if I did. I figured if I had to keep one secret, it was best to keep them all."

Chipper places his elbows on the table then buries his face in his hands. "She never trusted me. All this time and she never trusted me."

"That's not true," Preach says. "She trusted you with everything but her father's name. If I'm understanding right, she even gave you part of that."

Chipper shakes his head and again says, "She never trusted me."

"She trusted you enough to run to you when she was in trouble," I say, even though it hurts like hell to admit that she went to him instead of me. "I was sitting a few feet from the door when she came in the clubhouse after finding out Timmons was in Big Clifty. She ran right past me to get to you. When she needed somebody the most, she went to you. If that's not trust, I don't know what in the hell is."

We all sit there quietly for a moment before Chipper nods. "You're right. Even if you're not, it's my fault. I listened to Pop when I should have taken Timmons down."

I can't disagree, because I think he's right. I don't give a fuck what the old man had said. I would have taken Timmons' ass out on sight.

Timber slaps Chipper on his back. "Well, you'll have your chance to take him out soon."

Slowly, our conversation starts to fade as sounds of Kiss's *Heaven on Fire* blares out around the club. A moment later, one of the girls walks onto the stage and starts to dance. I take a drink of my beer and sit back to enjoy the show. I might not want to fuck any of these girls anymore, but that doesn't mean I can't enjoy their fine ass bodies.

The girl on stage is just getting to the good part when I feel a hand on my shoulder. I look up and see Krista standing off to my side. "Hey, Kidd. How about a private dance?" She asks, her voice coming out in a purr.

I shake my head. "Sorry, babe. Not tonight."

Not only is Jenna my woman, but I'm not interested in anyone else's ass rubbing against my cock, and this is Sarah's sister. The fact that she even thinks I may want her is fucked up.

She slides into my lap and wraps her arms around my neck. "Come on, just one little dance."

I grab her arms, trying to push her away without hurting her. "I said no."

Instead of getting up, the bitch wiggles around and somehow ends up straddling my lap. "I promise you'll like it."

With those words, she grinds her pussy against my cock. Want her or not, my dick knows a wet hole is close and starts to rise. "Get the fuck up, Krista."

She continues to grind into me. "It doesn't feel like that's what you really want me to do."

I'm a man. What man wouldn't start to get hard when some bitch, ugly or not, is grinding all over it? The difference between some men and me is that I won't cheat on my girl. I'm just about to push her away again when I hear a gasp. I turn and see Daisy standing a few feet away, holding our table's next round. I meet her eyes, and I know without a doubt she's going to tell Jenna. I stand up, tossing Krista to the floor, but it's too late. Daisy's already making her way out the door. "Fuck!"

I look down to Krista and shout. "I'll give you until pay day, because you're Sarah's sister. After that, I don't want to see your ass in Big Clifty ever again."

I turn and stomp out of The Kitty Kat, hoping I can find Jenna before Daisy does.

Jenna

I walk into the back door of The Kitty Kat, still fuming.

When I started getting calls saying that Kidd was getting a lap dance from Krista, I blew my fucking top. Kidd has 'forbidden' me to dance at the club, and I had every intention of doing what he said, but that all changed about an hour ago. A second after I heard that she had her hands on him, I decided he could go fuck himself. He could also stick his fucking rules right up his ass.

I rush to the dressing room and pull out my schoolmarm get up. I slide into my diamond thong and place apple shaped pasties over my nipples. After wiggling into my knee length pencil skirt, I put on my white cardigan. Finally, I step into a pair of red peep toe five inch heels and head to the makeup table.

I put my hair into a bun, holding it in place with two pencils, and then do my eyes in dark greys and cover my lips in cherry red. I grab a pair of the black framed glasses and pick up my ruler before heading to the side of the stage and making Skittles change the line-up. The other girls are just going to have to wait. I'm on next.

A few minutes later, the first cords of *Hot For Teacher* by Van Halen starts to fill the air and I strut onto the stage. As soon as I walk out, I pull the pencils from my hair and swing my head around, causing my hair to fan out behind me. I walk to the front of the stage and see a few of the boys.

"I know you've been a bad, bad boy, so I'm going to have to punish you," I say as I bend over and tap Timber's knuckles with the ruler.

"I've been punished by you before, baby. I liked every minute of it," he shouts over the music.

I smile towards him then turn to look at Reese. I blow him a kiss then straighten up and walk back up the stage. The cardigan goes, right before I slowly wiggle out of my skirt, and then grab onto the pole and start to spin.

Before I even get to the chorus of the song, strong arms grab me from behind. I'm thrown over a shoulder and hand comes down hard on my ass. I know instantly it's Kidd. "What the fuck!" I yell.

Shit. How in the hell did he get here this fast? Someone had to have called him. Then, I remember passing Krista in the hall. Guess grinding on my man wasn't enough for her, she had to rat me out too. That bitch and I will be having it out as soon as I can get the hell away from Kidd.

I hear the men all laughing at our little scene, and that just pisses me off even more. Kidd walks us down the hall and into my office. He tosses me onto the couch and starts pacing. "What the fuck?!" he yells. "I thought I said no fuckin' dancing."

I snort. "Yeah, just like I said for you not to have that bitch in your lap. Looks like neither one of us knows how to listen. Besides, I make lots of money dancin', more money than me just managing shit. You know I haven't been working at the club for a while. How do you think I pay for the online classes I take?"

His eyes narrow and I realize what I just said. Shit, no one knows I'm taking business courses. It was something I did on my own. Something I didn't want anyone to know about. At least not until I was done. I want to be able to run things professionally and maybe open a few more places. Plus, I want to do something that will make Chipper proud. Something that I know would have made Mindy proud.

"You're in school?" he asks, sounding surprised.

I nod, "Yeah. I decided to take some business courses, because I eventually want to open up a few more clubs around here. There's not much to do in Big Clifty except go to the dive bar out on highway 52 or come to The Kitty Kat. Whenever people want to do anything but drink beer or watch girls take their clothes off, they have to drive all the way over to Kansas City."

I stop talking for a second to think about what else I'd like to add around here. "More importantly, we need a decent hair salon. Maybe even a little spa. The strippers and club girls alone would keep one busy. We all hate having to drive all the way to Harrisonville or the city just to get our hair done."

I continue on about my dreams for the town, and by the time I'm done, I tell him about every plan I've ever made in the last two years. I look up and he's staring at me like he's never seen me before. I start to feel a little self-conscious. "What? You don't think I can do it?"

Instead of answering, he bends down and places his lips on mine. His arms tighten around me, and I hear the faint whisper of his voice as he says, "Baby girl, I am so fuckin' proud of you."

"What?" I whisper out. I'm sure that I didn't hear him right. Wasn't he was just pissed at me a few minutes ago? He shouldn't be telling me he's proud of me now. Fuck, I'm confused.

His head comes up, and he looks straight into my eyes. "I am so proud of you. You wanted something, and you went after it. You didn't come to any of us for help, and instead just did what you had to do to make it happen."

I shake my head. "I haven't done anything yet."

"You taking classes is the first step to making all of those other dreams come true. You stick with it, and when you graduate, I'll pay for you to get a salon set up in town."

I grab hold of his arms. "You can't do that. Those things cost a boatload."

"I'm the fucking president of the Renegade Sons. I can invest in anything I want to. Right now, I think you're the best investment I could ever make."

For some reason, I blurt out, "I love you."

"If you had asked me yesterday if I could have loved you more, I would've said no, but I would've been wrong."

He places his lips back on mine and gives me one of his slow kisses, the kind that makes my toes curl. I'm just about melt into him when I remember why I was so mad earlier. I pull back and gently push him back an inch or two. "Why was Krista crawling all over you tonight?"

He shakes his head and tells me what happened. When he's done, he says, "I don't understand why in the fuck she would even think about trying to get with me. I know you probably hate to hear me talk about her, but I was with Sarah for a while. What would Krista want with a man that had been with her sister, is what I don't get. I'm sure Chipper and I have shared a club girl or two, but no way would I want to be with someone that had warmed his bed for nearly a year."

Hearing him talk about Sarah doesn't hurt me like it did before. I guess I'm starting to understand that their relationship wasn't really a relationship at all. I hated Sarah for the longest time. Even after she died, I held on to my anger; not because she was with Kidd, but because she threw that shit at me on the day of Mindy's funeral. I don't hate her any more though. If anything, I feel sorry for her. "I don't know why she would do it. There's something about her. Something that's just not right. She's lying about her past, and she's definitely hiding something. I'm not sure what it is, but I know for a fact that she's keeping something from us, Kidd."

"I agree. I thought something was up as soon as I saw her,

but I just couldn't turn her away. It doesn't matter now anyway. I told her she has 'til payday, but then her ass is leaving Big Clifty for good."

I nod, placing my hand on his face. "I'm glad. We don't need her right now. If we're really going to try to make this work, then we don't need people trying to cause shit."

His face gets hard. "I agree. I don't want anyone causing us trouble. That includes Daisy."

I start to defend her, but he places his hand over my mouth.

"Don't even try to lie. As soon as she saw me, she ran out of here to get to you before I could even walk across the room. She didn't give me a chance to tell her what the fuck was going on. Her actions led you to get up on that stage, which is something that should've never happened." His eyes narrow, and his voice turns harsh. "It's something that better not happen ever again."

I jerk back, dislodging his hand. "You're right, she should've stayed around to hear your side of the story, but you're wrong if you think she was trying to cause trouble. She didn't call me to make me mad at you. She called me so I wouldn't listen to the bullshit when all the other girls called, and believe me, they did. Within five minutes of Krista climbing in your lap, my phone was blowing up with voicemails and text messages. Daisy was the only one that said I should talk to you. She told me that something didn't look right."

He looks at me and nods. "Fine, I guess Daisy's not a bitch after all."

"No, she's not. She's my friend. Other than Timber and Reese, she's my best friend."

He pulls me to him. "You mean other than me."

A slow smile creeps onto my lips. "If I remember correctly, you used to be a pretty good friend."

He kisses me gently and murmurs, "I'll be the best friend you ever had, and I'll be it for the rest of your life."

CHAPTER Twenty-One

Jenna

Daisy and I are driving home from the city. We've spent the day doing girly shit. It's not something I do often, but when I do it, I go all out. We went to Rocco's and got our hair done, got full body waxes, and we even stopped off at Měilì Nails to get manis and pedis. It cost us out the ass, but we look damn good.

Kidd didn't want me going into the city. He's on edge, because Timmons has been in town. I am too, but I can't let that dick control my life. He took enough from me when I was sixteen. I refuse to give him anymore. Kidd kept bitchin' until finally, I told him I needed a break, which is true. I'm not used to being an old lady. I am definitely not used to having someone by my side night and day.

It's only been a few days since he claimed me, but we've spent most of that time together. I've spent a few hours at The Kitty Kat or over at the apartments working with the girls, but other than that, he's been by my side. After I explained that I was starting to feel smothered, he agreed to let me go with Daisy, but made me take one of the brothers with me.

Needless to say, Rum has not been a happy guy today. I guess he's not as into nails and hair as we are, but he's been happier since Daisy showed him her new bikini wax. Granted, Daisy doesn't spread her legs for the boys, but she doesn't mind showing them her mind blowing body. She may be a tiny thing, but she's by far my best dancer. Guys come from miles around to see her dance. When "*Little Flower*" takes the stage, the crowd goes fuckin' wild.

I've never really had a woman friend before, but I love Daisy. We've really grown close since she started dancing at The Kitty Kat. I've known her for years, but I never thought of her as a friend before. Now, I rarely go through the day without talking to her.

When I see her looking into the visor mirror, I shoot her a wink and smile. "I love the pink tips. Wish they'd show up in my hair."

She smiles back and touches the tips of her hair. "My Mom's gonna flip the hell out."

"You're a grown ass woman. You need to get the hell out from under her thumb. You should move into the apartments with the other girls."

She closes the visor and looks at me. "I can't,"

"What do you mean?"

She leans back into her seat and closes her eyes. "Mom's been going to the gambling boat again. Dad doesn't know, but they're about to lose the house. They need the money I make to keep them afloat."

"What the fuck? You're supporting them?"

She shrugs. "I'm helping them out."

Yep, Daisy's mom is a bitch; even more of a bitch than I thought. "What's that got to do with you living in the apartments? You know the girls live there for free."

"I know, but if I lived there, I couldn't make sure stuff was actually getting paid at home. Sure, I could pay the bills and stuff, but how would I know if there was food in the house or other shit they need?"

I shake my head. "You could buy groceries and take them there."

She lets out a frustrated breath. "If I'm not there, I won't know if Dad's getting his pills. I have to keep them locked up and give them to him myself. If not, they'll disappear."

Maker had a bike wreck a few years back. He shattered his left hip and has been in pain ever since. "Is he taking too many, or is your mom selling the shit?"

312

She turns her head towards me and shakes her head. "She sells them before she even gets them home. Dad had to call the pharmacy and tell them not to let her pick 'em up anymore."

My hands tighten around the steering wheel. "He needs to throw her the fuck out."

Daisy doesn't respond, and we fall into silence as we finish our drive home. Ten minutes later, we pull into the compound. As soon as I do, I see Krista's car sitting out front. After last night, I didn't think she would have the nerve to show her face around here.

As we walk toward the clubhouse, I hear a party going on inside. From the sound, I'd say it's one hell of a party. My eyes narrow when I look back at Krista's car. Something tells me that I'm gonna be walking into something I'm not gonna like. I turn to Daisy. "Did you know they were having a party tonight?"

"No." She says, shaking her head.

Daisy's not really a part of the club, so she doesn't come to the clubhouse very often. Just like me, when she turned eighteen, she had a choice to make. Leave the club or become an old lady or a club girl. She chose to leave the club. Working at The Kitty Kat keeps her close though, and her friendship with me brings her to the clubhouse every once in a while.

We continue to the door, and Daisy walks inside before me. She struts her ass to the middle of the common room then stops and places her hands on her hips. I follow, but I don't give a fuck about struttin'. I'm on a mission. I want to find Kidd, and I want to find him now. He better hope that he isn't with Krista.

I look around the room and notice that a bunch of club girls are here, and even a few of the old ladies are around. Two of my girls are in the corner making out with each other, while Timber runs his hands over their asses. He catches my eye and winks, and then leads the girls down the hall.

Mary is on the couch, riding Holt. Fuck! That is something that I never thought I'd see, and something I never want to see again. Two oldies, all wrinkly and shit, bumpin' uglies. Yuck! I shiver as I turn away, hoping to get that image outta my head. I look around more, and see people getting it on everywhere. I bend my head towards Daisy. "What the fuck is going on here?"

Sure, these boys are bikers, and they've never been shy about where they got their nut, but... Well, this is like something from a bad seventies skin flick. Daisy starts to respond, but stops mid-sentence. Her body goes tight, and she stomps towards the bar.

I look to the direction she's heading and see that Preach has Leah bent over the bar, and he's pounding into her from behind. His hips buck against her, and he throws his head back and shouts out his release.

I look back to Daisy and feel my heart break just a little for her. No matter what she says, she's in deep with Preach. This shit has to be killing her. My eyes follow her, and I watch as she picks up a mug of beer from the bar and pours it over Preach's head.

Preach pulls away from the skank and turns to Daisy. He whips off the used condom and tosses it towards Leah. He starts to zip up as he yells at Daisy. "What the hell is your problem?"

Her body goes still, and I swear I can see her eyes filling with tears from across the room. "I hate you. I hate you so fucking much," she says in the coldest voice I've ever heard.

With those words, she turns around and walks out of the clubhouse. I whip my head over to Preach and give him my death glare, but I let it soften when I see how pale his face is. I swear it looks like he just had his heart ripped out of his chest. He stands there for a second more before chasing after her.

I'm still looking at the door when an arm wraps around my shoulders. "You best get your ass out of here, *wahine*."

I look up to Reese and scrunch up my nose. "What the hell is going on here tonight? I've seen a lot of shit around here over the years, but never anything like this."

"Some of the boys from the Lords came by, and they brought some weed with them. After it had been passed around a bit, they told us it was laced with *E*," he chuckles. "The only woman in the place was Mary. When the boys started looking at her like she was a piece of meat, I decided to call in some the girls."

I let out a short laugh. "That's good. Not sure Mary could handle you all."

He chuckles, "Doubtful."

I look around again, hoping to see Kidd, but don't. I also don't see Krista. "Where's Kidd?"

"When he realized it was going to be an orgy, he went to his room."

I nod then quietly ask. "Where's the new girl, Krista?"

He shakes his head. "Kidd told me to make sure she didn't come with the rest of the girls."

"Her car's outside."

He shrugs. "I haven't seen her, but when I called in to get the girls, I told Skittles to make sure that Krista kept her ass away from the clubhouse."

I lean up and give him a quick kiss on the cheek. "I'm going to go find Kidd."

I walk towards the hallway, stepping around naked bodies. With each step, I remind myself that Kidd wouldn't do anything with Krista. He promised me that he wouldn't do that shit to me.

When I reach his room, I hear murmured voices. It only takes a second to realize that Krista is in there with him. I have to stop myself from rushing in and going bat shit crazy, but I have to give him a chance to defend himself. I've seen too many old ladies just go off the rails on their man without knowing the full story. I'm more level headed than that shit.

I quietly crack the door open and listen to what they're saying.

"Why are you with her? Sarah hated her! Didn't you love my sister at all?" I hear Krista say.

Oh shit. Do I want to hear this?

"You know damn well I never loved Sarah. Why do you think Sarah was leaving? I told her straight up that she was a stand in for Jenna. She knew that since her first day in Big Clifty," Kidd says back.

"She's not good enough for you. She's cold. Even you call her Ice. Don't you want something warm?" I hear her say, making her voice sound like a purr. Women and their fuckin' purring. Why the hell do men like that shit? I'm not a fucking cat, and I don't purr.

I hear a long zip before Kidd shouts, "What the fuck are you doing? Put your damn dress back on!"

That's it! I swing the door open and see Krista plastered to Kidd, and Kidd standing as stiff as a board. I grab Krista by the back of the hair and throw her to the floor. The bitch's boobs are on full display, so I grab the small knife out of my back pocket and put the blade next to her nipple.

"Since day one, you have given me shit. Not only did you try mouthing off to me, you refused to stay behind the bar at The Kitty Kat like I told you. Then yesterday, you tried to get in with Kidd, even though I told you to keep your fuckin' hands off him," I say while running the flat of my blade over her nipple, not causing any damage, but scaring the shit out of her. "He turned your ass down, but you wouldn't take no for an answer. Now here you are, trying to get my man again. Do you really want to fuck him bad enough to die? I killed a bitch once just for slapping Chipper. What do you think I'd do to a skank trying to take Kidd from me?"

Talking about Cary's death sends a wave of nausea through me, but for the first time, I don't feel that guilt. Instead, I just feel angry; angry that this bitch just won't leave us alone.

"Jenna," Kidd says, placing a hand on my shoulder.

I ignore him and look into Krista's eyes, expecting to see fear, but instead I see disgust. It takes a minute for her reaction to click in my mind. "I know you don't really want him. The thought of doing Sarah's man turns your stomach. Doesn't it?"

When her face pales, I know I'm on the right track. "You don't want to be in Kidd's bed, but you're doing your best to get in it. I want to know why, and you're going to tell me. If you don't, I'm gonna take this blade, and for every minute you don't fuckin' tell me, I'm diggin' it in."

She doesn't respond, but looks behind me to Kidd. I feel

his hand tighten on my shoulder. He knows I'll do what I have to do to get the truth from her.

"Might wanna speak up, Krista. There's no stopping Ice once she starts," he says, sounding bored, his voice almost dead. I've heard that voice before; it's the voice he uses when he's doing club business.

She doesn't say anything, but I feel her body shaking. I start to dig the knife into her, slowly, but not yet drawing blood. I don't want to hurt her, but I'm willing to do what I have to. I also know that I can't leave this for Kidd. He feels guilty enough about Sarah's death. He doesn't need Krista's torture on his conscious too.

"T-t-t-immons," she suddenly stutters out.

I'm almost tempted to just shove the blade into her after hearing that name. I have a feeling what she's about to say is going to fuck with my head. More importantly, it's going to hurt Kidd.

Kidd

I pull Jenna away from Krista, and take the knife from her, before stepping around her and pushing her behind me. I let her play her game with Krista, but it's time to for me to step up. "What the fuck do you have to do with Timmons?"

Krista starts to scoot back, pulling her dress up. "He showed up almost two years ago, said Sarah had left some of her stuff at the Mateland clubhouse and he thought I might want it."

"It's been years since she was there. There ain't shit of hers in that place."

She nods. "I know that now."

"How did he even know where you lived? You told me that you were still in Iowa with your parents. Was that a lie too?"

"I lived on campus at Iowa State. I'm not sure how he knew where I was," she says, looking up to me. "I had never even met him before, but I wanted something of Sarah's. After she ran off, my parents threw everything of hers away. When she died, I didn't even have a picture to remember her by."

Her words cut through me. She sounds like that young girl I picked up from the airport; the one that was devoted to her sister. "So, you went to Mateland."

"Not right away. I had to wait until the semester ended," she explains. "When I showed up at their clubhouse, Timmons claimed me. The minute I walked through the door, he told everyone I was his."

I feel Jenna start to tremble behind me. She takes a step to my side and whispers out, "Did he hurt you?"

Krista looks to her, tears filling her eyes. "He hurt me every day."

Jenna makes a choked sound and buries herself into my side. "He used her to get to me."

She's right, but she's also wrong. Timmons used Krista to get to both of us. "Why did he send you here?"

Her eyes cut to me. "He wanted me to get Jenna away from the club, so he could take her. But then when he found out that you'd made her your old lady, he told me to have sex with you. I was supposed to make sure Jenna knew about it."

"Why the hell would you go along with this plan?"

Krista doesn't get a chance to answer, but instead Jenna does it for her. "She was scared."

"I didn't want to hurt either one of you, but he said if I helped, he'd let me go. You've got to understand, I can't go back there. I just can't go back to Timmons and Tug."

As soon as she says the name Tug, a memory sparks in my mind. "Tug? What the hell does he have to do with this?"

The fucker's been dead for years, at least that's what Killer told me. Was everything I was told in Mateland a fuckin' lie?

"He and Timmons are friends. He got out of prison a few weeks after I got to Mateland. Timmons likes for him to..." She trails off, but Jenna finishes for her.

"He likes for Tug to join in."

Visions of what Jenna must have went through sends bile

into my mouth. My God! What in the fuck is wrong with these people? Promise or not, Mateland is no longer part of the Renegade Sons.

Krista hangs her head and starts to sob. "I can't go back there. Please, don't make me go back to Timmons."

Jenna pulls away from me and gets on the floor beside Krista. She pulls her into her arms and starts to rock her back and forth. "You'll never set foot in that clubhouse again, and I promise Timmons will never touch you."

I look to the woman I love holding a woman that I thought I hated in her arms and say, "Timmons will never lay a motherfucking hand on any woman again."

I walk to the door and shout for Reese. Within minutes, he's there looking at Jenna and Krista, still comforting each other. "What the hell is going on? I thought Ice hated that bitch."

I ignore his question. "Call the boys together. Church in an hour."

He jerks his head towards me. "Are you going to tell me what's up?"

"I'll tell you when I tell everyone else. Too much shit to go into right now."

He nods and starts down the hallway. Before he disappears, I call out to him. "Send Mary up here. Tell her we need a safe room made ready for Krista. Also, send Rum up here. She'll need a guard. Tell Rum to watch her door, and end that orgy that's going on downstairs. The party is officially over. I want only members in the clubhouse."

I turn away and walk back to the girls. I squat down beside them and place my hand on Jenna's cheek. "I'm gonna let the boys know what's going on. Do you think you'll be okay on your own?"

She leans into my hand. "I'll be fine. You go take care of business."

I pull her into me and give her a soft kiss. "Love you, baby girl."

"Love you, too," she says against my lips.

CHAPTER Twenty-Two

Kidd

Sitting at the end of the table, I glance around the room. "We have a problem."

I spend the next ten minutes explaining all the shit that happened with Krista. Needless to say, the boys are pissed.

Timber pounds his fist against the table. "I know you're all comparing her to Ice, but you need to remember that Ice was just a kid when that shit happened to her. This bitch is a woman."

"Doesn't matter how old she is, no one deserves the shit Timmons did to her," Preach says.

Timber nods. "You're right about that, but you're not getting my point. Ice was stuck in that shithole. This bitch could have ran."

"You don't know that. He kept Ice under lock and key. He could've done the same thing with Krista," Reese adds, always the voice of reason.

Timber shakes his head. "She wasn't under lock and key when she got here. She could've came to any one of us, instead of playing his game. Hell, I hate the fuckin' cops, but she's not a club member. She could have went to the police."

Glad to hear my own thoughts are shared by at least one other brother, I say, "That's exactly what I was thinking."

Reese leans back in his seat. "You think she's playing you and Jenna?"

I shrug. "I don't know. Her fear of Timmons is real, but there's more to the story than she's telling."

"I don't really give a fuck," Chipper says in a voice only slightly lower than a roar. "She came here to help that sick bastard get my girl. As far as I'm concerned, she's a dead woman."

I nod in agreement. "I agree, but the hard part is getting Jenna to see the light. She sees too much of herself in this girl. She ain't gonna want to see Krista hurt."

"Too fuckin' bad," Chipper shouts.

I see the boys start to nod and know that Krista's days are coming to an end. "We'll deal with her later. For now, we need to focus on finding Timmons. I want his ass dead. I'm gonna call in the all the boys. I'm even gonna ask the Lords to keep their eyes open."

"You put a price on his head, you'll have every biker in the state looking for him," Preach says. "The Lords will help, but they'll be diligent if they know something's coming to them at the end."

I think for a second then say, "Twenty-five thousand."

Everyone nods as I look towards Preach. "Make it known that the man that brings Timmons in gets the money whether he's dead or alive."

"We got more trouble than just Timmons," Preach says.

I jerk my eyes to him and growl out, "What?"

"We put off dealing with the girls too long," he says then looks around the table. "Timmons had one of the dancers selling coke at The Kitty Kat. I know Ice is our first priority, but we can't let that shit fly. If word gets out that drugs are being sold there, we'll have the boys in blue breathing down our necks. With this shit going down, that's the last thing we need."

"Why the fuck didn't I know about this?" I ask, angry that I was kept in the dark again.

Preach looks to me. "Brother, you had your hands full dealing with Ice. I never meant to keep it from you, just didn't think about it again till Leah mentioned it to me earlier."

"I want drug tests done, and don't give them any fuckin' warnings. Whoever is doing that shit will be eighty-sixed, but of course, not before we have ourselves a little interrogation. Make sure Timmons is their only supplier."

We have fuckin' rules in place for a reason. Can't be fuckin' clear headed and be on drugs. I won't put up with that shit from my men, and I sure in the hell won't put up with it from the women. I don't need fuckin' crazy ass junkies in my club.

The guys all nod in agreement. I'm about to call the meeting when Reese leans forward. "We still need to deal with the Cali shit."

Fuck! I forgot about that. With all the shit going on with Jenna, I've let club business fall to the back court. I love my woman, but I'm president and it's my job to see that this shit gets done. For the first time since my time in Mateland, the Cali boys haven't got their blow. "Any word on the latest shipment?"

Reese shakes his head. "Nothing yet. I've called Brew three times. He says it's on the way, but he has no explanation of why it was over two weeks late."

"I want to cut the Mateland charter out. They're just a bunch of fuck ups. I promised Pop that I'd keep them on, but after this shit with Timmons, and now the late shipments, I'm done. I call a vote."

A minute later, it's official. The Mateland Charter of the Renegade Sons is dead. "I'll deal with letting Killer know when they get here this weekend. Any other business?"

Timber nods. "Got a call from my dad. The boys in Cali

want us to start running guns for them. They got a supplier in New York. They need us to pick them up and bring the shit here. Dad will send some boys up to bring them down to Cali."

Fuck again! "Why the hell did Digger call you about this shit, and not me?"

Timber shrugs. "He wants me to come to Cali. He mentioned the guns while he was spewing about me taking his spot."

He's quiet for a moment then looks to me. "I know it's not my decision, but I told him 'no' about the guns. I can't speak for everyone, but I think running the drugs is enough. It makes us a fuckload of cash, and the risk is minimal. You get involved with this, and it opens us up to a shitload of new problems."

I take a second to consider his words then look to the other boys and say, "I agree with Timber. That shit just brings too many fuckin' issues along with it. I know of other charters and clubs that run the guns, and they have nothing but trouble. The drugs we run keep us in the black. The legit businesses we have are even better. Plus, with Jenna wanting to get all those other legit businesses going, I don't see any reason to add guns, but I'm willing to vote on it."

Luckily, the vote swings my way. Surprisingly, it was close. Even more of a surprise, Chipper voted for the guns. "Meeting closed."

Ten minutes later, I walk into the bar and see Jenna talking to Rum behind the counter. I walk over to her and kiss the side of her neck. "I need you to get drug tests done on the girls. I want them done first thing in the morning. Don't give them any notice."

She nods. "We need to have the doc come in and do check-ups too. If the girls are doing drugs, we need to make sure more than just their blood is clean."

"If they test positive, there's no need for check-ups. Any one of those bitches that test positive, get rid of them. I don't care who it is. I want them gone," I say to her, leaving no room for her to protest.

She's stuck up for a few of the girls before, the ones she brought in from rough homes. I've let her have her way a time or two, but not this time. It's time to clean up the club.

Jenna just looks at me and nods. "Okay, but we still need to have the doc come in for the girls that stay. With the shit that was happening here a few hours ago, they might have been too wired to even think about protecting themselves."

It takes me a second to realize she didn't try to give me any shit about getting rid of the girls. I'm shocked really. I've never known her to just agree with me. "You do what you need to do."

She reaches up and gives me a kiss. "What did you decide to do about Krista?"

Shit! I don't want to talk about this right now, so I decide to skirt the truth. "Nothing's set in stone yet. We'll decide after Timmons is found."

"I don't want her hurt. She's been through enough."

Yep, I knew that was going to be her reaction. "She's not you, baby girl. She's a grown woman, and you were just a girl."

She wraps her arms around my waist and lays her face against my shoulder. "She was scared, Kidd. You can't understand, but I do."

I give her a tight squeeze. "Come on, baby girl. Let's get some sleep. We'll talk about all this shit tomorrow."

Jenna

As soon as I wake up, I call my girls in. Just like Kidd asked, I don't tell them what's coming, even though I feel the urge to give them a heads up. I hate to do this shit, but it can't be avoided any longer. I know I'm gonna lose some of my girls today, and the worst part is that I know most of them won't have anywhere to go. Kidd's right though, and if I let this go, things will end up right back where they were when I took over for Roxy. I'm not letting that happen.

By the time I get to the apartments, all the girls are there and are waiting in the lobby area of the apartments. I'm glad that

Kidd decided to go with my design layout. I asked him to make the bottom floor more of a lounge area for the girls, instead of the basic apartment layout we had before. The work took a few weeks, but it makes talking to the girls together a hell of a lot easier. Plus, having a place to hang out at home has kept the trouble down.

"Okay ladies, listen up," I say as I take in the group. "We got to get some shit straight."

As I'm talking to the girls and setting up a plan, a few of the boys walk in. The girls take in the guys behind me, and a few begin to look nervous. The rest just look confused as to why I've brought so many guys with me.

"We have a problem. Seems there are drugs floating around, and some of you are using. Also, I got word that a few of you ladies decided to spread your legs for more than just our charter. So surprise!" I say on a shout and grin. "It's testing time."

A few of the girls that looked nervous before now look scared. The girls that looked confused before now look angry. A few of the older girls are giving some of the newer ones knowing looks, almost as if they're happy to be getting rid of the scum. "This time, there are no more chances. I've stuck up for a few of you before, given your circumstances, but that's not going to happen this time."

I look around, making sure to make eye contact with each

girl. "Any one testing positive will be out of the club, so don't even think about asking for a second chance."

With those words, I walk over to the doc, who walked in with the guys. "Go ahead and set up in your usual room. I want you to give them all a pregnancy test too. I don't want to be kicking out a girl that's carrying a member's kid."

He shakes his head. "We've never done that before, so I didn't bring any tests."

"I did," Skittles says, sliding up next to me and holding two Big K bags. "I remembered you had them done when you took over for Roxy, and I figured you'd want to do it again this time."

I bump into her with my hip. "You always know what I need."

She smiles. "I can handle the pregnancy tests while the doc does his thing."

I nod before turning back to the girls. "Okay, girls. I want you to break up into groups of five."

I wait a minute while they get into their groups, and then motion towards them. "Leah's group, go with the doc. Yvonne's, go with Skittles for pregnancy tests. Daisy's group is with me."

I make my way to the bathroom and start handing out plastic cups. I have to watch each girl piss, not taking the chance they knew what I had planned and came prepared. Daisy is the last girl to come in, and I'm surprised to see that her face is pale. No way is Daisy doing drugs. She hates the shit. "What's wrong with you?"

She chews on her bottom lip for a second before responding. "Do we have to take pregnancy tests?"

Her question sends a shock wave through me. "Are you pregnant?"

She looks to the floor before answering. "I think so."

What the fuck? As far as I know, Daisy didn't spread for anyone. Hell, she could have told me she was a virgin, and I would've been less surprised.

"Who?" I ask, even though Preach's face keeps popping up in my head.

"You know," she whispers out.

"Does he know?"

"No," she says with a shake of her head. "I go to the doctor Tuesday. I figured I'd tell him after that."

Shit, shit, shit! This is not good. Even though I know Preach cares about her, I don't know if he cares enough. "Do you need me to go with you?"

"Nah, I'll be okay." She shakes her head again, barely holding back tears. "But I don't want everyone here to know. They will if I have to take a pregnancy test."

I take a second to think about it and say, "I'll let Skittles know what's going on."

She nods then takes her cup to the bathroom stall. A minute later, she hands it to me and walks out without saying another word.

A few hours later, I walk out of the apartments shaking with anger. Thirteen of my girls tested positive for drugs. Fuck!

CHAPTER Twenty-Three

Kidd

Jenna comes into the clubhouse looking pissed; even more pissed than usual. Seeing her walk in here dead on her ass reminds me that she sleeps here every night, just like I do. I let my apartment go years ago, but I never saw the need to get anything else. Now, I do. Staying at the club is okay when you're on your own, but now that I have an old lady, we need to get a place of our own.

Sooner or later, I'm gonna put a ring on her finger, and then I'll start planting my babies inside her. Kids need a home, and my kids are gonna have the best fuckin' home in the world. I know just the place. It's a little house on the same street that Mindy and Chipper's house is on. It may not be big, but it'll be perfect for us. Jenna will love raising our kids near the place Mindy called home.

I get up from my stool and make my way over to her. "What's wrong, baby girl?" I ask, taking her into my arms.

"You didn't hear yet?" She asks into my chest. I say nothing, but just shake my head. "Thirteen, Kidd. Thirteen of my girls tested positive."

"Fuck!"

She pulls back and looks up to me. "I can't believe they would do this shit to me. I know it's club rules they broke, but they were my girls. Most of them didn't have a home when they came to me. I helped them and I never once forced them to do anything that they didn't want to do. Still, they screwed me over."

Shit, I knew a few were gonna have to go, but I didn't think it would be that many. Hopefully, the boys are already rounding up those girls and taking them to the warehouse to get information on their suppliers. I hope it's just Timmons, but I can't be too careful.

"I'm sorry, baby. I know you care about your girls, but you can't control everything."

She shakes her head. "That's not even the worst part. The worst part I can't even tell anyone, 'cause it's not my secret to tell."

This doesn't sound good. She needs to understand there isn't going to be any secrets between us. "Ice, you can tell me anything," I say to the top of her head.

"I can't, because no one can know, Kidd. No one. At least,

not yet," she says, sounding desperate.

"Baby girl, I promise I ain't gonna tell anyone. I would never break my word to you."

She steps back and looks at me. "You're right, but Kidd, you can't tell anyone, no matter how much you're going to want to. Please promise me."

"I already did," I say, determined for her to tell me, but not willing to repeat myself. She needs to learn she can trust me on her own. I can promise shit until I'm blue in the face, but it won't help until she trusts me.

She looks at me for a while then seems to come to a decision. Finally, she leans up to whisper in my ear, "Daisy is pregnant."

I feel my body turn to steel. "What?"

She doesn't answer, just nods her head.

Stupid ass motherfuckin' Preach! This is going to cause seven kinds of hell around the club. Being a granddaughter of one of the originals, Daisy is held above most of the other girls. One of the brothers knocking her up, while he's still fuckin' around with club whores, is not going to fly.

"I'm going to kick his ass."

She shakes her head. "You promised you wouldn't say anything."

"I won't. I'll just kick his ass and let him figure it out later."

She starts to say something else, but I shake my head to quiet her. "Nope, don't want to hear it. Now, come on. We got somewhere to go."

Her eyes narrow before she asks, "Where?"

"You'll see when we get there."

****

Twenty minutes later, I pull into the parking lot in front of Ink Kings. Jenna slides off my bike, and I follow her. "Are you ready for this?"

"I can't believe you brought me here without asking."

She looks a little nervous, an emotion that I haven't seen her wear in years. "What's wrong? You agreed to get branded."

She blows out a frustrated breath and admits, "I don't like needles."

Oh shit! Some people just can't hack getting ink. The needles do them in. As bad of a motherfucker as Timber is, he had to be drunk off his ass before he got his colors. "We can get you drunk first, but you'll bleed worse."

Judging by the shade of green her face turns, that was the wrong thing to say. "I can get the tattoo, Kidd. Just don't talk about blood anymore."

I chuckle as I lead her inside. As soon as Greg sees us, he shows us back to a room. "I got your piece worked up. What do you think?"

He hands me a piece of paper with my new tattoo on it. I just nod and shove it into my pocket, not wanting Jenna to see it until it is done. "Let's get hers done first."

He leads Jenna to the table and gets started. As scared as she is, she doesn't even wiggle. She lays there with her eyes closed, and occasionally squeezes my hands. It takes nearly two hours, but it was worth it. Seeing my brand on her arm makes me proud; more proud of her than I have ever been in my life.

"You look fuckin' hot wearing my brand," I say as I pull her into my arms.

She looks up to me, pain still visible in her eyes. "I'm always hot."

I chuckle. "That's true."

"You ready, big man?" Greg asks while cleaning up his chair.

I nod to him and look back to Jenna just as her stomach growls. "Go next door and grab yourself a burger. You can eat and watch at the same time. This is going to take a while. No reason for you to starve while you're waiting."

"Sorry, man. No food in the tattoo room, so she'll have to eat out front," Greg says.

I lean down and give her a quick kiss. "Go on, baby girl. I'll be out as soon as I can."

After she walks out of the room, I pull my shirt over my head and climb onto the table so Greg can get started. My tattoo doesn't take nearly as long as Jenna's, mostly because he's been working on it for nearly two years. The fact that Jenna hasn't noticed it surprises the shit out of me.

When Greg is done, I jump off the table and walk to the mirror. "Fuck, man. It's amazing."

He nods as he pulls out his camera and starts snapping shots. "It's one of my best, if I do say so myself. I wasn't sure where you were heading when we first got started, but now that it's done, I love it."

I pull out my wallet and hand over a couple off hundreds. "Does that cover it?"

He nods as he leads me to the front. When Jenna sees me, her eyes start to search my body. "Let me see."

I shake my head. "You have to wait until we get back to the clubhouse."

Jenna

As soon as we walk into the clubhouse, Kidd pulls me down the hallway to his room. Well, I guess it's our room now. My old room is now officially Rum's, since he'll be receiving his cut soon. I was mad when I heard they'd given my room away, but I got over it pretty quick. No reason to be mad over something I can't change. Plus, I get to lay my ass down beside Kidd every night.

When we get into the room, Kidd pulls off his shirt and lays down on the bed, laying on his stomach. "Come tell me what you think?"

I climb onto the bed and straddle his thighs. The plastic covering on his back distorts the tattoo, but I can still make out my name in big block letters across his shoulder. A smile crosses my lips as soon as I see it, but disappears when I notice what surrounds it. Large icebergs are covering his entire back, and in the center is a diamond encrusted princess crown, none of which are new. I run my hands over the crown and say, "When did you get this?"

"I had the icebergs done about five years ago. I added the crown last Christmas."

"Why?" I choke out.

He slowly rolls over, being careful not to knock me off the bed. "The icebergs not long after I christened you, Ice. The princess crown came after I heard a few of the boys calling you the princess of the Renegade Sons."

This makes no sense. Why would he do something like that? "I don't understand. Why did you get them?"

He reaches up and cups my cheeks. "Jenna, I've always known you were mine. I couldn't get your name until you became my old lady, but I wanted to wear a piece of you on me."

My eyes water at his words. Yes, they brought fuckin' tears to my eyes. "Shut up!"

"What?"

I look in his eyes as tears begin to fall down my face. "I'm not one of those girly girls. I don't cry, and I don't do sappy, so you gotta stop making me cry by being all badass boy sweet."

A slow smile spreads across his face as he pulls me flat against his chest. "How about I stop being sweet and start being dirty?"

"Dirty is better than sweet," I say, burying my face into his neck.

He slowly slides his hands over my ass, digging his fingers between my cheeks. "How dirty?"

A smile crosses my face as I run my tongue from his collar bone to his ear. "As dirty as you want."

Before I can blink, he has me on my back and is removing my clothes. As soon as I'm down to my bare ass, he jumps from the bed and kicks off his boots. "Put your hand on your pussy baby, and get it ready for me."

I do as he says while watching him take off his jeans. As soon as his cock springs free, I decide to give him a present. I sit up and crawl to the side of bed, and then reach out and run my tongue across the tip of his dick.

He jumps back. "No, you don't do that shit."

Hearing him say that lets me know that I'm making the right decision. "I want to do it for you."

He shakes his head. "Hell no. It brings back bad memories for you, and I don't want that shit to be a part of us."

Just knowing that he cares enough to want this to be good for me, not only my body, but also my soul, makes me love him even more, so I pull out the big guns. "I want to do it. I want to have your cock in my mouth while I make myself come on my fingers."

Lust fills his eyes, and he takes a step forward. "Are you sure about this, baby girl?"

I reach out and wrap my fingers around his cock, the contact making my already wet pussy gush. "Oh, hell yeah!"

He smiles, placing his hands on my shoulders. "Then start working that pussy."

I immediately do what he says, using two fingers to rub slow circles over my clit. I put my weight on my other hand and use just my mouth to suck him in, taking him deep into my throat without once feeling an ounce of fear. Within minutes, his hips are bucking and pre-cum is leaking into my mouth.

What once was disgusting is now fuckin' delicious. Just the taste of him has me sending my fingers into my pussy, sliding them out as fast as I can. I continue to bob my head, taking him as deep as possible, until I feel his cock start to spasm. When he explodes in my mouth, I slam my fingers deep into me and moan my own release around his dick.

Kidd

I leave Jenna sprawled across the bed, dead to the world, and make my way down the hall. When I reach Preach's room, I swing the door open, not even bothering to knock. I see Preach passed out on the bed with a nearly empty bottle of vodka in his hand. I'm shocked as shit that some bitch isn't in bed with him, but then again, I guess no one is fuckin' the girls until the final STD test results are in.

I walk over to him and kick the bed. "Get the fuck up!" I shout, letting anger fill my voice.

Jenna trusts me not to say shit about Daisy, and I won't break that trust but this fucker is gonna get a beat down, even though he won't know why. I know I should take it easy on him, because he's gonna get even more of one when the brothers find out what the fuck he did. You don't fuck a member's kid, get her pregnant, and then treat her like shit. That just doesn't happen.

I know I fucked up with Jenna, but this asshole is even worse than me. I would've been by her side if she had gotten pregnant. I would have been there even if she didn't want me to. Preach is so fucked up when it comes to Daisy, I'm not sure how he'll react.

Daisy's all about the sweetness. She is nothing like Jenna; not that my woman can't be sweet, but she just seems to lean toward the bitch side more often than not. She used to be sweet, but that all changed when I fucked up. I used to think I wanted my sweet Jenna back, but over the last few days, I've discovered that I like having a bitch in my bed.

As sweet as Daisy is, she's stubborn. Every bit as stubborn as Jenna. It took me six years to get Jenna back, and I had to force her then. I'm thinking Daisy will fight it just as hard. I'm thinking she may never give him another chance. I can only hope I'm wrong.

I kick the bed again, and he still doesn't move, so I reel back and send the bottom of my boot into his ass. Finally, Preach rolls over, landing on the floor.

"Fuckin' floor," he mutters, trying to push himself up onto his knees.

I feel my eyebrows go up. Did he seriously just curse the damn floor?

"Get the fuck up!" I shout again.

He pulls himself up and leans against the wall. He then starts to walk back to bed, but stops when he sees me. For a few seconds, he just stands there and stares at me, in shock that I'm in his room. He tries to take a step towards me but stumbles and lands against the wall.

"Yo Pres, what's up?" he slurs.

I say nothing, just take my fist and crush it into his jaw. I don't let up on the beating until he's on the floor not moving. When I'm done, I rip off my t-shirt and wipe his blood off me, then walk to the door of his room and yell for a prospect. A minute later, Rum comes strolling down the hall.

When he sees Preach in a heap on the floor, he lets out a low whistle. "What the fuck happened to him?"

I ignore his question. "Call Doc and get his ass over here. Tell him to fix Preach up, but he's not allowed to give him a fuckin' thing for pain."

I start to walk down the hallway, but stop when I notice Rum just standing there, staring into Preach's room. "Hurry the fuck up. He's bleeding like a stuck pig. I just want him to hurt, not die."

A few minutes later, I'm sliding back into bed with Jenna. I barely get under the covers before she says, "You didn't kill him did you?"

I chuckle as I throw my arm around her. "Nah, just taught him a lesson."

"I don't think he knows about the baby, so I don't know if the lesson was needed just yet."

I give her a gentle squeeze. "Yeah, baby it was. When a man hurts a good woman, he pays for it."

I feel her body tighten, and I know where her thoughts have gone. "Yeah, I took an ass whooping for what I did to you. Actually, I took two."

"Who?"

I tuck her head under my chin. "Chipper, but quite a few of other brothers let me know if I hadn't been there VP at the time, they would have kicked my ass too."

"I'm sorry," she whispers.

"You have nothing to be sorry for."

I feel her wiggle into me, trying to meld her body to mine. "I'm not sorry you had your ass kicked. You deserved that, but I am sorry I wouldn't talk to you after that night. If I would've just listened to you, instead of being such a bitch, we wouldn't have lost the last six years. Those six years are what I'm sorry about."

I close my eyes, trying to block out the pain. No matter what she says, this shit is my fault. Not only did I break her heart six years ago, I also flaunted my shit around the club. Knowing my girl, she was probably pissed as hell when she saw me with the club girls. "You didn't do it. I did, and I don't want to ever hear you say you're sorry again."

"I'll say whatever in the hell I want."

I blow out a frustrated breath, causing her hair to tickle my chin. "If you try to fight with me over this, I will tan your ass."

"Sounds fun, but it'll have to wait until tomorrow night. I'm too sleepy to play right now."

"Night, baby girl," I say with a chuckle.

She giggles then yawns as her body starts to go slack. "Love you, Kidd."

"Love you too."

CHAPTER Twenty-Four

Kidd

I pull on my cut and look towards the bed. "What do you got planned for the day?"

Jenna sits up, stretching her arms over her head. "I asked Skittles to see if she could find any girls to come in for interviews. She texted me last night while we were at Ink Kings. She's got three coming in. I'll still need more, but it's a start."

"Where are you gonna do these interviews at?"

She crawls from the bed as she answers. "The Kitty Kat. I've done a few at the apartments, but some of the ones I hired bailed their first night. These girls need to know where they'll be working. They got to understand, it's not Hooters. It's a strip club."

For some reason, the thought of her leaving the clubhouse doesn't sit right with me today. I haven't let her go anywhere on her own since I found out about Timmons, but today I don't want her outside of the club. "Can you do the interviews here?"

"These boys have been pussy deprived for a day, so I don't think that's a good idea."

Shit! I should have known she'd argue about this. "Damn it, Jenna. Can you please just do the fuckin' interviews here?"

A puzzled expression crosses her face "I can, but why?"

I walk over to her and pull her into my arms. "I don't know, but I need you here today."

"Is something wrong?"

"No, I just don't want you leaving clubhouse right now."

She goes onto her toes and wraps her arms around my neck. "Are you sure nothing happened?"

I lean my head down, placing my forehead against hers. "No, baby girl. I just have to visit the Lords' clubhouse today, so I'm gonna be out of town. I need to know that you're okay. If you're here, I will."

She pulls back then brushes her lips across mine. "I'll do them here, Kidd."

Thank Fuck!

Jenna

I look over to Daisy and roll my eyes. She hides her laugh

with a cough and looks back to the brunette sitting in front of us. "So, you took ballet classes when you were in Junior High and you want to strip to your old routine?"

The chick nods her head, making her look like one of those stupid Taco Bell dogs that people put on their dashboards. "Yes, it would be soooo cool. It will bring a level of sophistication to the club. Who knows? It might even get you some new customers. Doctors and lawyers love the ballet."

I shake my head at her stupidity. "You do know The Kitty Kat is owned by an MC, right?"

"What's an MC?"

I barely hold in my sigh. "Motorcycle Club. You know, like the one you're sitting in."

She scrunches her nose and says, "I'm sure those kind of guys would like it too."

I've finally had enough, so I call over my shoulder. "Hey, Rum, come here."

A few seconds later, he's at my side. "Whatcha' need, Ice?"

"When you come to The Kitty Kat, what do you come to see?"

He snorts, thinking my question is idiotic. Which it is. "Tits and ass."

"Would you come to see ballet?"

"I guess, as long as the bitch doing it shows her tits and ass," he says with a shrug. "Oh, don't forget her pussy. Gotta have the pussy shot."

I smile at him and look back to the brunette. "Does you're routine include showing your tits and ass?"

"And her pussy!" Rum shouts as he walks away.

Daisy chuckles, "Yes, we can't forget the pussy."

The brunette's eyes keep darting between Rum and me, and she stutters, "I, I, I...."

I finally decide to take pity on her. "Just go."

As soon as the words leave my mouth, she's out of her chair and running towards the door. When the door shuts behind her, Daisy and I burst out laughing. Shit! That was fucking hilarious; a tinkerbell stripper.

When our laughter finally dies down, I look over to Daisy. "Well, that's two for two."

"But we still have one more. Maybe she'll be a winner?"

"Maybe, but right now, I gotta piss too bad to give a shit," I say as I stand up and start walking to the hall.

I barely make it a foot into the hallway when a hand wraps around my waist and pulls me into one of the storage rooms. Before I can even open my mouth, something hard hits me on the side of the head.

CHAPTER Twenty-Five

Kidd

"I don't care if your boys bring him in dead or alive. Either way, you get the money," I say to Miller, the Lords' president.

"I understand. Man fucked with my woman, I'd want him dead too," he says, sticking his hand out.

I reach for it and grab his forearm. "Thank you, brother."

A minute later, Chipper and I are climbing on our bikes. "I want you to stop by the warehouse on your way home. I don't know how much of a mess the boys made when they handled that shit with the girls. Take a look and see if we need to call in clean up."

"Yeah, I heard one of the bitches put up a fight."

I nod to him. "Yeah, she didn't want to give Timmons up. Stupid bitch didn't realize we already knew about him."

"It was more than that," Chipper says.

"What?"

He shrugs. "It was Leah, the one Preach has been fuckin'. Guess she thought sucking his dick meant she would earn a get out of jail free card. When that didn't happen, she got nasty and threatened Daisy. Told Preach that Timmons had a thing for little girls. She figured as small as Daisy is, that he'd probably like a piece of her. Then said, when she left, she'd make sure Timmons knew where to find Daisy."

"Oh, shit."

He nods. "Yeah, guess Preach blew her brains out right there in front of everyone."

Fuck! Wish I would've known that shit before I took my fist to him. Killing's never easy, but killing a woman… Shit, I don't even want to think about that. "I need to get to the clubhouse. Just let me know if I need to get some boys over to do clean up."

He lifts his chin to me then pulls away, me following close behind him.

Thirty minutes later, I pull into the clubhouse parking lot. I'm surprised to see so many of the boys' bikes on the lot. Guess everyone decided to pull Jenna duty today. Just as I'm walking towards the door, I hear Reese shout. "Get everyone on lockdown, right now. Ice is fuckin' gone."

It takes a second for the words to make their way into my

brain. When they do, I double over and shout out, *"Fuck!"*

I feel a hand on my shoulder and look up. Timber is looking down to me. "Get your shit together, man. We got to get Jenna home."

I slowly straighten up and walk into the clubhouse, doing my best to hide my fear. All my brothers freeze up as soon as they see me, each wondering what I'm going to do. I can't let them see that I have no fuckin' idea. "When's the last time anyone has seen her?"

Daisy pulls away from a group of old ladies that have converged in the corner; each one with tears streaming down their face. "She told me she had to go to the bathroom. That was about twenty minutes ago."

I look towards Rum. "Bring me Krista."

For some reason, I just know she's the key to all this. She can tell me what I need to know. I just need to get information from her.

His face goes pale before he responds. "She's not here, Pres."

"What the fuck do you mean, she's not here? I put you in charge of her ass."

He nods, "I know Kidd. I was watching her, I swear. I just came down to get her lunch, and Ice called me over to ask a question. I wasn't away from her door more than ten minutes. I made sure the lock was secure before I left her. She must've climbed out the fuckin' window."

That stupid bitch! She probably did this, and I put Jenna right in her hands by making her stay at the clubhouse today. I'm gonna put a bullet in the bitch's fuckin' head, and not even blink an eye afterwards. No one fucks with my girl.

Jenna

I wake up with pain pounding through my head. Shit! I slowly open my eyes and look around. My vision is fuzzy, but I think I'm at the club's warehouse. What the hell am I doing here? The question barely passes through my mind when Timmons walks up and crouches down in front of me. "Finally awake, Jenna. That's good. I wouldn't want you to miss any of the fun."

I have to stop myself from shrinking away from him. "What do you want?" I whisper out, causing my head to pound even more.

An evil smile crosses his face. "I want my old lady back."

I close my eyes to hide the fear I'm feeling from him. I can't let him see that I'm afraid. Even as a kid, it didn't take me long to figure out that he got off on my fear. "Well then, you better go look for her, 'cause I'm Kidd's old lady."

As soon as the words leave my mouth, he sends his fist flying into my face. The pain is so severe, I can't stop myself from crying out.

I hear him chuckle before he places his hand on my leg and starts running it up and down my thigh. "I missed you, sweetthing. It's gonna be so much fun having you back."

The feel of him touching my body makes me angry, so fuckin' angry. He has no right to lay a hand on me. I'm Kidd's woman, but even if I wasn't, Timmons should never touch me again. "Get the fuck away from me."

His chuckle turns to a laugh. "Oh, yeah. This is gonna be fun."

"Why?" I ask through clenched teeth.

"I told you, I wanted my old lady back."

I start to shake my head, but stop when the pain starts again. "No, you stupid fucker. Why the hell are you here now? If you wanted me so fuckin' bad, why did you wait so long?"

He straightens up and starts to pace across the floor. "The old man, he wouldn't let me come. Didn't want problems with the Big Clifty crew. My own fuckin' father let them take my woman away and didn't do shit about it, but that shit's changed now. Dear old Dad's got Alzheimer's, barely even knows his own name. Since your Dad is running the show now, I can do whatever the fuck I want."

I close my eyes again. This time to hide my pain. He did it to me again. My father gave me to a monster again. "As soon as they figure out I'm gone, Kidd will know you took me. There will not be a rock big enough for you to hide under."

He stops pacing and looks to me, another evil grin crosses his face. "But that's the beauty of my plan. See, right now, my ass is sitting in Mateland, at least that's what Brew's going to tell Kidd."

"Kidd already knows you're here."

He shrugs. "I was here, but I got home early this morning. I came down here to get my other bitch back, but when I couldn't find her, I left. Even if Kidd doesn't believe Brew, there'll be nothing he can do. The stupid fucker's still letting his dad lead him around by the balls, even though the bastard's dead. I know his dad told him to keep the peace with my father, so he won't lay a finger on me."

My God! Is this dick that stupid, or is he losing his damn mind? There's no way he can think Kidd would let someone take his old lady. "Kidd will kill you. I don't give a shit who your dad is."

"Bullshit. Kidd and Chipper have more loyalty to Killer than you. Why do you think no one came after me before?" Timmons says, sounding cocky. I don't believe a word he says. The guy's an ass.

"Mostly because Kidd never knew, but the minute he found out, he wanted you dead. Also, why the fuck is Kidd cutting the Mateland crew? Huh?" I say smirking.

His face pales. Guess he hadn't heard that bit of news before. Kidd hasn't actually told me that he's doing it, but I've heard enough mumbling around the club in the last two days to know that it's true.

"Between you, the drugs going missing, and all the money that your charter has lost the club, your charter is useless to the MC." I pause a second to let the words sink in before I shift into Ice mode. "When Kidd gets here, it will be buh-bye, loser."

"You fuckin' cunt! You did this shit! You fucked everything up!" he yells, reaching down to land another punch.

This time I'm ready though. I scoot back and scramble to my feet. "My fault? How in the hell do you think it's my fault? I'm not the fuckin' pedophile rapist sicko! You are. I've never done shit to you. It was you who took something from me when I was only sixteen; something that should have been Kidd's!"

He shrugs off my words as if they're nothing. "Old enough to bleed; old enough to breed."

Sick bastard!

"What about when I was eleven? Huh? I wasn't bleeding then. You remember that, don't you? When you crawled into my bed and made me put your cock in my mouth the first time!"

I scream.

"Who gives a shit? You were fuckin' hot even back then, and blowing me didn't hurt you. Hell, by the time I claimed you, you were taking dick like a pro," he says with a laugh. His anger is fading, but his disgustingness is coming out even more.

I can't take this anymore. I can't take listening to him talk about me like I was some whore he was training. If he's gonna kill me, I wish he'd just get it over with. "So what the hell are you going to do with me? With Kidd on your ass, you can't keep me for your old lady, so I'm not gonna do you much good."

"You're gonna die, but first we're going to have a little fun."

I sneer at him, letting him see every ounce of my anger. "You bring that little worm you call a dick anywhere near me, and I promise you that I'll bite the damn thing off."

"You can't bite shit when it's between your legs."

I smile, flashing him my teeth. "Try me."

He takes a small step back and stares at me, as if he's never saw me before. "What the fuck happened to you?"

"I grew the fuck up. Back then, you were dealing with a kid. This time, you got a woman on your hands," I shout. "Either kill me, or let me go. I want to get back to my man."

"No!" He yells, sounding almost manic. "Chipper took you

from me years ago. He should've never done that. Then Kidd tried to claim you as his old lady. Since they took you from me, I'm taking you from them."

"I wasn't yours!" I scream. "I was just a little girl!"

Timmons fires off a shot, hitting the wall a few feet above my head. "Shut the hell up."

I start to run, hoping to avoid the next shot, but freeze when I notice something from the corner of my eye. I start to thank God that Kidd has made it in time, but instead of seeing him, I see Krista slowly making her way into the room. What the fuck?

She's just a few feet inside the door when she bumps into one of pallets on the floor. Timmons turns towards the noise, gun drawn. He stares at her a second then slowly lowers his gun. "What the fuck are you doing here? I told you to stay at the clubhouse. You were supposed to send them after the Lords."

"They didn't believe me. They knew it was you, and they threatened to kill me if I didn't tell them where you were. As soon as they left me alone, I ran."

I know she's lying. If my guys thought she had anything to do with me be kidnapped, they wouldn't have let her out of their sight. That means she's running a game on Timmons. I just hope she was smart enough to include the boys in her plan.

"Fuck!" Timmons shouts, and then walks to her and knocks her to the floor. "You can't do shit right."

He then turns to me. "This one here has been my eyes and ears in the club. She had one simple little job. She just had to get you alone, but no, she couldn't do that. Couldn't get Kidd into her bed either, but I've had you both. I can't say I blame Kidd. You're a much better fuck."

While he talks, I notice Krista crawling towards me. My eyes narrow and I wonder what the hell she's doing. I can see a knife sticking out of the waist band of her pants. It's not a gun, but it's better than nothing. I try to stay focused on Timmons, so he doesn't know what she's doing.

He keeps on talking, and not paying any attention to her. "Even though she can't do shit right, at least she listens. Her stupid sister wouldn't do shit I said. Sarah was supposed to be my eyes and ears, getting me all the information she could about you, but she wouldn't give me shit. She was so in love," He says love as if it's a piece of shit he just stepped in, "with Kidd, that even though she hated you and couldn't have him, she wouldn't betray him like that."

He lets out a bark of laughter. "Look what happened. She ended up dead. All her loyalty earned her was a toe tag."

Maybe Sarah was a good person at heart. She was just so in love with Kidd that she was willing to hurt anyone that got in her way. At least she used her words to hurt me, and didn't put me back in this crazy motherfucker's hands.

"I decided to get my replacement, although this bitch really hasn't been all that much better. At least, she wasn't until I told her if she didn't do what I said, her daughter would die."

I go still. What the fuck? Krista has a kid? Then, memories of her mumbling through tears the other night pop into my head. She kept telling me she had to protect Sarah, but I thought she was just so lost in her fear of Timmons, that she was just losing it. Maybe the Sarah she was talking about is her daughter.

I see her trying to make her way around Timmons, and I know I have to do something to keep his attention. I swallow my fear and let the words flow. "Ok, enough with the fuckin' small talk. Let's get this over with. I'm bored."

Timmons aims his gun higher, pointing it right between my eyes. "Should I put it between your pretty eyes or shoot between those sexy tits of yours?" he says, talking to himself.

I know I've got to keep him talking, so I do something that I never thought I would ever do. I run my hands up to my breast and give it a squeeze. "You always did like my tits, didn't you?"

He eyes glue to my chest, and he runs his tongue over his lips. It's so disgusting that I have to swallow down the bile rising into my throat. "Yeah, I remember how you used to play with them. You would bite down on my nipples so hard, I would scream."

His free hand goes to his jeans and, I shit you not, the dumb fuck starts to stroke himself through the denim. I know I've got him now. If I can just keep him occupied until Krista gets close enough for me to reach the knife, I may make it out of here alive. "They were small back then, but they're bigger now. You could lay your dick between them and fuck them all night long."

With those words, Timmons takes a step closer to me and starts to lower his gun. As soon as I see it go down, I start to jump on him. Before I get the chance, Krista is between us with the knife pointing at him. A second later, I hear a gun blast and Krista drops to the floor in front of me.

I look down and see blood oozing from her chest. I freeze, staring at her and remembering the girl I killed. "Oh fuck." I say, swaying, yet trying to regain composure. I need to help her, but I'm frozen in place.

Finally, I drop down beside her and use my hands to try to stop flow. The entire time, Timmons rants about how she got in the way. He didn't mean to kill her. It was supposed to be me. I ignore him and try talking to Krista. "Come on Krista, fight. Stay alive for me. Your baby needs you," I say pleading.

When I say the word baby, Timmons goes nuts. He starts pulling on his hair, screaming that I made him kill the mother of his child. "You are going to die, bitch."

He raises his gun towards me, and I know this is the end. In my mind, I'm saying my goodbyes to everyone I love and praying that I get to see Mindy again.

Suddenly, the door to the room bursts open and Chipper comes in, gun in hand. "No motherfucker, you're gonna die," he says, then unloads his gun into Timmons.

As soon as his body hits the floor, Chipper is pulling me off the floor and into his arms. "Shhh, Jenna girl. Everything's okay now."

CHAPTER Twenty-Six

Kidd

I slam the phone down on Timber and prop my elbows up on the table, wrapping my hands around the top of my head. What the hell was I thinking, sending him to look for Jenna at Mindy's grave? I know she goes there when shit gets too much for her, but she wouldn't have left the club without telling someone with Timmons in town. I just had to check though. It was my last hope.

I can't take this shit. I feel fuckin' useless. I went to every known place I could think of, and even a few run down shitholes Jenna would never even step inside. I don't know where else to look. There is nowhere else to look. We've been everywhere... every-fuckin'-where.

I knew I should have kept more protection on her, but I would've never fuckin' thought she'd get taken right out of the clubhouse. The fact that Krista had something to do with it is even more mindboggling. Hell! Jenna could've taken her out with one hand tied behind her back.

"Pres!" I hear shouted.

I spin in the direction of the voice in time to see Preach run into my office. "Chipper found her. He's taking her up to the hospital to get looked at. Timmons is dead. Let's roll out."

The words are barely out of his mouth before he turns and runs back out of the room. I can hear him shouting for the rest of the members as I chase after him.

By the time we hit the road, every member of the club is following. Even the old ladies and club girls are riding along. I feel the anger and fear coming from them as we walk into the hospital. As we step into the emergency room, I see Chipper over in the waiting area and make my way over.

"Where's she at?" I clip out.

"They got her in the back. She was throwing such a fit that they made me come out here."

My fear multiplies at his words. "What the hell are they doing to her? Why's she throwing a fuckin' fit?"

He chuckles before answering. "They're just checking her over. I don't' think she's hurt, but you know my girl. If she don't get her way, she gets pissed."

"What in the hell is she pissed about?"

"She wouldn't stop bitchin' the whole way here about how

she was gonna piss her pants," he says, chuckling again. "When they threw me out, they were just letting her go to the bathroom."

I glare at him, not in the mood for a laugh. As far as I'm concerned, there's not one thing funny about this whole situation.

"She's fine, Kidd. She's just a little beat up, got a bruise or two, but that's all. She'll need you to keep a level head when she talks to you, man, because she's got a lot of shit on her mind right now. She'll need you by her side," he says.

"What the fuck did he do to her?" I growl out, barely keeping my temper reined in.

"It's not Timmons that's bothering her. It's Krista. She was there."

My body starts to shake with anger. "I fuckin' knew it. I'm gonna put a bullet in her fuckin' head myself."

He shakes his head. "No, man. Krista's already dead. She died trying to save Jenna, if you can believe that."

I'm tempted to not believe that shit, but what he says next has me wishing she was alive so I could kiss the shit outta her. "Jenna said, Krista got between her and Timmons, took a bullet in the chest for it. She has a kid, brother. Timmons was the dad, and he was threatening to hurt it. She was protecting her kid, but in the end, she protected Jenna."

Fuck! "Where's the kid now?"

He shakes his head. "I don't know, but I can tell you for sure that Jenna plans to find out."

Our conversation is interrupted when a man at the reception desk asks, "Is there anyone here for Jenna Chandler."

Jenna

I'm sitting on a hospital bed, about to start throwing another screaming fit, when Kidd walks in. He comes straight to me and pulls me into his arms. "Thank God. Thank fuckin' God."

I wrap my arms around him and whisper, "I'm fine, baby."

He pulls back and looks at me. I know the instant he sees the bruises on my face, because his whole body locks up. "What did that motherfucker do to you?"

I place my hands on his face and do my best to calm him. "He just hit me a few times, that's all. I swear he didn't really hurt me. I've been through worse."

I know I've said the wrong thing, when his face turns to stone. "I don't give a fuck what's happened to you before. You're my old lady, and I'm supposed to keep you safe."

"You did. You sent Chipper to me."

He frowns. "No, I just sent him over there to check shit

out. Thought we might need to do some cleanup. I looked everywhere for you, but I never even thought about the warehouse. Hell, I was fixing to ride to Mateland. I would have left you here all alone."

I pull him back to me, needing to have him close. "I was never alone. You were with me the whole time. No matter what Timmons said, I knew you would find me. I knew you would never stop looking."

He leans down and places his forehead on mine. "I was so scared. Never in my life had I felt anything like it before."

I'm about to tell him how much I love him when a nurse walks in. "Are you ready to go home, Ms. Chandler?"

I pull back and smile at her. "Hell yeah."

About an hour later, after tons of fuckin' paperwork, Kidd pulls his bike in front of an abandoned building not far from the clubhouse. "What do you think?"

I slide off the bike and smile at him. "I'm thinking this is not home, so I have no idea why you brought me here."

He climbs off and grabs my hand, pulling me to the building. He pulls some keys out of his pocket and opens the door. When we walk in, I see that it was once some kind of restaurant. "What is this place, and what the hell are we doing here?"

"How about this place for the new restaurant you wanted to open?" Kidd asks as we walk through the space.

"A restaurant?" I ask, confused.

He continues to pull me across the room and through another door. This one opens up to a huge empty space. "This here could be for the Spa you want."

He continues to motion around the room. "You could have a few girls doing hair here. Back there, you could have few more doing all that other shit you said that just blew out my other ear," he says on a grin.

"I don't understand."

He pulls me into his arms, a huge smile covering his face. "When I went to the Lords today, Miller asked me if I knew anyone that would take this place off his hands. His brother died a few years ago, and he inherited it. The place has been empty for a long time, but it's still solid. I thought it could work for what you need, and the price was right, so I bought it for you."

"It's mine?" I ask, surprised as hell.

He gives me a squeeze. "I bought it with club money, so it's the club's, but it's yours to do whatever the fuck you want with it. I planned to tell you about it later. After what happened today, I figured you could use some good news."

I feel tears come to my eyes, and I pull back and punch him in the stomach. "What the fuck did I tell you about being sweet?

I can't handle that shit."

He chuckles. "I love you, baby girl."

I move back to him and wrap my arms around him. "I love you too, Kidd."

CHAPTER Twenty-Seven

Jenna

I turn my head and look at the picture Daisy just hung. "I think it's straight."

"Good," she says, climbing down from the step ladder. "Just a few more, and we're done."

Tomorrow, we open the restaurant. Well, hopefully we do. First, we have to pass the final health inspection. "Yeah, we're almost ready."

Daisy and I have worked our asses off over the last month, trying to get this place ready. I decided to make her my assistant manager. Being pregnant, she won't be able to work The Kitty Kat much longer. To be honest, I don't think she ever really belonged there. Stripping just isn't her thing. She's one of those women that needs a house with a white picket fence and a man that treats her like a queen. She's just too sweet for the kind of lifestyle we live.

I'm starting to think maybe it's not for me either. I still want to be part of the club, but running the girls and The Kitty Kat never felt quite right. Getting the restaurant up and going has. Just knowing the salon is coming next, has me chomping at the bit to hurry the hell up.

I turned the girls and The Kitty Kat over to Skittles last week. It was kind of scary, leaving that part of my life behind, but I knew it was time. I helped her get the new girls she needed, but it's all hers now.

In total, we hired twenty-two girls. Not all of them were for her though; some will be working here at the restaurant. The ones working here will not be affiliated with the club in any way, shape or form. Yes, the club owns this place, but I don't want this turned into a whore house that serves food.

I look over to Daisy and notice she's quiet. "Have you told Preach yet?"

I haven't seen him beat up again, since Kidd did a number on him, so I'm guessing that would be a big fat no.

"No, not yet. I've tried, but every time I go to tell him, he's got some slut hanging all over him," she says sadly.

"You need to tell him before you start showing. Everyone's going to know soon. If he finds out on his own, it'll just make it worse," I say to her, trying to get her off her ass. She needs to tell him.

"I plan on telling him tonight. I don't care if he's with someone or not."

I nod. "I'm glad. Who knows? Maybe things will work out for the two of you."

"Nope, I gave up on that idea when I saw him with Leah only a few hours after I left his bed. After I say what I got to say to him, I'm done. I'll let him see his child anytime he wants, but there will be no me and him. After how he's treated me, I'm over his ass."

For once, she sounds sincere. For Preach's sake, I hope not. I know he loves her, but something's holding him back.

"I'll be with you, you know, when everyone finds out. I know him well enough to know he's not gonna let you just walk away, so if he says something fuckin' stupid, I'll make sure the girls don't touch him. His dick will wither away before he gets another piece of club pussy," I say, trying to make her smile.

She does smile, but it doesn't seem very happy. "I wish he could be more like Kidd."

I laugh at that, remembering how much of an asshole he was for years, but that's all changed now. He barely even lets me out of his sight these days. After all that shit went down with Timmons, Kidd told me he was never leaving my side again. I thought he was just talking out of his ass, but after about a week of him following me around, I got pissed. We had a huge blowout that ended with mind blowing sex. He now gives me a little space. Not much, but at least I can come to the restaurant without him breathing down my neck.

Between him hovering over me and his tattoo, all the girls are convinced that he's the most romantic man in the world. I swear some of the bitches even sigh when he walks by. The guys, on the other hand, have given him shit about it. He made the mistake of taking his shirt off while he and some of the boys were working on a bike, and everyone saw it. Some of the other members have their old lady's name tattooed on them, but no one except Kidd has it written across their back.

"You'll find your Kidd, someday." I just hope it's Preach.

Kidd

I look up from my desk just as Timber walks in. I lift my chin to him. "Hey, man."

"Talked to Dad. He said that Brew's been calling, trying to get the boys in Cali to join them," he says with chuckle as he sits down.

I have to chuckle to myself. Brew is an ignorant motherfucker, if he thinks Digger would cut ties with us to join the same club that's been fuckin' him over for years. I know he's just grasping at straws, trying to figure out a way to get his club out of this mess, but the Cali' boys are not the way to go.

"Dad said that Killer is out of commission completely. Guess they had to put him in a nursing home, so Brew is now president, and he named that fucker, Tug, VP."

I shrug. "I don't give a fuck. The whole damn club is just running on fumes As far as I'm concerned, Brew's just a walking dead man."

Brew and Digger never showed up in Big Clifty, and have never taken any more of my calls since. I sent some boys up there to let them know that their charter had been cut, but when they got there, the Mateland crew wouldn't even let them in. Hell, they were flying a new flag--The Mayhem Masters. I still plan on putting a bullet into Brew one day, but I'm not sure when I'll get the chance. From what I hear, he never leaves the clubhouse.

"I guess Dad has been talking to Killer's wife. He said that she's still got Timmons and Krista's kid, raising her as her own. Guess, her parents didn't want shit to do with it."

I nod. "I'm glad to hear that she's keeping her. She's a good woman, and she'll treat her right. Jenna's been bitching about making sure the baby had someone watching out for her. She keeps reminding me it ain't the kid's fault her dad was a stupid son of a bitch."

"I saw Jenna heading out a few minutes ago. I never see

her anymore, unless she's leaving."

It's been nearly a month since Timmons took Jenna, and she hasn't slowed down for a second. I knew when I gave her the building, she'd want to get it up and running fast, but I didn't think she would be so fuckin' busy that she'd forget I even existed.

I push away from the desk. "Neither do I, but that's fixin' to change."

Twenty minutes later, I walk into Jenna's restaurant and find her and Daisy hanging some shit on the walls. "Hey babe, got a house to look at today. You got time?"

She looks towards me and smiles. "Sorry, Kidd. We got to get the rest of this shit done, and then we have the health inspector coming in at one."

"Daisy can be here to talk to the guy. She's supposed to be the manager, let her manage."

Her eyes narrow. "She's only the assistant manager, and I want to be here to talk to the health inspector."

I know what she's doing. She's trying to stall on getting a house. When I first mentioned getting us a place, she threw a bitch fit. She claimed that I just wanted her out of the club. She said that she'd seen how some of the old ladies were treated, and she wasn't going to be one of them. There was no damn way she was going to let me install her in a house and forget her. I let her know that I thought she was a fuckin' idiot. How could I forget her when I couldn't stand being away from her more than a few minutes? We ended up having a huge blow out that led to the best fucking of my life. By the time it was over, she said we could get a house. Guess she changed her mind.

"Like I said, let Daisy handle it."

She starts to argue, but Daisy interrupts her. "Go ahead. I'll call you if there're any problems."

Jenna grumbles the entire way to my bike. Even after she crawls on, I can still feel the tension in her body, but that disappears as soon as I pull up to the house down the road from Chipper's. I cut off the bike and look back at her. "What do you think?"

A sweet smile crosses her face. "I think it looks like home."

"Slide off, baby girl. Let's go have a look."

By the time she reaches the front porch, she's making plans for the house. "We should paint it a really light yellow."

I just nod as I open the door. "I want to get a pool put out back. There's not a lot of room, but we could get an above ground with a deck out there."

"Oh, that would be awesome," she says, her voice sounding excited. "We can have cook-outs, and everyone can go swimming after they eat."

"I'm not sure I want to see Mary in a bathing suit."

She giggles, something I have never heard her do before. "I bet she'll wear a bikini."

I can't hold back my smile as I lead her from room to room. When we finally step into the last bedroom, she grabs my hand. "This would be perfect for the baby."

"Are you pregnant?" I ask with both happiness and a little fear in my voice. Yeah, I want her to be the mother of my kids, but I'd like to have a little time with just me and her first. I sure as hell want her having my last name before we add a kid into the mix.

She shakes her head. "No, I just thought…"

I pull her close to me, both relieved and sad. "You thought that someday we'd have a baby, and you'd be right."

She smile. "I love you, Kiddrick Jones."

I place my lips on hers, whispering against them, "I love you, Jenna Chandler."

Epilogue

Chipper

I pull into my normal spot and cut the engine off. I sit here for a few minutes, trying to build up my courage. I come here every week, every week for more than six years. Still, it kills me every fucking time. Finally, I slide off my bike and start to walk towards her. Knowing she's here tears my fucking heart in two. Why the hell it couldn't have been me instead of her, I'll never know.

I place my hand on the cold stone, feeling the familiar ache of her loss. "Hey, baby."

I pull the dried up yellow roses from her vase and replace them with the new ones I brought, just like I do every week. I then go down to my knees and pull the weeds away from her headstone. "It's almost summer now, and it's a real pretty day. The sun is shining, but there's just enough breeze to keep you cool. If you were here, we'd be at the lake. I'd be fishing, while you pretended to pay attention to your bobber, but we both know you'd be too busy talking about what our girl is doing to give a shit if you got a bite."

Finally, I go down on my ass and rest my head against her headstone. "I gave Kidd your ring last night. He's gonna ask Jenna to be his wife this weekend. Can you believe our girl is getting married? I know you said it would happen, but I was starting to think you were wrong. Guess I should've known better than that."

I wait a few seconds, hoping some miracle will happen and she answers. Of course, she doesn't. But in my head, I can almost hear the sound of her happy laughter. Yeah, my woman would be happy as shit that our girl was finally going to wear her ring. "You'll never guess what Jenna did. She's been taking classes online and getting some sort of degree in business. Silly ass didn't even tell me. She said that she wanted to do it on her own. Kinda pissed me off that she didn't want me to know, but then she said she wanted to surprise me when she was done. She wanted to do something that would make us proud. Can't be pissed about that."

I take a deep breath before going on. "Kidd bought that old building down on Streets Avenue for her. She's going to open a restaurant and some sort of place for the girls to get their hair done. She's named the spa something fuckin' stupid, but she's calling the restaurant Mindy's Café. Daisy's gonna run it, but they're using those recipes cards that you made up for Jenna.

She says, once everyone gets a taste of your sliced beef sandwiches, they'll be full of customers every day."

I run my hand over her name, Mindy Mae Jones. "She's doing good. No, our girl is doing fuckin' great. She reminds me more of you every day. I know she only had you for a little while, but you gave so much of yourself to her in that time that it made her who she is now. She's a good woman, a wonderful old lady, and I am so damn proud to call her our daughter."

I close my eyes and tell her the same thing I do every time I come here. "God, I miss you so much. Every fuckin' time I wake up, I reach for you. When I realize you're not there, it's like losing you all over again. I need you so bad. I can't stand living this life without you."

My words stop when I hear a car pull up and look across the graveyard. An older couple gets out and starts to walk to one of the graves. That's my cue to go. I don't share my time with Mindy with anyone, especially not strangers. I slowly push myself up and place my hand on the top of her headstone. "I guess I better get going. I'll see you next week. Love you, baby."

The End

Coming May 13, 2014
Daisy and Preach's Story

Renegade Reject

Daisy "Little Flower" Anderson has lived her entire life on the sidelines of the Renegade Sons MC. Her father is a member, and her mother a club whore turned old lady. Not wanting to follow their footsteps, she chose a different path; one that keeps her close to the biker family she loves, but out of the club.

Struggling to keep it together, she never thought she would have anything of her own, until she met Preach. He is everything she swore she didn't want in life. One night of passion leads to unexpected consequences, and she knows, now more than ever, it's time to move forward.

Garrett "Preach" Austin lived his life caught in his father's iron fist. He never thought he would want anything more than freedom from his past, until he met his "Little Flower". She shows him there is more to life than pain.

Preach has a secret; one that forces him to choose between Daisy and his brothers. Even though he loves Daisy, the

Renegade Sons are the only true family he has. He knows he can't have her, yet he can't let her go.

When Daisy moves on, Preach realizes what he's lost. Can he prove that he's the man for her, or is he too late?

More from Dawn and Emily

Love Songs Series by Dawn Martens and Emily Minton

Whiskey Lullaby (Book 1)

Julie Walker thought she found true love with Jase. Until he betrayed her in the worst way, with one of her best friends. Devastated and heartbroken she runs away, leaving behind her family and friends. She starts a new life filled with secrets.

When Julie meets Dean, she thinks he is the answer to all her prayers, but Dean isn't who she thinks he is.

Jase Gibson is a player. Even when he had the girl of his dreams, he still played. When he lost Julie, his life fell apart. He turned to whiskey and women, to fill the void. But, only Julie will ever make him whole.

Nine years later, Julie's back home, but she's not alone. What will happen when all of Julie's secrets are uncovered? Jase vowed that if he ever got her back, he would do right by her and never let her go. Will he let Julie's secret keep them apart?

When Julie's ex-husband refuses to be her ex, Jase must choose to help her or hang on to his anger.

Jase and Julie have to find a way to give their whiskey lullaby a happy ending.

AMAZON

Broken (Book 2) – Release TBA

Bethany has lived her whole life in the shadows, being repeatedly abused by her older brother, Dean. Living in constant fear of when and if it will ever happen again.

She is completely and utterly, Broken.

When her new friend, Julie, marries Dean, it all comes crashing down around her yet again and the abuse returns with a vengeance. Julie's hometown becomes their safe haven to escape from him.

Brandon has never gotten over the fact that their own mother, their flesh and blood, abandoned them when he and Julie were just children. His time in Afghanistan has left him even more scarred, inside and out.

Brandon feels completely and utterly, Broken.

When Brandon finally meets Bethany, he thinks that she might be the only woman on this earth that could be more than just sex. But, when he finds out that she is the sister of the man that almost killed the only family he truly has, will he turn his back on her or protect her?

Can these two broken souls find a way to heal each other?

Dawn Martens

Dawn Martens is a young, spunky Canadian Author, who is widely known for her best-selling "Resisting Love" series that she co-authored with Author Chantel Fernando. Being a wife to Colin, and a mother to two (soon to be THREE!) beautiful little girls (Sarah (6), Grace (3), Ava on the way!) hasn't stopped this Canadian Firecracker from pursuing her dreams of becoming a writer! She has also co-authored "Whiskey Lullaby" (book one in the Love Songs series) with her friend and fellow writer, Author Emily Minton; on top of serving as a mentor and support system for many Authors in the Indie community over the past few years.

2014 is shaping up to be a phenomenal year for Dawn, as the highly anticipated book two in the Love Songs series titled "Broken". She will also be releasing a brand new gritty MC series, "Renegade Sons MC," with Emily Minton, that will for sure take their avid readers on yet another mind blowing journey. Dawn's number one passion in life is the written word, and she's extremely thankful that she has to ability to share the ramblings from the characters inside of her head with the rest of the world! She also may or may not have the hugest girl crush on Author Kristen Ashley, who is her personal idol and helped inspire Dawn in the beginning of her Indie career.

She loves interacting with her fans/readers, you can contact her on FB -
https://www.facebook.com/martens.dawn

Emily Minton

USA Today Bestselling author, Emily Minton is a Kentucky native. Raised in Missouri, her family returned to Kentucky when she was a teen. She is proud to call the Bluegrass State home. She claims she bleeds blue--Wildcat Blue!

Emily has been married to her husband, David, for over twenty years. They share two lovable but irritating teenagers, Jess and Bailey. She is also the proud mom of a feisty terrier mix, Rae Rae.

Emily loves to read and has more books on her kindle than most people could read in a life time, but she intends to read every single one. Nope, no hoarding problem here! Her favorite author is Kristen Ashley, and she swears Kristen's book Sweet Dreams changed her life.

Many more stories are floating around in her head, and she hopes to get them all on paper before long. She loves sharing her dreams with her readers.

Find out more about Emily on Facebook.
https://www.facebook.com/AuthorEmilyMinton

33403591R00222

Made in the USA
Lexington, KY
25 June 2014